Credence

by Delphia Baisden

CREDENCE

Copyright © 2018 Delphia Baisden

Credence is a work of fiction. Names, characters, places, and incidents either are the product of the author's imagination or are used fictitiously. Any resemblance to actual persons, living or dead, businesses, companies, events, or locales is entirely coincidental.

Published by Delphia Baisden in the United States of America

Printed in the United States of America

First Edition, 2019

ISBN: 978-1-7320371-3-7 (ebook)

ISBN: 978-1-7320371-1-3 (paperback)

Library of Congress Control Number: 2018912450

Cover Art by SelfPubBookCovers.com/ BeeJavier

Edited by Keren Reed (kerenreed.com)

Proofread by Judy Zweifel (judysproofreading.com)

For my parents Lola and Oscar Baisden,

for setting the example for how love should be

One

James Morgan stood to the left side of the stage, his favorite guitar in his arms. The crowd was passionate and loud, cheering not only for Eden's lead singer, Theo Nichols, but also for him, their guitarist. And for David Rowan, their bassist. And for Phil Archer, their drummer.

Although James and his bandmates partied hard—including alcohol excess and drugs—James couldn't hope for a high more powerful than the one he felt playing for a crowd like this. He felt alive as the notes spilled from his hands as easily as breathing.

With the last chords of the final encore song played, Theo, James, David, and Phil came together in the middle of the stage, bowing, then waving and flashing "devil horns." After a few blissful moments of this, they turned, leaving behind a sea of cheers.

James jogged around behind the stage, using the tail of his T-shirt to wipe the sweat from his face. *Full arena, completely sold out.* He beamed with delight.

"Holy shit, did you see that crowd?" James turned as Phil bounded toward him. James dodged him, laughing.

"Yeah, I saw it!" *Nothing can feel as good as this, nothing*, he thought just as he caught Theo's eye. James flushed beneath the glow of performing for the past two hours. Theo winked at him, and James smiled, more out of habit than actual joy. He almost caught himself admitting that there was something that felt better than performing for a sold-out crowd, but he knew it was a lie. Suddenly, he was very thirsty for a beer. *Or two. Or ten.*

An hour later, after a shower and a change of clothes, beer in hand—the second of the night, the first having been consumed in the shower to calm the leftover adrenaline—James mingled with the band and crew. Alcohol flowed freely, drugs less conspicuously but just as much, and everyone seemed to be in good spirits. He looked around for Phil, finding him stumbling and laughing, engaged in a game of beer pong with David and some of the crew. James couldn't help but love him. Phil was probably the closest thing he had to a brother.

Just as he was about to try to weasel his way into the game, Theo entered the room. James looked back at the game, longing to just go and be normal, to have fun like he knew he should. *I'm still in my twenties. I'm in a successful band. I get to play guitar for a living. So why does it feel like there's always this wall between me and happiness?*

You know why, a different voice spoke up from the back of his mind. He downed the rest of his beer, willing that particular voice into silence.

"Hey, handsome." He heard Theo's voice low in his ear just as a cold beer bottle was pressed against his neck. He jumped. "Whoa! Easy there, spaz!" Theo handed him the beer.

"Thanks." Behind them, Phil whooped as his team won a round of beer pong. James smiled.

"Grow the fuck up."

James turned to Theo. Intoxication not only lowered his tolerance for Theo's comments, but also loosened his filter for responding to them. "He's having fun," James

Two

James found room 826 and let himself in. He stumbled, letting the heavy door close behind him. He leaned back against it, waiting for his eyes to adjust so he could find the light switch.

"Theo?" No answer. Once he'd turned on the light, he proceeded into the room. He fell back on the large bed, leaving one leg planted on the floor to combat the spins. He doubted he'd be able to get it up drunk, but he still wanted to fool around when Theo came upstairs. *Why would it matter whether you can get it up or not?* the voice chimed in. Ignoring it again, he reached into his back pocket, pulled out Theo's credit card, and laid it on top of his key card on the bedside table.

James lay there for nearly an hour, floating along the edge of consciousness. He tried to sit up when he heard the door, but the room began spinning and he had to lie back.

"Theo?"

"So this is where you've been." Theo came around the corner and crawled onto the bed with him. "Exactly how much of my money did you drink?"

Had James been any less intoxicated, the question would've bothered him. But in his stupor, he didn't care. "None," he said. "I can drink my own money, th-thank you very much."

"You're a cute little mess," Theo said, and James reached for him, pulling him into a sloppy, drunken kiss.

"And you taste like a bar."

"Aren't you drunk?"

Theo reached into his pocket and pulled out a small plastic bag of fine white powder. "Nope. I mean, I had a couple beers, but this is way better," he said. "I did a little before I came up here."

James's eyes grew heavy, the alcohol combined with the late hour taking their toll on him.

"Hey, come on." Theo tapped James's cheek a couple of times. "Stay with me. Big man like you should be able to hold his liquor."

With some effort, James refocused his eyes. "Sorry, 'm exhausted."

Theo kissed the corner of his mouth, his hand slipping down over the front of James's pants. "You come up here to sleep it off or fool around?" he asked, his voice in James's ear making James shiver. He reached over, pulling Theo on top of him.

"F-fool around." He pushed his torso against Theo's.

"F-fool around," Theo teased. He leaned down, crushing James's mouth with his. James kissed back, one arm snaking around Theo's back, slipping underneath his T-shirt, the other tangling in his long, dark hair. Theo rose up, removing his shirt as James continued to fight his intoxication, his eyes increasingly unfocused. He fumbled with Theo's belt buckle, laughing at himself until he looked up at Theo and found no humor in his expression.

"'M sorry. Maybe I should just sleep it off."

But Theo didn't move. "You're a real mess, you know that, James?" Theo's tone sobered him. "You're turning into a real goddamn drunk."

without removing his hat or glasses. Phil approached him.

"Mind if I join you?"

James didn't look up. "Don't know how much company I'll be."

"Come on, man, I'm sorry," Phil began. "I just worry about you when you get like you were last night."

"I know," James said.

Phil must have picked up on his unease. "You okay?"

"'M fine, Phil. Just tired and hungover. You know the drill." Phil nodded.

Theo came onto the bus.

"Bringing up the rear, as always," Phil muttered.

"Morning, Phil," Theo said.

"Morning, Theo," Phil reciprocated, but James could sense tension lingering between them. When Theo walked to the back lounge without a word to James, shutting the door behind him, James breathed a sigh of relief, feeling his own tension draining from his jaw and shoulders.

They'd been cooped up on the bus for most of the day when they parked at the hotel in the next city on their tour schedule. James bolted for the door. Phil looked around, but Theo showed no sign of emerging from the back lounge. He turned to go after James.

"James? James!" He caught up to him. "Are you sure you're alright?"

"I'm fine."

"Did you guys fight or something?"

"No, wh-why would you think that?" But Phil heard the nervous stammer.

"Brother, maybe you can lie to him, but don't act like

I can't tell when something's wrong," Phil said. "You don't have to tell me, but please don't lie to me." James shifted his backpack, and Phil noticed the bruise on his wrist, peeking out from the sleeve of a hoodie that should've been way too warm under the summer sun. "What happened there?" he asked. When James didn't answer, Phil's eyes went wide. "Did he—"

"Phil, don't," James said, keeping his voice low. "Not out here. Please."

James and Phil went upstairs to one of the reserved hotel rooms. "Beer?" Phil offered from the mini-bar, but James shook his head. "Alright, what happened?" James removed his ball cap and sunglasses. "What the fuck happened? Did he do that?"

"I was, you know, really drunk last night. And I... I went up to his room." James stopped, hoping Phil would decide he didn't want to hear the rest. But Phil didn't even blink. "He, uh, he wasn't up there yet when I first got there. So I lay down. When he finally came up, I was halfway passed out. He... We..." He faltered. "Are you sure you want to hear this, Phil? I—"

"James, you're my best friend. If he hurt you, I need you to tell me."

"He, um, he came in, and we, you know, we started fooling around. But then we argued. I don't really remember what about, but I remember trying to leave and he..." James paused, struggling with the words.

"Did he hit you?"

James nodded. "I think it startled me more than anything," James explained. "He's never done that before."

Phil took a deep breath. "And he's never going to do

it again," Phil said, "because you're going to break things off with him." James laughed grimly. "What? What is so damn funny about him hitting you?"

James felt a flash of rage and had to stifle his reaction. "Nothing. Absolutely nothing." *He doesn't understand.*

"Really? Because it looked like you were—"

"Phil—"

"No, he's not good for you—"

"Phil—"

"He's never been good for you, and if you can't—"

"Phil!"

Phil jumped. "Jesus, *what*?" James almost blurted it out before he realized he couldn't say the word. Phil narrowed his eyes. "Is there more?" James touched the side of his forehead, testing the bruise with his fingertips.

"He…he was different. He's always a little much, but h-he was rough with me," James said, his voice smaller, quieter. "We…we never, you know, went all the way before," he explained. "But last night, he…he…uh…"

"Did he force himself on you?"

James nodded, avoiding his eyes. Phil went quiet then, as if processing what James had just admitted.

"Please say something," James said.

"After we parted ways, I ran into Theo. We argued," Phil explained, and James read the guilt in Phil's face.

"It's not your fault, Phil." James frowned down at his hands. The bruise at his wrist peeked out from his cuff.

"It's not yours either," Phil said, standing. "And now, I'm going to go kill him."

"Phil!" James shot up. "No one can know. I mean it."

Phil looked at him in disbelief. "But he r—"

"Don't!" James's hands came up to his ears, as if intending to cover them if Phil continued. "Don't say it.

Don't say that word to me."

"Alright, fine, I won't say it. But we both know he did it. He struck you, bruised your face, fucked up your arm. You were blackout drunk. I won't say it, but that's what it is."

"I let him in. I—" He faltered, his eyes stinging.

"Stop that," Phil said. "You won't blame me, but you'll blame yourself?"

"I was lying on his bed, waiting for him."

"Not like that; not for that—"

"Then why couldn't I stop him?"

"It looks like you fucking tried," Phil snapped. "Look, if we were talking about a woman—"

"It's not the same—"

"It is the same! You said it yourself—you were fall-down drunk. You thought you could trust him. This isn't your fault. You're smart enough to know that." He paused, taking a deep breath. "What can I do for you, brother? Tell me how to help."

James sat down hard. "How am I gonna keep going with this tour?" He leaned forward, scrubbing his hands over his face.

"You don't. We pull out. We only have a couple more shows anyway."

"Like Ed is gonna go for that." Phil shot him a dark look. "How would I even begin to explain myself?"

"Just like I did. You're exhausted. Slam your foot down if you have to. I'll back you up." James's eyes welled with relief, his face falling. Phil sat down beside him, wrapped his arms around him. "I'm sorry, James," he said, holding him. James let go then, let himself lean on his best friend. "I'm so sorry."

Three

Kieran Jackson turned and caught James looking at him. The startled look in his face made Kieran wonder how long he'd been looking. Eden's singer made him uneasy, but their guitarist had caught Kieran's eye more than once in his cut-off T-shirts, and before this morning, he might've tried to flirt with him. But since learning that Eden was cutting the tour short... *Sure, maybe for them it isn't a big deal. But damn, when you're nobody...* Kieran's thoughts trailed off as he approached James.

"I don't think we've formally met. I'm Kieran Jackson." He held out his hand. James shifted the beer to his left hand and shook hands with him.

"James Morgan."

"I know who you are."

"Sorry," James said, flushing with apparent embarrassment as Kieran wiped his hand on his jeans.

"Heard about the tour ending after tonight," Kieran continued, eyeing the beer in James's hand. "Problems?"

James shrugged. "You're in a band. I'm sure you know how it goes," he said, taking a drink.

Kieran grew even more annoyed. He could tell by James's bloodshot green eyes, by the way he almost slurred his words, that James had already been drinking before the beer in his hand.

"You get in a bar fight or something?" Kieran

pointed to the bruise on James's forehead. James's face dropped at that, something like fear in his eyes.

"Fell into s-something," James slurred, and Kieran rolled his eyes.

"Gee, wonder why," Kieran said, turning away. James's hand on Kieran's forearm stopped him. "You got a problem with me or s-something?"

Kieran jerked away. "Yeah, actually, I do. I have a problem with asshole 'rock stars' who can't keep their shit together long enough to finish a summer tour," Kieran spat. "Maybe you fucks already made your money and don't care, but for us..." He trailed off.

"Look, I'm sorry," he said. "I'm sorry. We suck, I know." Kieran watched the embarrassed flush recolor his face, observed the way he wouldn't meet Kieran's eyes.

"Whatever, man," Kieran said, storming off. "Have a great fucking show."

James sat in his dressing room, buzzed, head in his hands. *What is wrong with me? Why couldn't I just finish the tour?* He looked around the little dressing room and realized how uncertain his life had become in the last twenty-four hours. *If I can't bear to be around Theo, how is Eden supposed to continue at all?* All at once, the room felt too small, the air too still. He stood and bolted from the room. But when he opened the door, he came face-to-face with Theo.

"James," Theo said, startled. He reached out to steady James, but James flinched away, hitting the wall behind him. "What the hell is your problem? What's this about ending the tour early?" He took a step toward James.

"I-I just thought, you know, we're all tired, I-I'm

tired — "

"Have you been drinking?" Theo looked him over in disgust. "Jesus, I can fucking smell it on you."

I'm bigger, I'm stronger, and I'm not near as drunk as I was last night.

"What the fuck is wrong with you?"

Why can't I just lash out, hit him, shove him, something? James was so preoccupied fighting himself, he didn't see Phil until he was grabbing Theo by the back of his shirt and shoving him against the opposite wall.

"Listen here, asshole," Phil growled. "If you ever corner him like that again, I swear to you, it'll be the last thing you do for a while."

"What are you talking about?"

"I'm going to say it one more time because you're too stupid to get something the first time. Come near him again, and I will kill you. I fucking mean it." He used his grip to take Theo and shove him down the hallway. James watched Theo right himself, watched as he turned and looked at both of them before stalking away. "You okay, James?" When Phil stepped close, James flinched, eyes darting to Phil's.

"'M sorry," he said, failing to keep the quiver from his voice.

"No, it's okay," Phil said. "I'm sorry. I came around the corner and saw him standing over you and…" He trailed off.

"I completely locked up," James said, absently testing the bruise at his temple.

"Come on, let's go outside, get some air," Phil said.

The warm evening air hit them, just cool enough to be pleasant. James took a deep breath, felt some of his color coming back as the tension drained from his face and frame.

"Wanna go check out some of these other bands like we used to?"

James nodded, walking with Phil to the stage. He stopped long enough to buy a beer from one of the roving vendors. Then they climbed the steps to the side of the stage and stood there, watching.

"Who're these guys?" Phil asked.

"Lost and Found," James said.

Phil turned to him. "You know them?"

"I, uh, ran into the singer earlier. He wasn't too happy about cutting the tour short," James said with a wry smile. He looked over at Phil and shrugged.

"Was he a dick about it?"

"Kind of. But I don't blame him, you know?"

"We don't have to stick around if you don't want to."

"No, let's stay," James said. "Kinda feel like I should."

As Kieran paused to take a drink of water, his eyes locked with James's for the second time that day. Instead of the righteously indignant frown James expected, he looked momentarily confused and flustered before turning back to the crowd.

"Damn, he's pretty good," Phil remarked. "Although I'm pretty sure he hates you."

"Probably." James turned for the steps again.

"Where're you going?" Phil called after him, likely hoping that James wasn't going for another beer.

"I have to take a leak, Mom. Is that okay?" And for a second, it was as if nothing bad had happened, like he was himself again.

"Sorry. I'll catch up with you in a few."

James did have to use the restroom, but afterward he went to the merchandise tables. Perusing the Lost and Found items—T-shirts, plastic wristbands, ball caps—he finally found what he was looking for. James picked up the band's only CD.

"How much?"

The young guy behind the table barely acknowledged him. "Five bucks."

It didn't feel like enough. James dug out his wallet and handed him a twenty. "Keep the change." James shoved the CD into the pocket of his hoodie, returned his wallet to his back pocket, and left.

Eden's final live show went as well as could be expected. James was nervous at first, but as always, he lost himself in the music and the energy of the crowd. He kept to his corner of the stage, too anxious to roam. He knew he might catch flack from their manager, Ed, or the media, or even Theo for being so stagnant, but he didn't care. This show was all that stood between him and putting as much distance between himself and Theo as he could.

Toward the end of the show, Theo approached him while singing, and James felt his jaw and shoulders tense. *Just keep playing*, he thought, keeping his face steady, breathing as deeply as he could without being obvious. *He can't hurt you in front of 50,000 people*, he reassured himself. He looked out into the crowd, and his gaze landed on a familiar face framed by familiar long, dark hair.

Kieran stood near the front, watching Eden perform. Their eyes locked, and for a moment James was as unnerved as Kieran had seemed earlier. He looked back down at his guitar, his face relaxing into a slow smile. When he looked up a few beats later, Kieran was gone.

At the end of the set, James removed his guitar and breathed a deep, cathartic breath. None of them waited to take a final bow, and that was just fine with him.

Phil caught up with him. "You did well, brother." He squeezed James's shoulder. James tensed, and Phil dropped his hand. "Sorry." James shrugged.

"I'm going to get my stuff and fly home to Orlando. I can't be on that bus."

"Can I come with you? I don't want to be around him either."

James nodded.

An hour later, they were waiting for their cab in the hotel parking lot.

"I told David we're taking off. He wasn't mad. You know him." It was no secret that while he was an excellent bassist, David had a voracious appetite for drugs. Most of the time, he seemed to live on his own planet. "You doing okay?"

"Not really," he said. "I don't think I can be a part of Eden anymore." He braced himself for Phil's reaction.

"I figured," Phil said, and James met his eyes in surprise. "We'll figure it out, man. I promise."

James found himself unable to say anything else. He knew if he tried, his voice might break and he might start crying again. *"You're a real mess sometimes, you know that, James?"* Theo's voice echoed in his head.

"James? You okay?" James stared at the ground, his breathing shallow. "Come on, brother. Let's sit down." But James remained rooted on his feet. Phil touched his arm, and James flinched away, snapping out of his trance. He turned to Phil, who had both hands up, palms turned out in surrender. "I'm sorry. You wouldn't answer, and I thought you were going to pass out. What happened?"

"I-I don't know," he said. His eyes darted around, expecting monsters to jump at him from the shadows. *Or Theo.* "Sorry. I'm just tired. I wanna go home."

Phil nodded just as the cab pulled up. "We're going."

During the drive to the airport and the flight home, Phil kept a close watch on James. Observing his fitful sleep on the airplane, it occurred to Phil what must have happened while they were waiting for the cab. James had a flashback. The thought made everything sink in for Phil. His best friend had been assaulted by a man who'd been emotionally abusing him for some time. All the signs were there. They've *been* there. The increase in drinking, the mood swings—always dependent on Theo's mood and how he treated James, the withdrawal from his friends and activities outside of Eden. The more he thought about it, the more he had to breathe deeply and intentionally to ease the red haze from the edges of his vision. *Look at what Theo did to him...* James, who used to only have a beer or two before shows to loosen and warm his hands, who interacted with and supported the bands they toured with, who enjoyed their juvenile drinking games after gigs, only getting drunk for fun instead of necessity. The man sitting next to him was a quivering shadow of that James.

Four

James lay sleeping in his bed when he heard the metallic clink of a lock being released, followed by the sound of a door opening. He sat up, scrubbing a hand over his face before peering around the room, allowing his eyes to adjust to the darkness before he stood. Once up, he padded around his bed and stepped into the hallway.

But it wasn't his hallway. It was a long, generic hallway, dimly lit by intermittent wall sconces. He started down one side of the hall, trying to remember from which side he'd heard the noises. He studied the doors as he walked, each of them the same, save for the numbers etched into metal plates next to each doorframe.

826. The number echoed in his mind, just beyond the reach of his understanding. Just as he came to it, all the lights in the hall intensified. He squinted in the newfound brightness, waiting for his eyes to adjust again.

He tried the door handle. It opened, requiring neither a key nor a key card. He stepped into a well-lit hotel room.

"Hello?" he called out. No answer. He walked farther into the room and found himself lying on the bed. Still processing what he was seeing, he heard someone at the door.

Again, he heard the distinctive slide and click of the locking mechanism. He turned and saw Theo come into the room. James stumbled backward, expecting Theo to see him. But Theo walked past him and toward the James lying on the bed.

"*Theo?*" *the other James murmured.*

"*So this is where you've been.*"

James felt a wave of nausea pass through him. No, no, please. He couldn't move as he watched Theo crawl onto the bed with him.

"*Exactly how much of my money did you drink?*"

He watched himself look up at Theo, drunk and docile and trusting.

"Come on, James, get up!" *Neither figure on the bed moved or indicated they could hear him.*

"*None,*" *he said.* "*I can drink my own money, th-thank you very much.*"

"*You're a cute little mess,*" *Theo said.*

James watched himself reach for Theo and pull him into a kiss. He closed his eyes against tears. "This isn't happening." *His voice shook. When he opened his eyes, things had escalated.*

"*You're a real mess, you know that, James?*"

James felt his sanity fray as he watched Theo hit him, watched an abbreviated version of their argument before Theo pushed him down onto the bed, shoving him over on his stomach. Just when he thought it couldn't get worse, Theo stopped. He turned, locking eyes with his. "See? Fuckin' mess." *He said it as he twisted the other James's arm behind his back, pinning him. The horror of it jarred him enough to make him run for the door.* "Where're you going? James!"

James jerked awake, snapping upright in his bed. Damp with cold sweat, he placed a hand over his chest, his heart hammering beneath his palm. He looked around before lying back down, only to feel how damp his sheets were with his sweat. Frustrated, he sat up again, swinging his legs over the side and pushing to his feet.

To his dismay, this wasn't his first nightmare. Or the

only version of the nightmare. Or even the worst version of the nightmare. In the week and a half he'd been home, he'd woken this way almost every night. Sometimes startled awake by his own shouting. Sometimes jerking awake so violently, he'd fall out of bed, scaring himself even worse. Sometimes just crying *no* over and over again until he finally woke up. In each instance, it took time to convince himself they were only nightmares. And then there were the truly cruel dreams, during which he'd wake up, convince himself everything was alright, only to lie back and find Theo next to him. Those were the worst of them because not only did they make it more difficult to convince himself that he wasn't actually back there, but they proved to him that it was over everywhere except in his mind.

Remembering those dreams, he turned back to his bed, making sure. *No Theo, I'm awake*, he thought with relief. He wondered if his mind would become more creative — would he get as far as the bathroom, only to see Theo standing behind him in the mirror? — before he managed to stop himself.

It was at this point he wanted one of two things. He either wanted to call Phil, or he wanted a drink. James knew his drinking was out of control, but he also didn't want to seek medical attention from a doctor or help from a therapist, like he knew Phil would suggest.

James walked to the bathroom. He turned on the shower, then stepped out of his boxers. As he waited for the water to heat, he caught his reflection in the mirror. He noted his short hair, mussed from his restless sleep and in need of a haircut. He saw the dark shadows beneath his bloodshot eyes, contrasting with the sallow tinge to his skin. He observed the way his once thickly muscled frame looked somewhat flabby and deflated from his alcohol consumption and general lack of healthy self-care. Worst of all, he saw that the bruises on his face and his wrist were fading. He couldn't reconcile the fact that while his body was healing, his mind still felt like an open, throbbing wound.

Just as steam began to fog the mirror, he reached into the shower and turned the water off. He went back to his room, found some passably clean clothes, and redressed. He checked his cell phone for the time. 10:36 p.m. on a Saturday. He stepped into his shoes, grabbed his wallet, and locked the door behind him.

Thirty minutes later, James sat at a bar on the far side of town. He was working on his third beer when someone sat down beside him. If he'd been any less intoxicated, the proximity would've upset him. Instead, he just sighed, avoiding eye contact.

"Hey, don't I know you?"

"I don't think so."

"You look real familiar." The man next to him tried to get a better look at him.

"'M not from around here," James lied. *Please just leave me alone.*

"Holy shit, are you James Morgan?" The man's breath reeked of beer as he spoke, leaning even farther into James's personal space. "You are! Holy shit, man! I'm a huge Eden fan!"

James made himself meet his eyes. "That's awesome. But look, man—"

"Let me buy you a drink," he interrupted, equal parts drunk and oblivious. He waved at the bartender. "Hey, I want to buy two shots of whatever he wants."

The bartender looked over at James. "What'll it be?"

Clearly not peace and quiet with my drink, that's for sure.

"Whiskey," he said.

"What kind?"

"The best kind! This is James-fuckin'-Morgan!"

The bartender looked at him, recognizing him at last.

Great, James thought.

"I thought you looked familiar," the bartender said, although he wasn't as excited at the realization as his drunken friend. He selected a bottle of whiskey that even James didn't drink because of its lavish price tag, and poured two steep shots. "On the house."

"Hey, that's even better!" He picked up his shot, nudging James. James picked his up and toasted with him before downing the shot. It went down smooth, blooming heat in his stomach. "So, James Morgan, what's next for Eden?"

James shrugged. "Not really sure," he lied. The extra kick from the shot made it easier to interact.

"I loved the last album, but the first one is still my favorite. How's Theo?"

James had to stop himself from cringing. "He's good," he said, forcing a smile.

"He's good? *He's good?* I'm probably the biggest fuckin' Eden fan I know, and I ask James Morgan how Theo Nichols is, and he says 'he's good'?"

James heard his irritation. "What do you want me to say?"

"What do I want you to say? Oh, I don't know, maybe thanks for being a fan? Maybe, hey, what's your fuckin' name? Is there something I can autograph for you? Hey, you know, Theo's doing great and we're working on new shit just for guys like you who stick around when everyone else calls our music 'fag rock'!"

James's adrenaline spiked, and he stood so quickly, his barstool toppled over with a loud clatter. He looked around, realizing that almost everyone in the bar was staring at them. He dug out his wallet, put some cash on the bar next to his unfinished beer.

"Man, fuck you. I always figured you for an asshole."

"You wanna know what's next for Eden? We broke up. That's what's next." James shoved his wallet back into his pocket. The man gaped at him as James grabbed his beer.

"Hey, you can't leave with — " The bartender stopped short when he saw James bring the bottle to his lips and tip it up, downing what was left. He placed the empty bottle next to the cash and turned to leave.

"I can see why. Who the fuck would want to work with *you*?"

James turned, taking a step toward the man, who in turn took a step back.

"Alright, man, enough," the bartender said. James noticed one of the barbacks watching him, wondering whether or not he should intervene. It then occurred to James that someone might call the police, might've already. He turned for the door.

"Where're you going?" the man called after him. James stopped, fists clenching at his sides, his stomach turning. *It's not his fault*, James told himself, taking a deep breath. He made himself leave the bar before the grip he had on his temper slipped.

Instead of trying another bar and risking it happening again, James drove to a nearby liquor store. He found the whiskey the bartender gave them and, along with a six-pack of beer, made his purchase without incident.

While in the store, he'd intended to take the alcohol home and drink himself into a stupor there. As he got back in his car and started in that direction, his thoughts returned to his nightmare, to the bed in which he had the nightmares. Once his sanctuary, his apartment had begun to feel like a cold, haunting prison. *Because you don't leave,* the voice said. *And where am I supposed to go? Phil's? To hear for the hundredth time that I should see a doctor, a therapist? That I'm drinking too much, not eating enough? That he's worried about me?* At the next red light, he pulled the bottle of whiskey from the paper sack. He opened it and took one long pull. He hissed as it seared down his throat, reigniting the heat in his stomach, making his eyes water.

"He should be worried," he said aloud as he recapped the whiskey. He was still lost in thought and the reinvigorated intoxication when the light turned green; the car behind him honked its horn. He dropped the bottle, pulling ahead, entering the highway. "Maybe I just need to drive, clear my head a little." *And maybe you should stop talking to yourself like a crazy person.* Feeling more and more unhinged, he turned on the radio. And for a few songs, he felt himself relax. *Yeah, this is what I needed.* He pulled out one of the beers, managing to open it without veering too far into another lane. He drank down a third of it before placing it in the cup holder. A familiar song came on the radio, and he turned up the volume, thinking it was another song he liked. It didn't dawn on him who the band was until Theo began to sing.

James couldn't turn the radio off fast enough, his fingers fumbling over the button several times before managing to shut it off. He tried to stifle his visceral reaction, tried to push the flashbacks away. Because if he began to have a meltdown while drunk, he'd have to pull over and call Phil after all. *No. No more calling Phil. No more dragging anyone else through this with you.* He reached under the seat, finding the bottle of whiskey. He uncapped it and took several swallows, not caring that he was driving down the highway. It made his throat and chest burn, made him want to gag, made him want to pull over and let it all come back up. Instead, he drank more, swerving as he did, missing the car beside him by inches. *Who actually cares about me? Not Theo. He couldn't have cared less about me.* He pushed away thoughts of Phil, of David, of his family. *What's the point? No band. No partner. I screwed this all up for Phil and David. And for the other bands touring with us, counting on us to keep it together, counting on me to keep it together.* He became aware of tears streaming down his face, felt the urge to whimper. Suddenly, it flashed in his mind's eye—Theo on top of him, inside him, pinning him so hard that his arm was sore for days.

"No! No!" he shouted, punching the steering wheel. "Get out of my head! Get out!" It ended as a sob, a plea. *"See! Fuckin' mess,"* Theo's voice taunted.

A pair of bright lights blinked in his rearview mirror; a semitruck, flashing its lights to make him move over a lane. But he didn't. Instead, he saw an opportunity. When he didn't get over, the truck moved to go around him on the left. With Theo's voice still echoing in his mind, and with the intoxication lowering his inhibitions, James made a split-second decision and jerked the steering wheel to the left.

The front end of his car struck the front of the semi,

causing the semi to slam into him. The impact sent his car rolling, turning over several times before landing on its top.

Five

A week later, James opened his eyes. At first, he thought he was waking up in his apartment. He lifted his hand to rub his face and saw the IV. He frowned at it, noting the hospital wristbands. He tried to sit up, but his head swam with dizziness so strong, he had to lie back down. Suddenly everything came rushing back to him. *I lived.*

"James?" He looked over and saw Phil rise from his chair, looking James over in relief. "Can you hear me?"

James nodded.

"I'll get a doctor."

"I need you to tell me what really happened," Phil said once the doctor left. James looked down, studying the tubes running from his hands and arms.

"I had too much to drink and got in an accident," he explained. "I'm not proud of it, but I took my eyes off the road for a second and veered into the other lane."

"I saw your car. I was there when the cops explained what happened. That wasn't just 'veered into another lane' and lost control. That was —"

"Phil," James said, looking up at him.

"I know when you're lying," Phil said, his voice rough. "It wasn't an accident, was it?" James's eyes fell, embarrassment — and a little fear — washing over him. "Fucking answer me!"

James jumped, looking up at him with wide eyes. "No!"

"No? As in, no, it wasn't an accident?" James looked away, feeling helpless. "No, it wasn't an accident," he said. Phil slumped into the chair next to the hospital bed, deflated, his eyes full of tears. "'M sorry, Phil," James said, his voice heavy with shame. "Why? Why didn't you call me? Or text? Something?"

"'M tired of being a fragile mess that you and everyone else have to coddle."

"Goddamn it." Phil wiped the tears from his eyes. "You were fucking assaulted." James shifted uncomfortably. "And before that, you were in an abusive relationship with the guy who assaulted you. You're going to be fucking fragile for a while, alright? No one expects you to be Superman. Especially not me!"

"'M sorry, Phil."

"James, I don't care if you need me to sleep in the same room with you and hold you when you cry. I just want you around," Phil continued, his voice shaking. "You're my best friend. I don't want you to be in pain, but I don't want to lose you either. And I know I'm not the only one."

"I just feel so messed up," he admitted. "I don't even know what I was doing with Theo. I guess I thought I loved him, but looking back..." He trailed off. "And after what he did, I can't close my eyes and not see it."

"You need to get help. No more shrugging it off."

"Will you help me do it?"

"Of course," he said. "You're gonna need my help anyway. They're gonna take your license away for a while, man. Believe me."

Alarmed, James met Phil's eyes. "Did I hurt anyone?"

"No. Just totaled your car and scared the hell out of the truck driver who hit you."

Phil let them into his apartment. It astounded him how physically unscathed James was, all functions normal. He knew James wasn't ready for it, but he swore to himself that one day he'd grab him and shake him and tell him how lucky he'd been to walk away from the wreck.

"Are you hungry? That hospital food looked awful."

"Not really," James said, shaking his head.

"James, you're skin and bones. Come on, I'll order anything you want."

James shrugged. "Whatever you want, I guess I'll eat some." He turned, heading for the bathroom. Phil sighed, grabbing a pizza menu from the front of his refrigerator.

James closed the bathroom door behind him, but didn't lock it. He didn't bother with the light, not wanting to look at himself. *The last time I looked at myself, I decided to get drunk and try to off myself.* He removed his sunglasses and ball cap. He turned on the sink and leaned forward, gathering cold water from the tap with cupped hands and splashing it on his face. The scratches and bruises all over his body stung and burned, but the most irritating were the marks on his face, and cold water helped soothe them.

After a moment, he chanced a look at himself in the mirror and cringed at his reflection in the dim light. Though the bruise over his temple from the assault had healed, there were several new bruises and scrapes from the accident. A dark, heavy bruise bloomed against his right cheekbone, accentuated by a cut bisecting his right eyebrow. A long scrape against his left jaw balanced his facial injuries, assuring that no matter the angle from which he viewed himself, he was reminded of what he'd done.

* * *

James shook Dr. Kate Evans's hand before sitting in the chair opposite her. He shoved his hands in his hoodie pockets.

"Tell me about yourself, James."

He shifted. "I just want to fix what's wrong with me."

"I understand. But first, I'd like to get to know you a little, if that's alright. You're twenty-eight?" He nodded. "You identify as male?" He nodded again. "And you are homosexual?" He swallowed, then nodded once more. "Are you open about your sexuality with your family and friends?"

"No. Well, my best friend, Phil, he knows. No one else." *Except...* He grimaced.

"I understand you've experienced some recent trauma. If you're ready, I'd like you to tell me about it."

James took a deep breath. "I tried to kill myself," he began. "I was drinking and driving. I got upset and tried to cause an accident." He lifted his gaze to her, finding her calm and composed. "Obviously, I caused the accident, but..." He trailed off.

"You're still here. I promise you, that's a good thing." The gentle but firm way she said it made him want to believe it. "I'm going to ask you a very personal question. Why did you want to end your life?"

"Because I..." He faltered. "I was kind of in a

relationship with a guy, and he, uh... You see—" He paused, unable to say it.

"It's okay," she said. "You can't shock me or hurt me by being honest. I'm here to help. Just take a deep breath and say it."

James tried, his breath hitching. "'M sorry," he said, leaning forward, placing his battered face in his hands.

"Take your time."

"He f-forced himself on me." He heard her get up and dropped his hands. He watched her pick up the box of tissues from her desk and place it on the coffee table between them.

"He raped you."

"I guess so."

"It wasn't a question. This person forcing himself on you is rape."

"I was drunk. Almost blackout drunk," he explained. "I was waiting for him in his hotel room."

"It doesn't matter," she said. "In fact, the element of intoxication makes consent even more difficult to establish. The fact that you were so intoxicated only means that he's even more responsible for keeping you safe and respecting your inability to give consent."

"Even if we were kind of in a relationship? And I was waiting for him in his room?"

"If we were talking about a woman, intoxicated, waiting for her boyfriend in their hotel room—if he tried to initiate sexual intercourse and she said no, would there be any gray area then?"

"Of course not."

"It's no different for you. You were raped by someone you trusted. How long had you been seeing this person?"

"We weren't technically seeing each other," he said, and she looked confused. "If I tell you who it was, it'll make more sense. You can't tell anyone, right?"

"I'm a doctor. I have to keep everything we talk about in confidence, unless it's an immediate threat to someone."

He sighed. "It was Theo Nichols." He waited for her to react.

"Your bandmate?"

"We weren't really in a relationship. We just kind of fooled around sometimes," he said, embarrassment heating his cheeks. "But we'd never gone all the way. Just, you know, oral, handjobs." He cringed. "Sorry."

"No need to apologize. It helps me to better understand your frame of mind," she said evenly. "Relationship or not, you trusted him?"

He shrugged. "He has a temper. And a strong personality. But I never thought he'd do" — he paused — "*that*."

"Maybe you didn't fully trust him, but you trusted him enough to let your guard down," she said. After a long pause, "James, what would you like to achieve with these therapy sessions?"

He looked down at his hands. "I just want to feel normal again."

"And how do you feel now that isn't 'normal' to you?"

"Weak. Overly emotional. Anxious."

"I know those feelings aren't your normal, but they are normal for someone who's been through what you have."

"I hate it."

"I know you do," she said. "But I believe I can help."

"I hope so."

"Tell me something you like about yourself." His eyes returned to hers at the change of subject. "I've only known you for a few minutes, and I can already pick out a handful of things I like about you."

"What are they?"

"It doesn't matter what I think. It doesn't matter what anyone else thinks. No one else was in the car with you when you decided to try to take your life. It starts and ends with how you feel about yourself."

"I didn't survive because I liked something about myself. I survived by chance. Jerking my car in front of a semitruck should've killed me."

"It's not my goal to make sure future attempts are unsuccessful. It's my goal to prevent future attempts from happening in the first place." Something in that clicked for him.

"I guess I like how I play guitar."

She smiled. "That's a good start. I know your band broke up recently, but do you still play?"

He thought back. "No. I guess I haven't since the last Eden show… It never occurred to me to try," he added, shocked.

"That's normal. Trauma and depression can stifle creativity. But if it's something you truly love, you should try playing a little every day. Writing new music may be difficult at first, but even just the act of playing through exercises or songs you like could help you. And that's your homework. I want you to try playing the guitar for a few minutes every day."

"Okay."

"As far as medication goes—"

"I don't want to be medicated." He said it suddenly,

without considering how desperate he might sound.

"I understand, but your doctor from the hospital said you're prone to nightmares. Sleep deprivation is one of the biggest factors in worsening depression. How about I give you something to take as needed instead of something you have to take every night? Would that be better?" He met her eyes as she continued. "The last thing I want is to take your choice away. I know that's been taken from you enough, and I don't want you to feel that way about your therapy."

Wide-eyed, he watched her as she wrote the prescription. "That's unnerving."

She looked up at him. "What is?"

"I didn't realize why I didn't want pills."

"You know more than you think." She tore off the prescription and handed it to him. "I want to know if it's not working or if you have any side effects. Okay?"

"Okay."

"I'll see you next week. Let me walk you out."

As James walked out of the room behind her, Phil stood up.

"Ready?" James nodded, but didn't speak. Putting his sunglasses on, he followed Phil out of the building. Late summer meant very little in Orlando, the heat continuing often well through the fall. In spite of the ever-present heat and humidity, not once had James gone out in anything less than a T-shirt, jeans, and a hoodie. Phil had begun to realize it was more out of shame than anything else, hiding the bruises on his body beneath the layers. Hiding his body in general.

Once in the car, Phil looked over at James. "You alright, brother?"

"'M okay," he said, even as his voice broke over the last word. He hunched over in the passenger seat, rubbing his forehead, his shoulders shaking. Unable to stand it, Phil leaned over and put his arm around James. "'M sorry, Phil."

"Don't be sorry. *I'm* sorry you have to go through this. But I am proud of you for getting help."

"It just feels like being ripped open, you know?"

"It'll get better," Phil said, pulling away.

"I h-hope so," James stammered. "I'm alright." Phil sat back in the driver's seat and started the car. "Can we go by my apartment?"

Phil looked over at him. "Why? What do you need?"

"I just wanna grab one of my guitars. Dr. Evans thinks it'd be a good idea for me to try playing some," James explained, looking mildly irritated.

"Aw, man, now I have to listen to you play?" Phil joked, breaking the tension, and James smiled.

"I guess you do."

Phil laughed. "Yeah, man. Of course."

Phil parked behind James's apartment building. When James didn't get out right away, Phil looked over at him.

"You alright?"

James met his eyes. "Yeah, I just..." He paused, looking up at the steps, the landing, the door. "I don't know what my problem is." He took a deep breath, moving to climb out of the car.

"You want me to go with you?"

James looked back at him, and Phil understood without James having to explain. "I'm going with you." Phil unbuckled his own seat belt and stepped out of the car before James could protest.

Phil had expected empty beer bottles and maybe open or empty liquor bottles. He'd expected James's apartment to reflect the state of mind he'd been in when he'd attempted suicide. But his apartment was as neat and clean as ever. A few books on the coffee table, one open and facedown. A couple of dirty glasses in the sink. The lack of disarray was eerie.

"I'll be right back." James was gone less than a minute before he came back, guitar hard case in hand. Judging by the size and shape, it was one of his acoustic guitars. Though still paler than normal, James seemed more hopeful than he'd been prior to his therapy session. "Let's go."

Six

A year and a half later…

The midmorning sun bore down on James as he rounded the corner, dropping down to a slow run, then to a walk. He wiped sweat from his face with the tail of his cut-off T-shirt. Though winters in Florida weren't usually devastating, he'd still been stuck on treadmills for the past couple of months. He relished the heat and humidity, the way the fresh air coursed over him as he ran. He jogged up the steps to his apartment and let himself inside. Locking the door behind him, he placed his keys on the hook beside the door and went to the refrigerator. He took a bottle of water from the shelf and drained nearly half of it in two long pulls. Just as he'd begun to catch his breath, his cell phone rang.

"Hey, sleeping beauty," Phil teased. "You still up for company today?"

James laughed. "Wasn't sleeping. I went for a run."

"Oh, right," Phil said, as if he'd forgotten. Phil knew everything, had been there every step of the way during his recovery. "Well, David and I are ready when you are."

"I just have to shower, and I can meet up."

"How about that deli across from the studio?"

"Sounds good. Give me twenty minutes."

James came through the door just as they'd found a table.

"There he is!" Phil said.

James smiled. "Hey."

David stood up. "Hey, man!" They hugged briefly, all smiles and backslapping hugs. "You look great. How're you doing?"

"I'm doing better. How about you?" They sat at the small café table.

"Oh, I have a feeling we're doing about the same because of the same kind of shit."

To an extent, that was true. But he knew David's struggle was with drug addiction for addiction's sake. Not trauma, nor depression, as had plagued James and fed his alcoholism.

"One day at a time."

"Tell me about it," David said, almost to himself. "So what are you guys up to? Are we just jamming, or…?"

James and Phil looked at each other.

"You tell him," Phil said. "It was your idea."

James rubbed the back of his neck. "We want to try to reform a band."

"Man, I don't really think I can work with Theo again, if that's what you're working up to," David said, sighing heavily.

"Why?" James frowned, unable to remember much from that time, other than his own problems with Theo.

"So, I know I look dumb, but even I knew there was tension between you and him," David explained.

"And you still want to work with me?"

"James, you clearly weren't the problem," David continued. "He made us all miserable with his moody ass."

You don't know the half of it. "No Theo," he said.

"We do need to find a singer, though. God knows I can't do it," Phil said, attempting to lighten the mood.

"Me neither," David said.

"I don't really want to," James said. The three of them thought in silence long enough that the waitress brought their orders. James looked at the sandwich and drink placed before him, then to Phil.

"You order the exact same thing every time," Phil said, popping a chip into his mouth.

James chuckled, picking up one half of the sandwich and taking a bite. "I can't really think of anyone, to be honest." As James chewed, he ran through the bands they'd worked with in the past. Suddenly, a name dawned in his mind, and it must've shown on his face.

"What? Did you think of someone, or are you choking?"

James swallowed the bite in his mouth, washing it down with a drink of his diet cola. "That last tour we did, they opened for us," he said. "Something about being lost—"

"Lost and Found?" David asked.

James snapped his fingers. "That's it!"

"Yeah, I remember them. Their singer was a wiry little guy. The fuck was his name?"

James pulled his cell phone from his back pocket, even though he already knew his name. He typed Lost and Found into the Internet search function. "Jackson. Kieran Jackson."

"I do remember him. He was good," Phil said. But James had momentarily been distracted by the pictures included with the search results. Long, brown hair and baby-blue eyes. *Yeah, Phil, I remember him too.* "Are they still together?"

James looked up. "What?"

"Lost and Found? Are they still together?"

"Oh." James scrolled past the pictures and tapped on a link on one of their social-media pages. "Nope. Split about a year ago. Doesn't look like he's active."

"Let's see if Ed can dig up a phone number, and we'll give him a call."

Thoroughly pleased with the prospect of reforming a band, if nervous about reaching out to Kieran after all this time, James hadn't been home long when he heard a knock at his door. He peered through the peephole. Phil. He opened the door.

"Hey, what's up?" James asked, and Phil arched an eyebrow. "What?"

"Can I come in?" James stepped aside, letting him in. "So you remember Kieran Jackson, huh?"

"Yeah, he was a great singer," James said. Phil narrowed his eyes, and James found that he could no longer stifle his smile. "It might also be because he berated me for being a drunk and ending the last tour early. But who's counting?"

"Uh-huh," Phil said. "Wouldn't have anything to do with him being so pretty, would it?"

James put his hands up in surrender with a smile. "Alright, he's pretty," James conceded. "But even you thought he was good."

"He was good, but listen—"

"Here we go," James said, crossing his arms over his chest, preparing for a lecture.

"Don't 'here we go' me. I just got my best friend put back together," Phil said shortly.

"You think I'd let that happen again?"

"That's not what I'm saying and you know it. I don't think you *let* anything happen."

James grimaced. *Sometimes I do.* A year and a half of therapy, as well as distance from Theo and the pressures of touring, had done a lot for him. But that old doubt still cropped up from time to time.

"You think I'd suggest a singer for the band based on attraction? Do you really think I'm that shallow?"

"I never said that."

"Then what are you saying?"

"I just don't want you to get hurt again, James."

"Last time was a hell of a lot more than just getting hurt."

"I know it was. And I almost lost you because of it." It was out of character for Phil to talk to him that way. He knew how much Phil cared for him, but Phil almost never expressed himself so directly.

"I know," James said with a sigh. "Please, just trust me. I know that's asking a lot, even now."

"Alright. But if he's even remotely an asshole, it's a no from me. Okay?"

"I don't even know if he'd be interested, you know? In the band or me."

Phil shot him a look. "I can't tell if you're being your normal, self-deprecating self, or if you mean you're not sure if he's interested in men."

James snorted, then admitted, "A little of both, I guess."

"Look, I know you were swimming in the bottle back then, so maybe you don't remember, but I saw the way he looked at you when we were watching him perform."

James lifted his gaze to Phil's, hopeful. "He looked at

me?"

Phil rolled his eyes. "Yeah, he did. I was embarrassed to have seen it. Felt like I was watching something I shouldn't be, you know?" James laughed. "But seriously, please be careful. I wouldn't say it if I didn't care."

"I will."

* * *

"Could you turn that shit down?" Kieran asked, more bite than humor in his voice.

"Okay, grumpy ass!" Adrienne turned down the car radio.

"I don't know how you still listen to that," he said.

"I know, I know. Eden's dorky, and I'm a dork for listening to them. I got it, Kieran. For the thousandth time." She looked over at her twin brother, smirking.

"What?"

"Just trying to figure out if the bristles are only for me, or if you're going to be a dick to every customer you talk to this morning."

He rolled his eyes. "I'm a fucking delight with customers."

She snorted as she pulled into the parking lot of the popular chain coffee shop where they worked together. As they exited the car, Kieran's phone began to ring. He pushed his sunglasses up on his head and squinted at the screen. He didn't recognize the number, and normally, he would've let it go to voice mail. But something about the time of day and the weird area code piqued his curiosity.

"Hello?"

"Hi, is this Kieran Jackson?"

"It is. Who's this?"

"It's James Morgan. We toured together a couple years ago. Do you remember me?"

Kieran's eyes went wide.

"Yeah, man, I remember you. How are you?"

"Good." James paused, and even over the phone, Kieran felt the awkward tension between them. "I'm sure you heard—Eden broke up."

"I did. I'm sorry for that."

"Yeah, me too. But hey, listen, what're you up to these days?"

Kieran chuckled. "Not much, to be honest."

"Well, uh, David, Phil, and I want to make music again, but we need a singer. Obviously."

Kieran felt his heart skip. "You want me to replace Theo?"

"*Who is that?*" she mouthed. But Kieran didn't acknowledge her at all.

"No, not in Eden. Eden's done. We want to start something new together. Would you be interested in auditioning for us?"

Kieran came back to himself, looking around at the coffee shop, at the shitty car he and Adrienne shared while his was in the shop, and made a split-second decision. "I am. I... I am. When?"

"How soon can you fly to Orlando?"

After nailing down his audition date, Kieran ended the call, looking down at his phone in disbelief.

"Who was that?" Adrienne asked.

"You wouldn't believe me if I told you," he said, rubbing his hand against his mouth.

"Tell me. Tell me!"

"It has to be a joke," he thought aloud.

"Kieran, I swear to God—"

"James Morgan," he said.

"Shut up." Her eyes darted from his cell phone to his face. "You're fucking with me. Ha-ha, very funny."

"No, Addy. I swear."

"Look, I know you hate listening to Eden, but—" Kieran sat down on the curb next to the car. "He wants me to come to Orlando and audition for a new band he's putting together."

Something in his face must've convinced her that he wasn't joking. "Holy shit." She sat down next to him.

"That really was James Morgan," he said, almost to himself.

"Look who's starstruck." She nudged him, likely trying to snap him out of his daze.

"I'm not starstruck."

"I can practically see the stars dancing around your head, you look so stunned," she joked.

"Stunned is a better word," he said.

"Are you going to do it?" Kieran looked over at her, uncertain, and suddenly they were children again, his eyes searching hers for guidance. "I think you should. I think it might be a really good thing for you."

He nodded, chewing his lip. "I think I will."

"Oh my God, my brother is going to be in Eden!"

"Keep your voice down," he said. "I don't know if I'm supposed to tell anyone."

"If you want to borrow any of my CDs, you know, to get a feel—"

"Shut up," he said, smiling in spite of himself.

After their shift, Kieran and Adrienne left the coffee shop together.

"I think we should celebrate," she said.

"It's just an audition," Kieran said.

"With—"

"With Eden. I know, I know." He couldn't help but laugh with her.

"I think it's awesome they remembered you," she said, and Kieran shrugged. "Come on, you can be excited. I swear it won't ruin your cool."

He sighed. "Of course I'm excited. I just..." He paused. "Should I tell them about the tinnitus?"

He watched the realization hit her, that he wasn't just playing it cool because of his prejudice against Eden. "How bad is it these days?"

He shrugged again. "Not bad. But I've been much less active and a lot more careful."

She pulled into the parking lot of their favorite bar and grill. "Then just keep being careful and keep an eye on it. But for now, I'd say just let it ride. You don't even know if you've got the job yet," she said, and he nodded. "Come on, let's celebrate."

James,

I'm emailing to confirm my interest in your offer for an audition. I was a bit taken aback when you called, and I just wanted to assure you that I am, in fact, interested. My flight is supposed to arrive on Wednesday at 11:30 a.m. I'll be at the studio shortly thereafter (wish me luck for no delays).

Thank you for this opportunity,
Kieran Jackson

Kieran,

Thanks for confirming your interest. I know my call was out of the blue, so no worries.

See you Wednesday (good luck for no delays),
James

Kieran's cell phone pinged. Adrienne perked up.
After reading the email himself, he let her read it.
"That is too cool."
Kieran took a drink of his beer. "Yeah, I guess so," he
conceded. He put the beer down, covered his face. "What
did I just agree to?"
"An audition to work with some awesome
musicians," she reassured him. "Theo was the joke of the
band, not the others."
He ran a hand through his hair. "Why me?"
"Because you're good. I hate to tell you this because
I know it jacks up your ego, but you're actually one hell
of a singer and guitarist," she said. "They —*he*—must've
remembered that."
"I'm not so sure," he said.
"What else could it be?"
He sighed. "I never told you this because I thought
you'd yell at me," he started, "but before the last show
with them, I actually ran into James. And I was kind of a
dick to him."
Her eyes narrowed. "What do you mean?"
"Oh, you know, in my usual prickly manner. I pretty
much told him how pissed I was and that it must be nice
to not have to care about missing a couple of shows," he
explained.
"Maybe he liked your honesty?" she offered. "That
was almost two years ago. Maybe he forgot."
He shot her a look. "I doubt it," he said. "Aw, man,
it's already awkward, and I'm not even there yet," he
groaned.

* * *

James lay in his bed. He couldn't believe he was about to step back into making music again. He was a little surprised Kieran had so easily agreed to audition for the band. He wondered if he still looked the same. Something about his long, dark hair pulled at James, made him want to touch it, to bury his face in it. Frustrated, he turned over on his side, facing the wall.

"How the fuck am I going to do this?" he murmured to himself with a heavy sigh.

Seven

Kieran stood over his battered suitcase. He kept stopping to reread James's email, reassuring himself he hadn't made it all up. *Why would he call me? I was an asshole to him. And he was half drunk when he watched me perform.* He wondered if James was still a drunk. He'd sounded with it on the phone. Maybe he got sober over the past couple of years. Kieran remembered the red-rimmed eyes, the glassy, drowsy look in them as James spoke to him, oblivious at first to his anger. *And that pretty shade of green.*

"Shut up, Kieran," he muttered. *There's no way he's gay.* During the last show, James had looked right at him in the crowd before peering down at his guitar, a slow, sexy smile pulling at the corners of his mouth. Kieran closed his eyes, willing the memory away.

"Hey," Adrienne said from the door, startling him.

"Hey," he said.

"Everything okay in here? I heard you mumbling to yourself." She leaned against the doorframe.

"I'm fine," he said.

She came into the room, plopping down on the bed next to his suitcase. "Nervous?"

"No," he said, a little too defensively.

"You know, I wouldn't judge you if you were," she said. He shot her a look, but continued packing. "You don't always have to play aloof, Kieran. I know you have to be excited. I promise I won't make fun of you for it."

He closed the suitcase and sat down next to her. "Alright, maybe I'm a little anxious," he admitted.

"I understand. I can't imagine doing what you've done. Sometimes, just talking to people at the coffee shop makes me nervous."

"It's not that," he said. "It's my hearing."

She reached for his hand, holding it between hers. "If you're careful, your hearing will be fine," she reassured him.

"What if they can tell? What if—"

"No one can tell."

He looked away. "You're not a musician, Addy."

"I'm telling you, no one can tell. I didn't know until you told me about it."

He sighed. "Maybe you're right."

"And you know, as far as most people would be concerned, you're an upgrade from Theo by default."

He smiled, looking over at her. "I thought you loved Theo," he teased, nudging her.

"Nope. James is the babe," she joked.

Sometimes, we really are twins.

"You're ridiculous," he remarked.

"What? He is!" She narrowed her eyes at him. "But I'd venture to say you already knew that."

"Shut up."

"I knew it!"

"You didn't know shit," he said.

"No one gets that irritated with a band unless it's personal. He doth protest too much!"

"I swear to God, if you don't shut the fuck up," he said, his cheeks flushing.

"Oh, baby brother, is it awful to know that someone

can see right through you?"

"We're thirty-three years old. How long are you going to keep pulling the I-was-born-a-minute-earlier shit?"

"It was two minutes. And forever."

He rolled his eyes, but couldn't help but love her. None of his other friends would be this excited for him, and right then, he needed someone to remind him this was supposed to be exciting and not terrifying.

Kieran sat in a window seat during his flight. He tried to relax, to enjoy the scenery, but he kept getting lost in his own thoughts. Without telling Adrienne — because he knew he'd never hear the end of it — he'd sneaked her Eden CDs into his room, burned them onto his laptop, and transferred them over to his iPod. He'd then carefully replaced them, hoping she wouldn't notice.

While he'd had them, he flipped through the liner notes. In the booklet of their first CD, there were pictures of each band member. *Wasn't that part of what bugged you about him? That he was handsome. And talented. And, even through the drunken haze, he was a nice guy.* He sighed heavily, wincing with mortification as he remembered how he'd tried to pick a fight with James, only to see him hours later from the side of the stage. *Being a nice guy and watching my shitty band perform.*

Kieran listened to the songs he remembered, trying to get past Theo's voice. He respected him for what he was, but his voice never failed to make Kieran cringe. What he did notice while listening was the music — though too cinematic for his taste, it was damn good.

A couple of hours later, Kieran pulled up to the studio in his rental car. Everyone else in shorts, he stepped out of the vehicle in jeans and a black T-shirt, his hair fluttering in the warm, humid air. He locked the rental, took a breath, and walked up to the studio. He opened the door, and there he was.

"You made it," James said, extending his hand, and Kieran took it.

"I'm way early, sorry," Kieran said.

"It's alright. We just got back from lunch," James said before seeming to realize how insensitive it sounded. "Sorry, I know you just flew in. Are you hungry?"

"I'm fine, thanks," he answered.

"Did you get the material I emailed you?"

Kieran blinked in confusion. "No. When did you send it?"

"Last night. But no worries, it was just a couple of sound files and lyrics for the songs we want you to sing," he explained. Kieran flushed, frantically looking through his emails on his phone.

"Shit. I'm sorry. I didn't see it."

"Hey." James touched his shoulder. "No big deal. We're not do-or-die, Kieran. You're fine." Kieran tensed, and James dropped his hand.

"I'll go listen to these and come back when you were expecting me," he said.

"You can use the conference room. I promise we'll leave you alone."

Kieran shifted. "Okay," he said.

"Come on, back here." Kieran followed James to the small conference room. "If you need anything, let me know." Kieran nodded. "I'll come back in about an hour?"

"Sounds good," Kieran agreed. James turned, closing the door behind him. Once seated, Kieran rubbed his hands over his face. *Get a fucking grip.*

About an hour later, Kieran emerged from the conference room. He found James, Phil, and David in the front of the building. His stomach twisted anxiously. He cleared his throat, and they looked back at him.

"Hey. Ready?" James asked.

"I am," he answered.

"Kieran Jackson," James said, turning back to Phil and David. "This is Phil Archer and David Rowan." Kieran shook their hands.

"Nice to meet you," David said, pumping his hand. Kieran then turned to Phil, extending the same hand.

"Thanks, guys, for the opportunity," Kieran said. James then led them down to the recording suite.

Back in the conference room, James sat at the head of the table, Phil and David on his left, Kieran on the right.

"Initial thoughts?" James asked the two on his left.

"Impressed," David said. "Sorry, bud, but I don't really remember you. But that was damned good."

"Thanks."

"Phil?" James prompted.

"Also impressed," Phil said. "Although I do remember you. So I already knew what to expect." Phil turned to James. "What about you? He was your idea. What do you think?" James shot Phil a look Kieran pretended not to see.

"It was great. Honestly, the best we've auditioned so far," he said. Kieran observed the fading blush in his cheeks and wondered if he'd been wrong to think James was straight. "I'd like to listen a couple more times to what we recorded, but don't leave town."

Kieran fought the smile tugging at his lips. "I won't."

Kieran drove to his hotel in silence. Normally, he'd listen to the radio, or plug in his iPod and listen to music. But exhausted mentally and physically, he felt the beginnings of a headache. Part of it was the waning nervous tension from the audition, and part of it was that he hadn't eaten since before the flight in.

He checked into the hotel and found his room. He dropped his duffel bag on the floor and let himself fall face-first onto the bed. He wanted to sleep but knew if he fell asleep without eating, he'd wake up with a migraine. He dug out his cell phone and searched for vegan delivery options close to the hotel. Forty-five minutes later, he had two tofu-sushi rolls and had to force himself not to inhale both immediately. As he ate, his cell phone pinged.

Hey, jerk, you make it there okay?

Yes, Mom.

Can I call, or are you too busy becoming a rock star?

He rolled his eyes, calling her. "You know, you're a little late on the draw. My plane got here hours ago," he sassed.

"Forgive me for having to work like the lowly, talentless peasant I am," Adrienne shot back.

"Shut up."

"So, how'd it go?"

"Really well, actually. The consensus was they were impressed and that I shouldn't leave town."

"Are you singing or being held on suspicion of murder?"

"Their words, not mine." *James's words*, Kieran thought.

"How do you feel about it?"

He sighed. "I think it went well, but I'm not gonna lie, I'm still nervous."

"Don't pout. They said they were impressed. What did James think?"

Kieran bit his lip, remembering the blush, remembering what Phil had said. *"He was your idea."*

"He said I was great. And Phil said it was James's idea to have me audition. What do you make of that?"

"I'd say that's pretty damn awesome, Kieran. James was the standout of Eden. All joking aside, you've heard them—"

"Regrettably," Kieran interjected.

"Whatever. The point is, he's amazing, and to have him remember your voice and still like it two years later, that's something. Aw, I'm proud of you, little brother!"

He laughed. "I hate you."

"Hate you too," she returned.

* * *

The next day, James sat in the studio with Ed, their manager, listening to the recordings. Once they were finished, Ed leaned back in his chair, eyes wide, looking over at James.

"Holy shit."

"Right?"

"Where'd you pick this guy up from again?"

"His band opened for us on the last Eden tour," James answered.

"They broke up too?"

"Yep."

"That high note, man, he soars like a damn bird.

Where has he been all our lives?" *Tell me about it*, James thought. "What do we think?"

"David and Phil liked him."

"And you?"

"I think he's great. I'd like to offer him the spot," he said. "What do you think?"

"I think he's different enough from Theo to make the new sound stand out. What about personality? Is he a hothead like Theo?"

James steeled himself against the inevitable comparisons. "I don't think so. He's a smartass, from what I remember, although he was on his best behavior yesterday."

"Smartass we can handle," Ed said. "It's the over-the-top hothead shit I can't stand."

"Me neither," James agreed. There was so much more to it, so much he'd never told anyone besides Phil and Dr. Evans. Agreeing that Theo was just some run-of-the-mill jerk made him feel empty.

"Alright," Ed said, standing up. "I'm on board. We'll draw up something formal next week, but feel free to offer it to him whenever."

James smiled. "Thanks, Ed."

Kieran had just stepped out of the shower when his phone began to ring. He wrapped a towel around his waist as he grabbed his phone from the nightstand. *James.*

"Hello?"

"Hey. Interested in grabbing dinner?"

Kieran felt his heart pound. "Of course. Wh-where?"

"Meet me at the studio in an hour, and we'll decide then. Sound good?"

"Sounds great," he said.

"Alright, see you soon," James said.

"Bye." Kieran hung up, sitting on the edge of the bed, looking absently down at his cell phone. *I've got the job*, he thought, his hand coming to his mouth. *I've fucking got it.* After a moment of pure excitement, he snapped out of it and began dressing.

Kieran pulled into the parking lot, and James came outside, jogging up to his car. Kieran got out.

"I'm early again."

"I'm beginning to sense a habit," James said with a smile. "But I'm ready to eat. Let's take my car." Kieran followed him.

"Just us?"

"Yep. That okay?" Kieran nodded. *Maybe I don't have the job*, he thought as they climbed into James's SUV. "What're you hungry for?"

"Uh, actually, I'm glad you ask," Kieran said. "I'm vegan."

James snorted. "Of course you are."

"Yeah, yeah." Kieran laughed with him.

"It just so happens that my favorite pizza place has a vegan pizza," James said. "Does that work for you?"

"Sounds great." They rode most of the way in awkward silence, Kieran too afraid to ask about his fate.

"So," James began, sipping his diet cola. "I didn't bring you out for dinner because I'm a nice guy."

Kieran fidgeted with his straw wrapper. "I didn't think so," he said, feeling his stomach drop.

"I let our manager listen to your recordings."

Kieran met his eyes. "Oh yeah?"

"Yep."

"And?"

James smiled. "He liked it. A lot. He gave me the okay to offer you the job, if you'd like to be part of this band. So I'm offering you the part, if you want it."

"Damn it, James." Kieran laughed, sitting back in his chair. "The whole ride here I thought you were taking me out back to shoot me," he joked.

"I could tell," James admitted.

"If I'm being honest, I'm surprised you called me for this at all," Kieran said, and James looked away as if embarrassed. "I was such an asshole to you last time."

"I remember," James said. Kieran rubbed the back of his neck. "I figure I deserved it. We screwed you guys out of those last shows."

Kieran shrugged. "We wouldn't have been any more successful with three more shows anyway. I was being a bitter asshole."

"You *were* pretty pissed." James seemed to be teasing him. *Is he teasing?* Kieran wondered. "But anyway, I felt bad, so I came down and watched your set." Kieran studied him. "I was embarrassed, thought I could at least be respectful enough to watch the last show. You guys were good, really good. Phil thought so too." Kieran was taken aback by James's candor. "Which is why we called. Would you like the part?"

"I would."

Once in his car and headed back to the hotel, Kieran called Adrienne.

"What're you wearing?" she asked suggestively.

"You're so fucking weird." But he couldn't hold back his laughter.

"Wow, you actually laughed at one of my jokes. You

must be in a good— Wait, why are you calling me?" He could hear the excitement change the quality of her voice.

"I've got the job," he said. He then had to hold the phone away from his ear as she screamed in joy.

"That's so awesome! I'm so happy for you, Kieran," she finally calmed down enough to say.

"Thanks," he said. "Which means I probably won't be back until after the album is finished."

"Right, of course, Mr. Rock Star," she said. "But you still have to call and tell me everything."

"As long as you keep it to yourself," he conceded. He knew she'd be excited for him and with him, and at the moment, he needed it. Doubt and worry, only occasional echoes before, had begun to threaten in earnest.

"You're the only one I annoy with my guilty-pleasure band, so you're set there," she said. "Any idea what they're going to call the band?"

"No clue." He hadn't realized until she said it that he hadn't thought to ask. "But hey, I'm gonna get off here so I can get some sleep. I just wanted to let you know the plan."

"*The plan*," she teased. "You know, it's okay to say you called to tell me how excited you are that you got the part. I promise, I won't laugh at you."

"I am excited," he admitted. *And scared. And nervous. And completely out of my element.*

Eight

It'd been a few days since he'd accepted the lead vocals, and Kieran couldn't shake his excitement as he headed for the vocal ISO booth. He rolled his neck and shoulders, trying to release as much tension as he could before he warmed up his voice. James came out of the far ISO booth.

"Hey, didn't hear you come in," James said.

"As the new guy, I'm trying not to be overly obnoxious. Not really sure when my probationary period is up," Kieran quipped.

James snorted. "I'm heading out. Have a good one."

"You too."

Kieran looked into James's booth and saw the guitars. Beautiful, well loved, and well cared for. *Don't*, he thought as he entered the booth. *Don't touch his stuff. You have no idea how he feels about that.* But the pure magnetism was too much. He touched the headstock of one, completely black. Though he taught guitar lessons back home, he hadn't played a guitar for pleasure or for making music since Lost and Found broke up. He didn't even keep his own in his apartment anymore, he'd been so disenchanted. Before he knew what he was doing, he picked it up and sat down, holding it in his lap.

"Aren't you the sexiest thing I've seen in ages?" Although, thinking of the man the guitar belonged to, he wasn't sure that was true. He shifted, sliding his fingers over the strings, feeling the fretboard beneath. He plucked a chord and jumped, realizing it was still on and plugged into an amplifier. "Fuck," he swore, heart pounding.

James got all the way home before realizing he'd left his cell phone at the studio. He could almost let it go for the night, but Kieran was there working on his vocals. The possibility of him picking up James's phone and going through it made him uneasy. He couldn't remember if he had the Lost and Found album on it, not to mention any conversations between himself and Phil during which Kieran might've come up. Begrudgingly, he turned back for the studio.

He pulled up, then jogged up to the door. As he let himself in, he heard the music. Not the prerecorded stuff, not Kieran warming up or singing. He heard beautiful, bluesy guitar music. He paused in the hallway, frowning. At first, he thought Kieran was playing a CD. Maybe he'd ordered in his dinner and was listening to music while he ate. But something nagged at him as he approached the recording suite, observing the open door to the ISO booth he'd used. Peering around the doorframe, he saw Kieran just before Kieran saw him.

"I'm sorry," Kieran started, hurriedly putting the guitar — *his* guitar — back as he'd found it. "I shouldn't have. I just... It was — "

"You played all that?"

"What?"

"Just now, when I was walking in? That was you?"

"It was."

James blinked. "Kieran, that was amazing. I had no

idea you could play like that."

Kieran's eyes narrowed. "You're not pissed at me for touching your stuff?"

James shook his head. "If I'd come back and you were destroying my stuff, yeah, then I'd be upset." He reflected again on what he'd just heard. "Why didn't you tell me you could play like that?"

"I guess I thought you knew. I had a guitar in my arms the day you and Phil watched me."

He did, James thought. *And you were so drunk and out of it, you almost don't remember.* James felt the flush of embarrassment creep up the sides of his face.

"Hey, it's alright. I probably wouldn't have remembered me either, to be honest."

James met his eyes. Kieran had been such an ass that day, and he was still somewhat bristly. But the warmth in his gaze and the kindness in his voice just then disarmed James.

"I remember," James said. "I just don't remember everything, I guess."

"No big deal," Kieran said. "I'm sorry I touched your stuff. Won't happen again." He moved to exit the booth, but James placed a hand on his shoulder, stopping him.

"Play any you'd like. I don't mind."

Their eyes locked, and it almost happened. Kieran's gaze dropped to James's mouth, and he very nearly leaned in to kiss him. James saw the heat in his eyes and snatched his hand away. He spotted his cell phone and grabbed it, shoving it into his back pocket.

"James—"

"I'm late. See you tomorrow," James said, slipping away.

James climbed into his SUV and pulled away as quickly as he could because he really was late to meet Phil for dinner. *Oh my God. Oh. My. God.* Feeling the heat in his cheeks, he looked at himself in the rearview mirror, finding himself flushed. *Great.*

He almost kissed me, James thought as he drove. Part of him felt giddy at the thought that Kieran was attracted to him. It'd been a long time since he'd felt that from someone. *Maybe never...* He still struggled with whether or not Theo had been attracted to him, in spite of what Dr. Evans said.

"I was just available and willing," James had told her.

"With all the influence and power he had as your band's front man, you really believe he couldn't have found other available and willing partners?"

James shrugged. "He also knew I wouldn't say anything," he countered. "Because I didn't want to jeopardize Eden either."

He'd hated the brief hesitation in her face that day. Because if it was true, that meant the only man he'd ever been with hadn't been attracted to him at all. And just like that, the excited flush in his face gave way to the sickly pallor that plagued him during the early days of his recovery.

"Hey, I was starting to think you'd stood me up," Phil joked. "You alright?"

"Yeah, fine," James said a little too quickly, and Phil narrowed his eyes. "I'm fine, Phil."

"Alright." Phil gave in, putting his hands up. "So what took you so long?"

"I left my phone at the studio," James said, picking up the sweating glass of diet cola and taking a drink.

"Kieran already there?" Phil asked.

"Don't," James said.

"It was just a question," Phil said irritably.

James looked at him hard. "Just don't."

"Look, I may not be quite warmed up to him yet, but that doesn't mean you can't be."

"I don't really want to talk about this right now."

"Did something happen?" Phil's tone grew concerned, and James's eyes darkened.

"Do you think that's funny?"

"You need to calm down. You know I would never joke about that."

James looked away. "I'm sorry. I'm sorry, I just..." James hesitated. "I think he almost kissed me, and it caught me off guard."

Phil's eyes went wide with surprise. "Just now?"

James nodded. "I went back to the studio to get my phone, and I caught him playing one of my guitars. He thought I would be upset, but Phil, he was really good."

"Seems like I remember him being pretty good," Phil said.

Well, that makes one of us.

"So you caught him playing and he almost kissed you?"

"No. He probably thought I was going to lay into him for touching my stuff. He went to pass by me, and I stopped him and told him it was fine, I didn't mind him playing them. And Phil, for a minute, I really thought..." He trailed off.

"Is that something you think you'd want?"

"I don't know if I'm ready —"

"That's not what I asked."

"You know I'm attracted to him," he muttered.

"That's not quite what I asked either," Phil persisted.
James sighed. "I don't know. Maybe."
Phil tried to contain his smile. "Does that mean you'll finally admit that heart isn't quite dead?"
James rolled his eyes. "No. It just means my dick isn't quite dead." Phil laughed with him, even though he knew better.

* * *

Over the next few weeks, the album—already largely written before Kieran was hired—was completed. Kieran and James managed to keep their distance, but there were still moments when they couldn't avoid the increasing tension between them.

Now the band sat around the conference table with Ed.

"Alright, guys, I think I can say confidently that the album is finished." Kieran watched Phil, David, and James smile, clapping each other on the back with sighs of relief. When James turned to him, Kieran realized how hard it'd become to hold his gaze.

"Good job, man," James said with a smile. "I listened to the whole thing, and you sound amazing."

"Thanks," he managed in the face of such praise. *And handsomeness.*

"So, what exactly are we calling this band?" David asked.

James looked over at Ed.

"James and I had an idea," Ed said.

"And?" Phil prompted.

"What do we think of True North?" James asked, and Phil frowned, seeming to think it over.

"Why True North?" David asked.

"Because after paradise was lost, after everything was lost, we all had to find our way back to our True North."

Kieran was taken aback by the role his old band played in naming this band.

"Is that too cheesy?" James asked.

"I like it," David said first. "I really do."

"Me too, actually," Phil affirmed. "Rolls off the tongue."

"What do you think?" James asked Kieran.

Kieran looked around at them. "I get a say?"

"You're the singer, weirdo," Phil said. "Of course you get a say."

Kieran smirked. "I like it too," he said, feeling his place in the band gain permanence.

"Then I guess you're True North," Ed said. "We're going to call the album that too, since we don't know how fans are going to react to the new lineup and sound."

Kieran downed another shot with Phil, wincing as the tequila warmed his throat and chest.

"You know, for a little thing, you can drink," Phil teased.

"Yeah, yeah, I'm the runt, very funny," Kieran said. "You want to pick on me for being the oldest too?"

"How old are you?"

"Thirty-three."

"Shut up!" Phil feigned shock. "So what now? You gonna hang around here for a while, or are you headed back home?"

Kieran shrugged. "I kinda think I should stick around for a little while. See how the album does, in case you guys need me or something."

He looked over at James, who was seated alone at a table, drinking diet cola as his bandmates and people involved with the album production celebrated its release.

"He doesn't drink anymore?"

"Nope."

"Why?"

Even in his intoxicated state, Kieran could sense Phil's tension at his question. "You know what, none of my business. Sorry, I get chatty when I'm drunk."

"It's kind of nice. You're a ball of anxiety normally," Phil remarked with a chuckle.

"You try walking into a successful band as the new guy," he said. "See how relaxed you are." He looked back at James again.

"You should go talk to him," Phil said. "I bet he'd get a kick out of drunk-Kieran."

Kieran turned back to his beer. "I don't want to breathe booze all over him if he's sober."

"Suit yourself."

Kieran eyed him suspiciously. "If I didn't know any better—"

"You know, you're not quite as dumb as you look."

Kieran laughed. "Fuck you, Phil."

"Trust me," Phil said, standing up. "Just go."

He watched Phil walk over to the pool tables; then Kieran tipped his beer up, downing the rest of it so he wouldn't have to take it with him.

"Hey." Kieran plopped down in the chair across from James.

"Hey," James said.

"Phil thought you'd find drunk-me funny," Kieran said.

James's eyebrows rose, and he looked over his shoulder at Phil, who tipped his beer in their direction. *Jerk*, James thought.

"I told him it was rude, since you're not drinking."

"I don't mind," James said, turning back to him. "How drunk are you?"

"I probably shouldn't drive," he answered, clearly meaning it as a joke.

James felt himself tense. "I'll take you home," he said, then backtracked. "Back to your hotel." He felt himself flush. "You know what I mean."

James saw the shift, saw him lean forward, his shoulders turning slightly inward. Kieran pushed his hair behind his ear on one side. *What I wouldn't give...* James thought. *The first thing I'd do is find out if his hair's as soft as it looks.*

"Thanks," Kieran said, bringing him out of his thoughts. "Sorry. I guess drunk-Kieran lost his groove."

"That makes two of us," James remarked with a smirk.

"S-sorry." Kieran stumbled, and James steadied him, laughing with him. He'd expected drunk-Kieran to get on his nerves, but he didn't. James sensed Kieran held back when sober. But intoxicated, inhibitions lowered, he was more genuine.

"You know, I don't know about funny, but drunk-Kieran is pretty fun," James said. "And he certainly has a harder time remaining upright."

"I was rather interested to see what drunk-Jamie was like."

The use of the shortened name caught James off guard. "He was an idiot. You wouldn't have liked him. Come to think of it, you didn't."

"Oh fuck, don't remind me," Kieran said with regret. "I was such a prick."

"I understood why."

"I don't get that. Theo seemed like a spoiled brat, but you, I gave you every reason to hate me, and you still called."

"What can I say? I'm a nice guy."

"Too nice. You'd almost never know you were in a successful band."

"Careful there, Kieran, someone might think you're not quite the too-cool hipster you pretend to be, talking about Eden like that."

Kieran leaned in, placing a playful finger over his own lips. "Shh, don't tell anyone. I can only be pretentious when I'm sober," he joked.

James chuckled, overwhelmed by the man's drunken charm.

"Here you are," James said, steering Kieran to his hotel room door. Kieran began patting his pockets. Having observed him put the key card in the pocket of his hoodie, James retrieved it for him and held it up.

"I knew it was there," Kieran said with a smirk. But when James met his eyes, the teasing humor melted away. Suddenly, Kieran leaned in and pressed his lips to James's. James gasped, eyes wide, but before he could fully react, Kieran pulled away. "Shit, I'm sorry. I'm... I didn't mean to," he stammered, turning red. He looked up at James, then quickly turned away, letting himself into his hotel room.

James lay in bed, staring at the ceiling, replaying the evening over and over in his mind: Kieran hanging on to him as they walked, stumbling and giggling. Kieran fumbling for his key card. James reaching into his pocket to retrieve it. Their eyes locking, as they had many times over the past few weeks. Only this time, Kieran kissed him. Nothing passionate or even very romantic, but it'd taken James's breath away. *Maybe I'm not completely broken.*

Nine

Kieran was the last to arrive at the studio the following morning for the meeting with Ed. He was hungover — sunglasses on, paler-than-usual skin. Over their respective coffees, the band joked about the previous night's shenanigans.

"Hey, kid. Rough night? You look a little green," Phil said, sitting down next to James, across from Kieran.

"Fuck you, man. I'm older than all of you," Kieran said.

"And still, he doesn't know better," Phil teased, then turned to James. "Do you ever sleep?"

James shrugged. "Not really."

Kieran excused himself to the restroom. The hangover wasn't helping his nerves. The dread of knowing what he'd done, of knowing it was only a matter of time before he was kicked out of the band, made him even more nauseous.

Once in the bathroom, Kieran pulled off his sunglasses, exposing tired, red-rimmed eyes. Not only had he thrown up a couple of times during the night, he'd also cried a few frustrated tears. *Fucking idiot. The only chance you have at getting back in, and you blow it.* He might've been drunk, but the look of pure horror on James's face after he kissed him was seared into his memory. *Of course he was horrified*, he berated himself. *He's the guitarist for goddamned Eden, and you came on to him.* Just as he began to descend into an anxiety attack, he heard a knock at the door. *Fuck.* He felt the adrenaline surge into his nervous system. And then an idea hit him. *If I play it just right —*

"It's me. Can I come in?" James called.

Kieran took a deep breath. "Door's open," he answered. James came inside, pulling the door closed behind him. He turned to Kieran, who was standing at the sink, washing his hands.

"You looked a little sick. Thought I'd better check on you," James said.

"Yeah, thanks for taking me back to my hotel last night," Kieran said, turning off the sink, letting his hands drip for a moment. James was watching him in the mirror.

"Of course," James said.

Kieran pulled some paper towels from the dispenser, drying his hands as he turned to James. "I hope I didn't say or do anything offensive." He looked at James's eyes as he said it, forcing himself to remain calm and aloof. James blinked, and for a moment, Kieran would've sworn he saw disappointment cross his features.

"You didn't," James said. After an awkward pause, James must've realized he was still holding the water and aspirin he'd brought for Kieran. "These are for you." He shrugged, dropping the tablets into Kieran's palm and handing him the bottle of water.

"Thanks," he said as James turned for the door and left. Kieran waited for it to close behind him before he leaned against the wall, exhaling a breath he hadn't realized he was holding.

James stalked down the hallway and pushed through the back door. Everything felt too close in the studio — the walls, the sounds, everything. *He doesn't remember.* It stung like hell. *You actually thought he wanted you? No one wants you. And even if he did, do you think he'd still want you after he finds out about your past?* Usually, he could combat the negative self-talk before it took hold, but Kieran's lack of memory gave it credence for the first time in a long time.

"Gentlemen, I hear we had a pretty good time last night after I left?"

"We know this one did," David said, clapping Kieran on the shoulder.

"Good. Anyway, good news. We have a small festival tour in the works. Are we up for that?"

"Absolutely," Phil said, then turned to James.

"Are we ready for that sort of thing?" James saw the look on Phil's face at his lack of enthusiasm. He didn't dare look over at Kieran.

"All we have to do is rehearse," David chimed in. "Make sure Kieran's ready."

"You seem a little doubtful," Ed said.

"No, not doubtful. We just haven't done this in a while," James said, shrugging. "I guess I'm a little nervous."

"David's right," Ed said. "We need to rehearse, re-feel each other out."

James stifled a cringe at Ed's choice of words and said, "Right, you're right. I'm in." He chanced a look at Kieran then, who'd peered up at him at the same time. James forced a smile before looking away.

After the meeting, Phil caught up with James in the parking lot.

"Alright, spill," Phil said.

James looked at him. "It's nothing."

"Brother, it's all over your face. What happened?"

James shrugged. "When I took Kieran back to his hotel, I...we..." He hesitated. "He kissed me."

"Ho-ly shit." Phil frowned. "I don't get it. I figured that'd make you happy."

James looked away. "He was drunk. He doesn't remember."

"He doesn't know he kissed you?"

"He apologized for anything inappropriate he may've said or done. And the way he said it..." James trailed off, shaking his head.

"Well, that doesn't mean he isn't interested. It just means—"

"No," James interrupted. "It just means I should leave it alone."

"Oh, come on, you don't believe in all that fate crap," Phil said. "Look, *I've* seen the way he looks at you."

"It doesn't matter. *I* shouldn't be getting involved." He rubbed a hand over his face. "What am I doing?"

"Breathing again," Phil said. "Maybe trying to live your life again."

"I'm too fucked up for this—"

"Stop it. I don't want to hear that anymore. You've been through some shit, but that shouldn't stop you from living. You've had a thing for him since you first saw him. I remember." James looked doubtful. "Personally, I don't see it in his skinny ass and stringy hair, but apparently you do."

James smiled a little. "You're also straight."

"There is that." Phil smirked. "Don't write him off just yet. He's the new guy. Maybe he thought jumping in bed with the boss was a bad move."

James snorted. "I am not the boss."

"Well, you're not *my* boss."

* * *

As the old Eden tour bus pulled onto the road, Kieran could hardly believe he was actually on it. Before, it'd been old, rusted minivans and trailers jammed with their instruments and equipment. Not so for True North.

Apart from the initial cooling between them, James hadn't completely shut down on him. He could see in James's eyes that he remembered the kiss. What he couldn't see was whether or not he'd liked it. And after pretending he didn't remember, Kieran couldn't ask.

He plopped down across from James at the small table to the right of the aisle.

"What're you reading?" Kieran tilted his head, trying to read the cover of the thick book in James's hands.

"*The Talisman*," James said.

"Any good?"

James nodded, looking up at him. "I've read it and the sequel a few times." Kieran looked at the cracked spine, noting the worn cover and pages, and smiled. "What?" James asked.

"Didn't figure you for a bookworm."

James shrugged. "Gotta do something to pass the time. These long rides used to kill me."

"Yeah, I get carsick if I'm not careful," Kieran said, and James eyed him warily. "Don't worry, I took something. I'm not going to throw up on your book."

James chuckled. "You'll get used to it."

Their first show went off well. Better than well. They'd all been nervous about performing live with Kieran, but he'd fit so well, it'd felt nearly effortless.

"How'd I do?" Kieran asked, sitting down across the bus aisle from James and Phil.

Phil looked over at James, feigning doubt. "I don't know. Those high notes, I'm not sure they were quite high enough," Phil teased, and James rolled his eyes.

"You did great," James said, and Kieran smiled.

"And you're no fun," Phil said to James. "You did fine. I know I haven't been that comfortable onstage in years."

"Me neither," James admitted.

Registering the seriousness in James's voice, Kieran looked up at him. But James's gaze was inward, leaving Kieran to wonder.

"Man, it feels good to be back at it!" David bounded onto the bus last.

"Where did you manage to get drunk between the stage and here?"

"Shit, there are only about a dozen roving vendors and half a dozen stands selling booze," David said. "Come on, guys, let's celebrate!"

Kieran looked to James, but James didn't look disappointed or upset.

Phil rose. "You mind?" he asked James.

"Go for it. Have a few for me," James said, then looked over at Kieran. "You too. Go on. I'm going to go find something to eat." Kieran agreed, though it didn't seem fair. James had offered him this job and had been nothing but kind. And now he had to stand by while his bandmates celebrated without him.

Kieran headed back for the bus before the others. Phil and David gave him a hard time, but he felt guilty for leaving James alone while they were out partying. He ascended the steps—this time only slightly buzzed—passed through the front lounge and the bunk area, and came to the door to the back lounge. Finding it ajar, he pushed on it just as James was pulling. Kieran stumbled forward, and James caught him, bracing Kieran's shoulders with both hands.

"Easy," James said as Kieran's hands landed against his chest. He looked up at James, near laughter, when their eyes met. Kieran leaned in, but James turned his head to the side. "Kieran, you've been drinking again."

Kieran drew in a sharp breath, his arms tense under James's hands. "I know," he said. "Apparently, it's the only time I have the balls to make a move."

James blinked. "You remember?"

Kieran flushed. "Remember being a drunk ass and kissing tequila and beer all over you? Yeah, unfortunately I do." James recoiled. "No, not unfortunately like unfortunately that I kissed you. Just, unfortunately, I kissed you, a sober person, while I was drunk and reeking of alcohol and—" He stopped, running his hands through his long hair. "And I'm talking too much. This is why I don't usually drink."

"Hey, look at me," James said, and Kieran met his gaze. "How much have you had?"

"A shot of tequila and a beer."

"You're not drunk."

"Not-not quite, I guess," Kieran said. "Although right about now, I wish I were—"

James pulled Kieran to him, closing the space between their bodies. "Hey, Kieran? Just shut up for a second."

And just as Kieran realized he was going to, James leaned down and pressed his mouth against his. James kissed him tentatively, one hand slipping into the hair at Kieran's nape. Kieran felt the tension drain from his body, replaced with desire, need even. He felt James's other hand rest at his side near the waistband of his jeans, sliding his thumb under the hem of his T-shirt, stroking bare skin. Kieran had to stifle a groan. *Goddamn, am I that desperate?* But it'd been so long since he'd been touched or kissed, and with so much tenderness and passion, he couldn't help but react, tensing at the touch, and James broke their kiss.

Kieran looked up at him, all flushed and wanting, and reached for him. "Kiss me. Kiss me, please," he breathed, his hands on James's shirt, pulling him near again. James let himself be pulled back in and crushed his lips over Kieran's once more. When the kiss broke, he lingered close, he and Kieran looking at each other in warm, dazed shock. James began to pull away.

"Kieran—"

"Look, I'm sorry. I'm sorry. I've probably way overstepped," he said.

"You didn't," James said. "But we can't do this." He paused, then corrected himself. "*I* can't do this."

"I respect that," Kieran said. "But to be fair, you kissed me."

James looked like a man who was starving, too afraid to eat for fear of getting sick. "I know," he said. "I just... I'm not good at this." At that, Kieran almost filed him under "nervous straight guy who's experimenting." But then James added, "The last time I did this, I got hurt pretty badly."

Kieran's eyes snapped to his. "The last time? You've done this before? With a guy?"

James frowned, confused. "Yeah, with a guy," he said. "I'm gay. Why would I kiss you if I wasn't into guys?"

Kieran blinked, unable to keep the shock out of his face. "You'd be surprised by how many pretty-much-straight guys come on to me," he said. "And anyway, you're the guitarist for Eden. I just assumed..." He trailed off.

"I just don't think I would be able to give you what you want."

"James, I'm not going to pressure you into anything. The last thing I want is to make you uncomfortable. I'm truly sorry about before. I shouldn't have acted like I didn't remember kissing you." A lock of Kieran's hair fell against his cheek as he looked away in shame. When James reached up and pushed it back behind his ear, Kieran's eyes fluttered. But just as he leaned into James's hand, James pulled away.

"Trust me, you don't want to get involved with this mess," he said.

"Who said anything about getting involved?"

"That's something I really can't do," James said.

Kieran frowned, then rolled his eyes in understanding. "No, that's not what I meant. I'd like to get to know you. Clearly, there's more to you than I realized."

"I'm the least interesting person I know," James said.

"That may be because you're actually the most interesting person in your life."

"That makes no sense." James laughed, and Kieran saw his way in.

"It does, actually. If you're the most interesting person in your circle, then obviously, you wouldn't know it. Because you're used to you," he explained.

James shook his head. "What is it about me? *You* could have anyone you wanted."

"Maybe I like a challenge," Kieran teased, and James gave him an incredulous look. "Alright, you got me, you're an excellent kisser. It's my weakness."

"Now you're just making fun of me," James said.

"That actually may be the most honest thing I've ever admitted."

"And you got that off one kiss?" James countered.

"It was two kisses, actually," Kieran retorted matter-of-factly. "Both exceptional."

"They were?"

"Mm-hm. Which is why I refuse to accept this moody, I'm-too-damaged bit." James didn't back away as Kieran came to him. He lifted his hands to James's shoulders, holding his gaze. "And look, maybe you've been hurt. But that doesn't mean you should close yourself off forever. If you're not interested in me, I accept that. But I think you are."

"I have to go slow. Really slow. It's going to get old real fast."

Kieran shrugged, then joked, "Sexually frustrated is like my default setting." He watched the smile warm James's green eyes, and felt his knees go weak. *He's a knockout, and he doesn't even know it.*

"I'm serious."

"I know," Kieran said. "I can do slow. As long as you'll kiss me sometimes. Kissing's okay, right?" That made James laugh, and Kieran felt something in him shift even more than it already had.

Ten

"What's with the goofy grin?" Phil asked.

"Nothing," James said, picking up a guitar to test out.

"Yeah fuckin' right. I haven't seen you look like that since —"

James felt the smile fade. "Thanks for reminding me," he said with an edge to his voice.

"Sorry, man, I'm sorry. I didn't mean anything by that."

James shrugged. "It's fine."

"So what's making you the blushing bride?"

"'M not blushing," he said, fighting his smile again.

"I swear to God, James, if you don't tell me —"

He dragged Phil to the side. "Jesus, shut up. I kissed Kieran."

"Oh yeah? Think he'll try to remember this time?"

James saw the doubtful expression on his face. "Funny."

"I'm not trying to be funny," Phil said, and James turned to walk away.

"Forget it."

"Wait." Phil caught him. "I'm sorry, okay? I'm sorry. I just… I thought it was really shitty when he came on to you and then tried to pretend like it didn't happen."

"He did remember. He just got scared."

Phil's eyes widened. "So he lied?"

"He was scared. You have no idea what it's like to come on to a guy and then think you misjudged the situation."

Phil sighed. "I guess that's fair." He peered up at James. "Look, I'm sorry for being skeptical. But do you have any idea how close we came to losing you last time?"

"If you're going to throw that in my face every time I'm interested in someone—"

"What? You won't be friends with me? You'll kick me out of the band?" Phil huffed. "I just don't want you to fall in love with another guy who treats you like shit."

"Oh my God, I'm not falling in love!"

Phil rolled his eyes. "Yeah, but you will."

"I barely know him."

"Have you looked at him?"

James couldn't help his smile. "Thought his skinny little ass and stringy hair weren't your thing."

"Yeah, but they're yours," Phil countered.

"Trying to imply I have a type?"

"No, that would imply Kieran looks like a dumbass. Even I can see Kieran's prettier than that. Just be careful, okay? Please?"

James nodded.

James flinched when he heard the door open behind him.

"Just me," Kieran said, coming in and shutting the door.

"Am I being too loud?"

"Nope," Kieran said. "But I could hear you warming up. Er, trying to warm up."

James frowned. "Trying to warm up?"

"Relax. I'm not trying to boss you around," Kieran said. "But I can hear vocal strain from a mile away."

James tried to stifle the smile forming on his face. "That bad?"

"Not bad, but let me show you a couple things, okay? You don't have to use them if you don't want to, but let me show you."

"Alright, singer extraordinaire, show me your ways."

Kieran approached him. "Stand up straight." James hadn't realized he was slouching. "Good, but relax your shoulders." James tried but inadvertently fell back into a slouch. "No, okay, here." Kieran stepped around behind him. James felt himself tense and hoped Kieran hadn't noticed. He felt Kieran put his hands on his shoulders. "Stand up straight." James felt Kieran's breath on the back of his neck. "Good. Now, I want you to tense your shoulders and neck as much as you can."

"Are you making fun of me?"

"Nope. I'm serious," Kieran said, and James did as Kieran instructed and tensed his upper body. "Hold it for a second," he continued. "Now release." And to James's surprise, his body felt more relaxed.

"Huh, that's interesting."

"Yep," Kieran said, stepping closer. "Now take a few deep breaths." James started to take one. "Not from your chest."

"And where exactly am I supposed to breathe from?"

Kieran snickered at the mild irritation in his tone. "When you sing, you want to breathe from your belly," Kieran said. He reached around James's waist, placing his hand over James's stomach. "Take a deep breath, but don't move your chest. Breathe from your stomach."

James took a deep breath and found that not only did it feel more natural to breathe that way, but he could get a deeper breath. "Good," Kieran murmured, and James sensed how close Kieran was, how his voice had changed.

Kieran lingered behind him, wrapped around him, his instructions having ceased. It took James a moment to realize that the close proximity wasn't making him uncomfortable, didn't make his skin crawl. He wanted to place his hands over Kieran's, wanted to lean back into him. Just as he was thinking of all the things he wanted, he felt Kieran lean in and nuzzled the back of his neck. His breath hitched as Kieran continued to press soft, delicate kisses against his nape.

"Kieran," he whispered, his hands coming to Kieran's, pressing against them.

"'S that feel good?" Kieran's lips brushed against James's ear as he spoke. James nodded, biting his lip as Kieran nipped at the curve of his ear. James whirled and backed Kieran up against the wall behind him, crushing his lips against his.

"You," a kiss, "sneaky," another kiss, "bastard."

Kieran smiled against James's lips. "Hey, those were all good tips," Kieran said. "Just so we're clear."

"Noted," James said, leaning his forehead against Kieran's. "Did you lock the door behind you?"

"Wha—" James stalked away, bolting the door before coming back to him. "Jamie, we don't have to—" James reached down, lifting Kieran against him, his hands gripping under his thighs. Kieran wrapped his arms around James's neck, his legs locking over his hips. James carried him over to the worn-out sofa and plopped down, careful not to jar him too much. Kieran, breathless, hopefully from the excitement of being kissed senseless, gasped when James reached for his belt.

"I want to touch you," James said. Kieran nodded, and James undid his pants. When he wrapped his hand around Kieran's erection and freed it, Kieran tried to stifle a groan. James stroked him, enjoying every hitching breath and grateful noise he made. Kieran pushed James's shirt up. Gentle hands with calloused fingers ran along his bare torso. James raised his arms, and Kieran removed the shirt.

"You're so fucking sexy," Kieran breathed, and James leaned forward, kissing Kieran again.

"I want your hands on me," James said. He took one of Kieran's hands and pressed it against the front of his jeans. Kieran undid James's jeans and reached inside, freeing his aroused member. James closed his eyes, forcing himself to breathe. *This is okay. Kieran's okay.*

"Goddamn, Jamie." James opened his eyes to see Kieran gaping down at him. James looked down at his own cock, then back up at him.

"What?"

"What? What do you mean, what? That thing is impressive, that's what." James laughed, trying to hide his sigh of relief. Kieran took him in his hand and began stroking him. He bit his lip as James began matching his movements. Kieran leaned in, kissed James's throat. James gasped against Kieran's ear, his warm breath sending goose bumps down Kieran's arms, across his chest. He wanted Kieran, wanted to do things with him that he hadn't desired in a long time. *Not since...* Suddenly, James wasn't in the dingy little dressing room anymore, nor were the hands touching him Kieran's...

James dozed on the bed in a hotel room, many months and

many miles from the final one. He floated in and out of sleep, his rest unaffected by alcoholism and stress. The only thing stealing his sleep at the moment was Theo.

James had known he was gay for most of his life, but hadn't had much romantic attention due to his shy, reserved nature. So at twenty-five, when Theo flirted with him, teased him, James found himself drawn in.

He heard the snick of a key card, then the mechanical turn of the door handle, and smiled to himself. Theo stopped, leaning against the wall for a moment, fidgeting with the card before looking over at James.

"You awake?"

James nodded, rising up on one elbow. Theo came to the bed. He balanced one knee on the mattress, looking down at James, and James flushed under his gaze.

"Come here," James said, working to keep the tremor out of his voice. He reached for Theo's hand, and Theo let him. He settled on the bed beside James so they faced each other, then slid closer.

"You ever been with a guy before?" Theo asked.

"No." Theo smiled, and James felt some of his nervousness fall away. "Have you?"

"Here and there a little. Nothing serious," Theo admitted.

Looking back, James had come to realize that this was probably the most honest – and most vulnerable – Theo had let himself be with James. Theo reached for James, pulling him close, nuzzling his cheeks, his jaw, not quite kissing. But it didn't matter. James loved it. He reached for Theo, shaky hands smoothing up and down his back. He felt Theo's hands at the front of his pants, undoing them, reaching inside, and for the first time, another man's hand touched his bare flesh. James looked at him for a beat before Theo seized his mouth, pressing a hard, bruising kiss against his lips. James reached for the front

of Theo's jeans, wanting to reciprocate.
    "James," Theo murmured…

"James?" James blinked, and brown eyes were replaced with blue, along with a different face, time, and setting. "Are you okay?"

"I'm sorry," James said. He realized Kieran wasn't touching him anymore, realized that he wasn't touching Kieran either. He looked down and saw he'd gone flaccid. Mortified, he tucked himself back into his jeans. Kieran did the same without complaint or even annoyance, shifting over to sit beside him. James wasn't sure what he would've preferred — irritation, or the look of tentative concern Kieran wore.

"You left me there for a minute," Kieran said. "Where'd you go?"

"Did I say anything?"

"No, you just zoned out."

James couldn't look at him. "I didn't mean to scare you."

"You didn't scare me," Kieran said softly.

"Told you I'm a mess."

Kieran put an arm around him, leaning his chin on James's shoulder. "Slower," Kieran said. "We just have to go slower, I think." James looked over at him. "What on earth have you been through?"

James shook his head. "I can't. 'M not ready."

"Okay," he said. "But when you are, I'm here."

* * *

"James, can you hear me?"

"I can." After the stunted encounter with Kieran,

James emailed Dr. Evans to see if she could fit him in for a quick phone session. Using Phil's hotel room for privacy, James sat on the floor next to the door. He hated hotel rooms enough, but he knew he wouldn't be able to have this conversation near the bed and focus.

"Your email sounded urgent. What happened yesterday?"

James took a deep breath. "The singer we hired for the new band, Kieran. I'm... I'm really attracted to him," he began. "And he's into me too."

"That sounds like good news," she said, excitement coloring her tone.

"Yeah, well, I...I don't know yet. Yesterday we, uh, we were kissing and, you know, things heated up," he explained. "We, um, we were touching each other" —he felt his face heat—"and I think I had some kind of attack or flashback or something."

"I see. I know this is difficult, but can you explain a little more? About the attack?"

"Well, um, Kieran and I, we were touching each other, and I just, all of a sudden, all I could think about was Theo. Like, before the rape, before the bad stuff. I got caught in this old memory and couldn't snap out of it."

"I understand. Was it a specific memory?"

"It was," James said, fighting the urge to let it replay in his mind.

"It likely was a flashback. Not a traumatic memory?"

"It's traumatic when you put it in context, but by itself, no, I guess not."

"Are you comfortable telling me about the memory?"

James sighed. "It was basically what Kieran and I were doing, just a different setting. And instead of Kieran, it was Theo."

"Ah, I see. Something triggered it, then. Can you think of what may have triggered it?"

"I don't know. I hope him touching me isn't enough to make that happen. Because if so, I'm screwed."

"I promise, you're not screwed. You're normal. This is normal for someone who's been through what you have, especially at the hands of someone they once trusted and cared for." James recoiled at that. "What were you doing or thinking right before you slipped into the flashback?"

"Like I said, we were touching each other. And I was thinking about how long it's been since I felt that way. Like I wanted to be touched."

"I see," she said. "Reflecting can be a powerful tool. And you're good at it. But when you go into moments of sexual vulnerability like that, it's best to try and stay in the moment."

"It's hard," he admitted. "It's so hard not to compare. I want this to be different. I don't want to fall back into something like that."

"I can already tell you, that's highly unlikely. How did Kieran react to your flashback?"

"He was completely fine," he answered. "He didn't get upset or annoyed at all."

"See, that already tells me he's better for you than Theo ever was, even at his best. But flashbacks are going to happen. Anxiety attacks, panic attacks, they're part of life for you, and you shouldn't be ashamed of them. I know it's difficult when your potential partner isn't aware of your triggers."

"Should I even get involved with someone if they don't know?"

"That's a difficult question to answer. Ideally, no. But I know you don't feel ready to share that part of your past yet, and I can't blame you. In its entirety, it's very heavy. However, I do think it's good for you to step into dating and slowly reclaim your sexuality. My only advice is to advance slowly. And as you're ready, with Kieran, with any partner you choose, be honest."

James sighed. "I don't know how I'll ever be ready," he admitted.

"If I could show you how far you've come, you wouldn't be so unsure," she said. "Keep those things in mind, and try to stay in the moment."

"Alright. Thank you, Dr. Evans."

"Of course, James. Good luck."

* * *

Unable to find James, Kieran approached Phil.

"Hey. Can I talk to you for a second?"

Phil eyed him. "Sure. What's up?"

"I, uh, I know you and James are close, so I have to think you know what's going on between us."

Phil frowned, his eyes questioning. Kieran felt his eyes widen just as Phil broke into a laugh. "You're too easy."

Kieran put his hand over his chest, relief flooding his senses. "Don't fucking do that," he said, laughing.

"Going awful far out on a limb, assuming he'd told me," Phil said.

"Well, I'm about to go out even further," Kieran said. "I know you're probably just going to tell me to fuck off, but" —he paused, took a breath— "did something happen to him?"

Phil narrowed his eyes. "You're right. You can fuck off with that question."

"Look, I... I'm beginning to really care for him, and I can tell he's been through something."

Phil frowned. "Why are you asking me this?"

Suddenly, Kieran felt awful, like he shouldn't have said anything at all. "Forget it. Please don't say anything to him. I just, I thought..." Kieran sighed. "I don't know what I thought. I just don't want to misstep and lose him."

"He needs patience. That goes as much for his mind as it does for...other stuff."

"I'd never push him. I just, I feel like there are things I'm working around that I can't even see, you know?"

"That's amore, my friend," Phil said, and Kieran laughed. "He likes you, a lot. Just take it easy."

"Okay, sure," he said. "And, Phil? Please don't tell him I asked."

"I'll think about it."

Eleven

Kieran felt the tension between them when they were close. When James would accidentally meet his gaze, he would flush and look away. Kieran wanted to go to him, to tell him he wasn't upset, that he was still interested. But he couldn't get him alone long enough to gather the courage to do so.

One night after a show, as Kieran climbed the bus steps, he heard excited voices shushing each other from within. He reached the top step and saw Phil and David, along with much of the crew, crouched down, attempting to hide from view. A birthday cake sat on the small dining-area table.

"Oh fuck, it's just Kieran," one of the crew said.

"Yeah, it's only me," Kieran said playfully. "Who's this for?"

"James's birthday is tomorrow," Phil said. Kieran felt his stomach sink. *Damn it.* He felt like a shitty…whatever he was to James. "Was he behind you?" Kieran turned, peered out of the windows, and saw James coming across the parking lot.

"Yep, here he comes. Get down," Kieran said, playing along. He looked around at them, all grown men, some tattooed, some bearded, all crouched down to surprise James. Something about it spoke of the kind of person James was and the kind of love and respect he garnered, even as shy and reserved as he could be. Kieran heard his footsteps on the stairs and watched Phil, who had the best view of the door. All at once, everyone sprang up.

"Surprise!"

Kieran turned, observing the startled but happy expression on James's face as he took in his friends and the cake. He looked as pleased as Kieran had seen him in days.

"Jesus, you scared me," James said, hand over his heart.

"Oh damn, that's true. We probably shouldn't have startled the old man," Phil teased.

"I'm still the youngest," James countered. Kieran looked around again and realized for the first time that that was true. Not by much, but James was the baby of the group.

Kieran watched James cut the cake, handing everyone a piece. When he finally took his own, he looked to Kieran, finding that his hands were empty.

"Sorry, here." He held out his piece to Kieran, turning back to the cake.

"No, that's okay," Kieran said, trying to be discreet.

James frowned at first before it must've dawned on him. "Oh," James said.

Phil looked between them. "What?"

Kieran felt the attention shift to him. "I-I'm vegan," he said, waiting for the jokes. He'd been able to keep it to himself—apart from the pizza he and James had shared weeks ago when James offered him the vocals.

"Shit, sorry," Phil said. "I didn't know."

Kieran shrugged. "It's James's birthday, not mine," he said. "No worries."

The next day, after some searching, James found a bakery in the town in which they were staying. He looked down at the cakes and pastries, each of them so beautifully decorated, it would almost feel wrong to eat them.

"Can I help you?"

James looked up at the young man behind the counter. "Yeah, uh, the website said you had vegan stuff."

"Of course. Over here." He led James to a separate case filled with baked goods as delicious-looking and artful as the others. It was then he realized he didn't know what Kieran liked. Chocolate? Vanilla? Spiced?

"Not buying for yourself?"

"That obvious?"

"Not to perpetuate a stereotype, but you don't look vegan to me," he joked, and James laughed.

"'M not," he admitted.

"Girlfriend?" James shook his head. "Boyfriend?" His eyes snapped up at that. The guy winked, and James broke into a smile.

"Something like that," he said. "Any recommendations?"

"Our cakes are pretty popular," he said. "Can't really go wrong if you get a slice of chocolate and a slice of vanilla. He's bound to like one of them."

James smiled to himself. "Alright. One of each."

James knocked on Kieran's hotel room door.

"One sec," Kieran said.

"Open up. This coffee is hot," James called playfully.

The door opened, and James's eyes went wide. Kieran stood there naked, save for the towel wrapped around his waist. He was still wet from the shower, his long, dark hair dripping, his skin flushed.

"I was going to get dressed real quick, but when boss-man says open up..." Kieran shrugged.

James felt himself flush as he tried desperately not to stare at Kieran's body. "I can come back," he said, turning, forgetting all about the hot coffee in his hands, but Kieran reached out, catching his arm.

"No, it's fine. Come in. Just, let me put some clothes on."

James followed him into the room. He tried—and failed—to not stare at Kieran's ass wrapped in the towel. Kieran went back to the bathroom to dry off and dress. James placed the coffee cups and cake box on the dresser. He sat down in one of the armchairs next to the desk, trying not to think about Kieran naked, only separated from him by a limited distance and a door. *Why can't I just be normal? If I wasn't so messed up in the head, I would've charged through that door, picked him up, and carried him to the—*

His head snapped to the bed. And that's when he realized he'd just walked farther into a hotel room than he had since—

The bathroom door opened, and Kieran came out. Dressed in jeans, a plain black T-shirt, his hair toweled off but still damp, he was incredibly sexy.

Kieran stopped, frowning at the coffee cups and cake box on the dresser. "What's this?" He looked over at James.

"I felt kind of bad about last night," James explained, taking the cake box out of the paper sack. "So I found some vegan cake."

"You didn't have to do that," Kieran said, shaking his

head. "It's your birthday, not mine."

"I know," James said. "Still didn't seem very fair, you know? You were part of surprising me too."

Kieran gave a half smile. "Actually, I wasn't." James frowned, confused. "I just got to the bus before you. I had no idea today was your birthday."

James shrugged. "Still." He handed Kieran one of the coffee cups. "Green tea." Kieran took it. James opened the cake box, revealing the two pieces inside. "Which one?"

"Chocolate," he said. James took one of the paper plates from the sack, along with a plastic fork, and placed the chocolate piece on it. He handed it to Kieran, then moved to close the box.

"Oh, no no no, you're going to eat that one," Kieran insisted. "I'm not going to eat cake without the birthday boy." James frowned at him. "Man. Guy. Whatever, you know what I mean."

"But it's vegan," he said.

Kieran rolled his eyes. "I promise you won't automatically fall protein-deficient," he joked. "I insist. I know stuff like this isn't cheap." James conceded, taking the piece of vanilla cake from the box and putting it on a plate.

They sat together at the hotel room desk. Kieran took a bite of the chocolate cake. "Damn. That's not bad," he said, covering his mouth as he spoke.

"Really? You can tell me if it's terrible," James said.

"It's really not. Try it," he said, pushing his plate over to James, and James took a bite from Kieran's piece. His eyes widened with surprise.

"Wow, that's really not bad," he said.

"Told you," Kieran said.

James turned to his own cake and took a bite. "Mmm,

this one's good too. Although the chocolate kind of blows it out of the water."

"Then here, trade me," Kieran said, but James shook his head.

"Nope, I bought it for you. Besides." He paused, with a teasing smirk. "Wouldn't want to catch vegan, you know?"

Kieran snorted. "You already ate after me."

"I know," he said. "I can already feel my muscles wasting away. Am I turning yellow yet?"

Kieran nudged him with his shoulder. "Shut up. I'm not yellow."

They finished their cake in comfortable silence. Kieran was pressing his index finger to the crumbs on his plate, bringing them up to his mouth a few at a time. "I've wanted to talk to you." James looked over at him. The glow from their laughter had faded from Kieran's face; he looked back down at his plate, chewing the inside of his lip. "I just want to say, I'm not upset about the other day. Not even a little. I know I don't have the full story, but I can tell you've been through something. The last thing I want to do is make you feel pressured into anything."

"It just...wasn't very fair to you to have me freak out like that in the middle of..." James paused, looking over at Kieran, then back down. "You know."

"Fair? James, you don't owe me anything. You don't owe anyone anything—"

"Yeah, but it's still pretty messed up to get halfway through something like that and then zone out."

James chewed his lip in frustration, an embarrassed flush creeping into his cheeks. He was beginning to have thoughts of retreating when Kieran placed his hand against James's nape, stroking his thumb over the bristle-short hair.

"Hey," he said. James looked over, and the warmth Kieran managed to convey with his cool blue eyes disarmed him. "Stop being so hard on yourself."

James searched Kieran's face. "You barely know me. How can you be so understanding?"

"I don't know if you noticed last night, or if you ever do, but the people around you adore you. No one ever gave a shit about anyone's birthday in any other band I've ever been a part of. At first, I thought it was just because you're the one who pulled it all back together, but it's more than that."

James attempted to shutter himself from the sweet words. "You're making me out to be a prince."

"I don't know another person who would've gone out of their way — on their own birthday — to get another guy a piece of cake because he couldn't eat with the group."

"You're not just 'another guy,'" he said, and Kieran smiled.

"No?"

James looked over at him, at his blue eyes, his slightly pink mouth. "No," James said, leaning in. He pressed his mouth against Kieran's before trailing kisses across his cheek, down his jaw, nuzzling tenderly at his throat. Kieran must have been so caught up in being kissed senseless that he seemed shocked when James dropped from his chair to his knees in front of him.

"James — "

He began undoing Kieran's jeans. "It's my birthday, and I've thought about you every second of it." His lips brushed against Kieran's as he spoke. He reached inside Kieran's jeans, finding and stroking his member, eliciting a gasp that dissolved into a groan.

"You don't have to—" Kieran croaked.

"I want to," James murmured in his ear. "It's my birthday." He nipped Kieran's earlobe. "I've had my cake..." He paused, stroking Kieran's cock. "And now I want to eat you." Kieran whimpered, arching into James's touch. "'S right, babe. Get hard for me." James stroked him, pausing to draw his thumb against the tiny slit at the tip, sticky with precome.

James paused to study him, taking in the flushed, well-above-average cock as he gripped him once more. Kieran squirmed under his gaze. "James—*ahh*," Kieran gasped as James leaned forward and took the deeply pink tip in his mouth. He swirled his tongue around the head, drawing a firm line against the slit. James felt Kieran slump back against the chair as he mouthed up and down both sides, enjoying the way Kieran moaned and squirmed. He cupped his balls, rolling them, poising himself. He peered up to find Kieran panting, head thrown back in pleasure. He then took Kieran entirely, feeling him slide past his mouth, down his throat. "Oh Christ." James drew back, repeating the motion again, and again, and again.

James felt Kieran's hand on his shoulder. He nearly panicked, thinking Kieran might grab his head and start bucking. *Theo used to do that, and I hated it*, James thought, fighting to remain present. *Because this is Kieran in my hands, in my mouth.* Kieran passed a hand over his head once, running his fingers through James's short hair, encouraging but never rough with him. He could feel Kieran's legs quivering. His hands cupped Kieran's perfect ass as he continued, increasing his pace.

"Close," he panted. "I'm close." But James didn't let

up or change his rhythm. Instead, James slid one hand beneath his balls, between his ass cheeks, finding his hole. He didn't penetrate, only stroked the tip of his index finger back and forth over it as he continued to suck him off. "Coming, I'm co-OOH." James held still, Kieran buried deep in his throat, pulsing as he came. Kieran gripped the armrests of his chair, moaning. James waited a few beats before pulling back. He looked at the temporarily ruined man before him. "I tried to warn you," Kieran said, embarrassed.

"I know. But I don't mind. I don't expect the same from you, but I know how good it feels." *No, I don't. But I can imagine*, he countered himself. *Look at him.* He tried to get up, to get a drink of water before he tried to kiss him. But Kieran grabbed the front of his shirt, pulling him up and crushing his mouth against James's, and James wrapped his arms around him. "You like tasting yourself on me?"

Kieran chuckled. "Is that weird?"

"No. It's hot," James admitted. "You're hot. Answering the door in a towel." James smirked. "Happy birthday to me."

"I feel kind of shitty. It's your birthday, and you're the one bringing me cake and other…" He paused, as if searching for the right word. "Favors."

James pushed Kieran's mussed hair back from his face. "You're not just 'another guy,' Kieran," he reiterated.

"Neither are you, Jamie."

James looked down at Kieran's knees, feeling the weight of the moment passing between them, hearing the echoes of a thousand words neither of them was ready to say.

Kieran moved to nuzzle at James's cheek, his jaw. "And, birthday boy, if you'd like me to return the favor…"

James pulled back far enough to look him in the eyes. With some regret, he shook his head, self-consciousness creeping back into his face.

"Hey, it's okay," Kieran said, leaning his forehead against James's. "But just so you know, that offer doesn't expire." James snickered as Kieran pulled him into another kiss.

Twelve

After James left, Kieran slumped back in the armchair and let himself relive it. James, kneeling in front of him, kissing him, talking dirty to him—*who would've guessed sweet, reserved James was the type?* Kieran's body, though well sated, responded to the memory. He cupped himself through his jeans, aching for more.

His cell phone rang, tearing him from his thoughts. He stalked over to the nightstand to retrieve it. Adrienne.

"Hey, rock star," she teased.

"Hey…" He paused, trying to think of a smart comeback and failing. "You."

She snorted. "What, are your brains already obliterated from your rock 'n' roll shenanigans?"

No, just from having my brain sucked out through my cock by James Morgan, that's all. "Very funny," he said.

"How's the tour going?"

"Great, actually. The bus is nice. They say I'm doing well. I can't complain."

"So, what're they like? To tour with?"

"Fine. No one really parties hard. I mean, Phil and David and some of the crew drink after shows, but it's nothing excessive."

"I'm going to be that fan girl and ask, what's James Morgan like?"

She'd probably expected a laugh or a sarcastic

remark, but he faltered. "H-he's, um, he's great," he heard himself say.

"Well, no kidding. I meant as a person."

"He's a nice guy. Kind of reserved, quiet. But sweet."

"Sweet? Are you feeling alright? You don't even describe sweets as sweet."

He needed to tell her, to tell someone. It wasn't misplaced attraction or ignorant lust anymore. *"You're not just another guy,"* James's voice echoed in his mind.

"If I tell you something, do you promise not to repeat it to anyone?"

Silence. Then, "Oh my God," she said finally. He could imagine her, idly doing something, maybe putting away groceries or fixing herself a cup of tea while chatting with him, when it dawned on her. He could see her blue eyes, so much like his own, go wide with the realization. "Kieran—"

"Adrienne, I'm dead serious. No one can know."

"I won't say a word, but, Kieran…" She paused. "He's, oh wow, he's gay?"

"He is."

"Damn. I mean, I don't mean anything by that," she stumbled. And then the other part of the realization hit her. "So wait, he's interested in you?"

"I'm as shocked as you are," he admitted.

"No, dummy, that's not what I meant. Just…" She hesitated. "Are you sure that's a good idea?"

"This isn't like—" He faltered again. "He's nothing like Jude."

"Just because he's not like him doesn't mean he couldn't be using you—"

"He's not," he said, cutting her off. "Trust me, he's not."

"So what, did you just call to tell me that my celebrity crush has the hots for you? Wanted to rub it in a little?" she teased.

"You called me!"

"Fair," she said, and he laughed.

"But seriously —"

"I won't tell a soul. I promise," she said. "Please be careful."

"I will," he said. "Love you."

"God, he must really be something else. *Love* you too."

He snickered.

Kieran lay back on the bed, the euphoria from James's attentions dissipating rapidly after the mention of his ex.

Jude Adams had been the rhythm guitarist for Lost and Found for almost a year before he was picked up by another act. He'd also been Kieran's only serious boyfriend. Certain that Kieran would support him, he hadn't given leaving Lost and Found a second thought. But Kieran had been hurt by Jude's readiness to walk away from the music they'd created. It felt like he was walking away from Kieran too. In the end, after many heated arguments, paired with less and less tenderness and understanding, they broke up, both personally and professionally.

He understood his sister's hesitation at him getting involved with another bandmate. *Hell, I should probably be more apprehensive myself.* But then he thought of James's green eyes, the way he'd responded when Kieran reached out and stroked his nape, the way he glowed when Phil and David and the rest of the crew clamored around him, and he couldn't make himself back away.

* * *

Phil watched James and Kieran during sound check. It was increasingly obvious that something was going on between them. Something good, but serious. *Surely, James didn't fuck him. Not this soon.* Phil watched them catch each other's eyes a few times, only to look away, one or both of them flushing, stifling smiles.

When they finished and Kieran went back to the dressing rooms to warm up his voice, Phil saw his opportunity.

"Hey, James," he called over.

James looked up as he put away his guitar. "What's up?" At first, he sounded carefree and light, but after reading Phil's face… "Oh jeez. What, Mom?"

Phil rolled his eyes. "Come on. Let's go find a quick bite to eat."

"The show —"

"Our set is in two hours," Phil interrupted. "Come on, don't make me drag you out by your ear."

They found a small sandwich shop a block away from the venue. After ordering their food, they sat down at a table.

"Alright, I think I'm ready for the lecture," James said.

"I'm not lecturing you," Phil said. "I just want you to be careful."

James looked across the table at him. "He's not like Theo," he said with a quiet fierceness that gave Phil pause.

"I'm not saying he is."

"What exactly are you saying, then? A couple weeks ago, you were telling me to go for it. 'Breathing again,' I think is how you put it."

"I don't think it's a good idea for you to rush in either."

"I can't rush in," James said with an edge. "You know that."

Phil sighed. "He came to me, you know? A few days ago."

James's startled gaze met his. "What for?"

Just then, the woman who'd taken their orders brought out their food. "Can I get you anything else?" She looked back and forth between them.

"No, thank you," Phil answered for both of them.

"Alright, enjoy," she said, returning to the counter.

"He wanted to know if you'd been through something traumatic."

James's eyes went wide, the color draining from his face. "And you said?"

"I told him it wasn't my place to tell him about your past."

James sighed, pushing his plate back, his appetite clearly gone. "You tell him no, Phil. You always say no." He rubbed his forehead.

"Look, I'm not saying tell him the full story tomorrow. But I don't think blatantly lying is a good foundation to build on."

"What'd he say?"

Phil shrugged. "Said that was fair. Said he just felt like he was maneuvering around things he couldn't see."

James laughed bitterly.

"I didn't tell you this to upset you. I told you because

I think you need to know that." Phil paused, then with a sigh, "I think he's starting to have feelings for you." An odd mixture of hope and apprehension colored James's expression. "I want you to be ready for that, because I think he's good for you. But I don't want you to push yourself if you're not ready. Because he's also one talented fucker, and I don't want to lose this band over hard feelings." James nodded. "Come on, son, eat something. Your color doesn't look so good."

To Phil's relief, playing along with the joke elicited a weak smile. He watched as James slid his plate back in front of himself, picked up one half of the sandwich, and took a bite. They ate for a few minutes in silence.

"I think I'm ready."

Phil looked up at him.

"I wasn't sure before" — he looked down at his plate, seeming to choose and measure his words carefully — "but he makes me feel safe. Does that make sense? I mean, when he kissed me, I wasn't sure. But he's so patient. I really get the sense that the slowness doesn't bother him."

"Just observing you guys in public, I'd say that's true," Phil said. "He never seems frustrated or irritated with you."

"It's kind of strange for me," James said. "I keep expecting him to reach his limit, you know?"

Phil knew. Because James felt that way about everyone since everything that'd happened to him. Because of his alcoholism, though dutifully kept in check, and his PTSD, though made manageable by therapy, he believed everyone should — and did — think he was a burden.

"You should see the way he looks at you," Phil said, and James flushed.

"Shut up." He took a drink of his diet cola.

"All dopey," Phil continued. "Although, come to think of it, that may just be his face."

James snorted. "His face isn't dopey."

"No, but yours is when you talk about him," Phil countered. "What, did he give you a birthday BJ or something?"

"No." James paused. "I gave him one."

Phil inhaled his soda and began coughing. "That," Phil managed to say between sputters, "is just a little bit more than I needed to know."

James smiled. "Don't ask questions you don't want the answers to."

Phil wiped his eyes. "Duly noted. Asshole."

Kieran heard a knock at the door and smiled to himself. He opened it.

"Hey there," James said, all warm green eyes and disarming charm. "Still warming up?" Kieran shook his head. "Then let me in," he said, softer. There was something intimate about the way he said it. Kieran felt his body react, felt the flush creep up from the collar of his T-shirt. He stepped aside, letting James enter the dressing room. James handed him a warm to-go coffee cup. "Green tea, no honey."

"Thank you," Kieran said. But he could see the hardness in James's features. *Fuck, it was too much. I knew it.*

"I wanted to talk to you about something," James said, and Kieran's throat tightened. This was the last thing he needed before a show. "I know you asked Phil about me and my past." His adrenaline spiked. *Goddamn it, Phil.*

"I'm sorry, I just —"

James stepped forward, drawing Kieran's gaze back to him. "I'm not mad. I'm really not. I just..." He looked down, then around the room, taking a deep breath. "You're right. I have been through something traumatic. And I know... I know it's unfair to keep you in the dark, but I'm not ready to talk about it yet."

"I respect that," Kieran said. "And I'm sorry I went to Phil."

"Look, I'm new at this. The last time I did this..." He trailed off. Kieran felt something in him shift again, like it had back in the hotel room when he'd reached out to stroke James's nape to soothe him. "If at any point my high-maintenance self gets to be too much —"

"You're not high-maintenance," Kieran reassured him. "How dare you have baggage and boundaries after thirty years of life," he teased.

"Twenty-eight."

Kieran gaped in humorous disbelief. "Are you serious?"

"I'm twenty-eight today," he said.

"Christ," Kieran swore, only half kidding.

"I can't be that much younger than you."

"Try five years younger," Kieran said, and James feigned shock. "Not a word."

"I was just going to say you look good for your age," James teased.

"Ha-ha."

James reached out, pushed a lock of Kieran's hair behind his ear, grazed his cheek with warm, calloused fingers. Kieran couldn't stifle the smile spreading on his face.

"I'm sorry," James said, pulling him into a brief kiss.

"I don't want to tell you what to do or how to act."

Kieran leaned his forehead against James's. "You're not. You're — rightfully — putting me in my place. I overstepped. I just..." He paused, taking a breath, trying to find the right words. "I don't want to do the wrong thing and ruin this."

"You won't," James said.

Kieran leaned in and brushed his lips over James's. "Don't let me."

"I won't."

After the show, the band sat in the front lounge of the bus, watching the TV. Ed had gotten word that they were going to be mentioned on the news, and they wanted to see it. James was eager to hear what was being said about the new band, and he could sense Kieran's excitement, though he tried to hide it. To Kieran, it was all completely new.

"And now — you know them as the music-making part of the award-winning rock band Eden. But James Morgan, Phil Archer, and David Rowan are back at it with a new singer, Kieran Jackson." The clip cut to some footage from an Eden music video, fading into a recent live video from a True North show. *"Meet True North. Eden and True North manager, Ed King, states that he is thrilled with the commitment of the newly formed band and that their sound is 'out of this world.' News of the new band comes as a bit of a shock to Eden fans after Eden's abrupt breakup almost two years ago. But much of the reception for the new band has been enthusiastic, with increasingly warm fan support and pleas for them to add more tour dates. Even Eden singer, Theo Nichols, sounds positive about the new music from his former bandmates."* And suddenly, there he was on the screen.

"I've heard it, and I think it's great." James felt adrenaline flood his system, felt the nausea wash over him, and hoped he wasn't as pale as he felt. He didn't hear the rest of the newscast. All he heard was the rush of his pulse in his ears as he fought to maintain his calm.

Kieran was looking around at his bandmates. "Awkward," he joked, and Phil snorted.

"They would ask his dumb ass what he thinks," David remarked. *"I think it's great*; give me a break." David stepped away to take a phone call.

"Who gives a shit?" Phil said as he retired to his bunk.

James caught Kieran studying him and gave him a tight smile.

"So, what *does* Theo think of all this?"

"I could care less," James answered, trying to keep the strain out of his voice.

"Couldn't."

James met his eyes, annoyed. "What?"

"Couldn't. You *couldn't* care less. Could implies there's still room for you to care."

I wish that were true. "Honestly, knowing him, he probably hates it," James said. *And me.* Sometimes he wondered if Theo even knew or understood that he'd done something wrong. Sure, Phil had violently called him out before their last show. But did Theo believe it? Or did he think James was being stupid?

"He probably really hates me, huh?"

James looked up at him, saw the self-consciousness in Kieran's eyes, the way he frowned, biting his lip. James almost reached out, almost cupped his cheek right there in the middle of the front lounge. He watched Kieran sense it, saw the sting in his eyes when James stopped himself.

"Now, that?" James managed to say, looking away, shutting himself off from the clear disappointment in Kieran's face. "That, I really couldn't care less about."

Thirteen

The following day, Kieran startled awake at a knocking on the side of his bunk, knocking he felt more than heard. He lifted his head, confused by the ringing in his ears he hadn't noticed the night before.

"You awake in there, sleeping beauty? I'm not opening the curtain, but you have to get up. We're here," Phil said. Kieran swung his legs out of the bunk and pushed the small curtain aside. "Morning, sunshine."

"Morning," he said, pulling on his T-shirt.

"Be glad it's only me," Phil said. "James might've come in there after you."

"Ha-ha," Kieran shot back, noticing how warped his own voice sounded in his ears. *Did you really think it was going to be different? That your ears would magically heal?*

"You alright?"

"Yep, fine," he said, realizing he'd zoned out. He slid out of his bunk, grabbed his duffel bag, and headed for the hotel.

Kieran stopped mid-note and swore. Warming up was usually a tedious activity he felt indifferent to. But on days when his tinnitus was bad, it was torture. Cupping his hand near his face didn't work. Being loud didn't work. Being quieter made no sense at all. With Lost and Found, he would've just pushed through; no one gave a shit anyway. If he had a guitar lesson back home, he'd reschedule. But now, with True North? He was desperate. Just as he was about to give in to a panic attack, a knock came at the dressing room door.

"Kieran?"

Shit. Kieran wondered if James had heard him. It seemed so silly that just a few weeks ago he'd been worried about being kicked out of the band for coming on to James. He doubted James would be as understanding about his waning hearing as he'd been about that. He opened the door.

"Hey," Kieran said, trying to sound casual. *Not that I can hear myself to know…*

"You okay?"

Kieran shrugged, avoiding James's eyes. "Yeah, why? I sound like shit?" He winced at the scathing edge he'd said it with.

"N-no, not at all," James stammered as if caught off guard by Kieran's tone. "You just sounded frustrated."

Kieran sighed. "Sorry. I didn't mean to snap."

"It's okay."

Kieran ran a hand through his long hair. *I should tell him. I should just get it out.* He felt the tension creeping into his shoulders.

"Hey." James reached out and cupped his cheek. "It's okay. You're allowed to have a bad day." Kieran pressed his hand over James's, and James drew closer. "You've been working so hard. Don't think I don't see it. And not just because I like looking at you." Kieran reveled in James's tenderness. *And you're lying to him. You're lying to probably the sweetest, most understanding man you've ever been with, let alone worked with.*

"James—"

Another knock at the door startled both of them. James flinched away, jerking his hand from Kieran's cheek.

"Hey, I was looking for you guys," David said.

"What's up?" James's voice was steady, but Kieran could sense the fresh tension coming off him.

"They want us to go on early. One of the other bands couldn't make it," he said. "Are you guys ready?"

"How soon?" James asked.

"They said about half an hour."

James looked over at Kieran, and feeling put on the spot, Kieran nodded. "Sure, I'm ready," he lied.

James turned back to David. "We'll do it."

Kieran placed the monitors in his ears, carefully adjusting the sound. After James had left him, he'd finished warming up as best he could. But the tension from talking to James, the adrenaline spike from almost telling him the truth, combined with the persistent ringing in his ears, had induced a headache like he hadn't had in a long time. *What if I fuck up?* He adjusted the wires and then the pack on the back of his jeans. *What if I fall out of key and everyone can hear it but me?* He knew that True North was already under special scrutiny because of their past as Eden, and he even more so as their new singer. He stopped at the side of the stage and leaned against one of the larger amps. It was too hot, the sun too bright on his back and neck. He pulled his sunglasses from their perch on top of his head and down over his eyes, feeling the panic attack descending. He tried to breathe through it, tried to calm himself.

"Kieran?" James called to him. He tried to turn to James, to give a thumbs-up, but taking his hand off the amp caused him to swoon.

"Kieran?" James called out again, removing his guitar from his shoulder. He jogged over and managed to catch Kieran before his legs buckled. "Hey, you alright?"

"I'm gonna be sick," Kieran said, holding on to James weakly.

"Alright, come on." James walked him down the steps behind the stage and to one of the big trash cans. Kieran let go of James and braced himself over the can with both hands. He tried to maintain his composure, but the heat, the tension, the headache escalating into a migraine, was all too much. He began to heave, embarrassed as James remained at his side. He helped steady him, pulling back his long hair and tucking it into the collar of his shirt. "It's alright, let it out." And he did. James turned away, keeping his hand on Kieran's back. He pulled his sunglasses off, and James touched his forehead, his cheek. "You're way too cold to be sweating like this. Phil!"

"No, James, I'm okay. I just don't feel —" He stopped, heaving again.

Phil watched the whole thing. He watched the way James held Kieran up as he walked him to the trash can. He watched the way James tucked his hair back, holding him steady, talking him through it. He'd chuckled to himself. *He's so in love, and he actually thinks he's being discreet about it.* But then he heard James yell for him. He turned just as Kieran slumped against James.

"Shit." He took off toward them. "What's wrong with him?"

"I don't know," James said.

"Sit him down." Phil helped him seat Kieran on the

125

ground. "Did he throw up?"

"Yeah," James said, kneeling behind Kieran, propping him up.

"Kieran? You feelin' bad, brother?"

Kieran nodded.

"He's cold, Phil. And clammy."

"How much water have you had today?" Phil asked, and Kieran shrugged. "Alright. Keep him upright. Here." He handed James the water bottle in his hand. "Make him drink some, and pour the rest on his neck."

"Alright, I'm gonna pour some of this on you," James warned as he leaned Kieran forward. Just as the water hit his skin, the tension seemed to drain from his body and he passed out.

"I'll get a paramedic and be right back." Phil took off around the stage.

Phil watched James sit in the corner of the hospital waiting room, chewing his nails. He carried an unopened bottle of water over to him, handing it to him along with a packet of aspirin.

"He's alright, man, just dehydration," Phil reassured him. James tore open the packet and washed down the pills with the water.

"He flat passed out," James said, holding the cold, sweating bottle in his hands. "Scared me a little, I guess."

"James?" James turned to him, his eyes as intense as Phil had ever seen them. "You really do have feelings for him, don't you?"

James looked away. "Now's really not a good time for the lecture—"

"I'm not lecturing," Phil cut him off. "You don't have to sit here and shrug off your feelings for him. Not with me." He gripped James's shoulder, and James sighed, nodding.

James and Phil filed into the hospital room.

"Hey," Kieran said, feeling foolish in the hospital bed and gown.

"You look better," Phil said. "You looked like death warmed over a little bit ago, no offense."

Kieran gave a wry smile. "Gee, thanks." He looked over at James, who stood off to the side, hands shoved in his pockets. "I haven't been completely honest with you guys."

"What do you mean?" Phil asked, eyes narrowed.

Kieran took a deep breath. "It's my hearing. I have tinnitus."

James and Phil looked at each other, then back at Kieran.

"I guess I don't know what that means," James admitted.

"Ringing in my ears, pretty much constantly."

"Then how do you sing?" Phil asked.

"I'm not deaf. It's just harder, especially with more use," he explained. "It's a big part of why I wasn't active when you guys called. It got so bad toward the end with Lost and Found, I really thought I was going deaf."

"Aren't there things you can do, or already do, to help it?"

"Just, turning the monitors down, both in the studio and onstage. Not blowing out my ears listening to music. Wearing earplugs to shows I go see. But I have bad days, no matter what I do."

"Is that what happened today?"

Kieran nodded.

"Why didn't you just tell us?"

Kieran chewed the inside of his lip. "I was going to—"

"Yeah? When?"

James shot Phil a look. "Give him a break."

"He's been lying this whole time. I just want to know when he was planning to tell us."

"Look, I'm sorry, okay? You're right, I lied." He looked down at his hands. "I just wanted this to work. I wanted to get back in so bad, and you called, and—" He felt the room grow hazy, felt his pulse in his stomach, in his gums.

James sat on the edge of the bed beside him. "Hey, come on. Relax." He turned to Phil, but Kieran was too woozy to see the look that passed between them. "I'm not mad."

Kieran looked up at him, James's eyes wrought with a sweetness that drew Kieran in, made his chest ache. "You should be. Phil's right."

"No, Phil's not right," Phil said. "You should've told us the truth. But..." He sighed. "Alright, look, I'm sorry. I like you. I think you're right for the band." Kieran looked from Phil to James, then back. "But, man, let me tell you both something. If you guys think you're hiding this thing between you, you're both deluded. Especially when he thought you were dying."

"I didn't think he was dying," James said, cheeks flushed. "I just thought something was really wrong."

"I'm going to go do some damage control," Phil said, moving toward the door. "When we get back home, we should all have a meeting about this. Just so we're on the same page." James looked up with wide eyes. "No, dummy, about his hearing." Kieran snorted.

"Yeah, right now, the most scandalous thing is the fact that True North's singer can't actually hear. I can't wait for the jokes," Kieran said.

"Alright," James said.

Phil left them, pulling the door closed behind him.

James reached for Kieran's hand, looking him over with gentle concern.

"I'm sorry. I was going to tell you right before the show —"

"It's okay," James said. "I'm really not mad."

"You think David or Ed will want to kick me out?"

"I doubt it. But if they do, I'll fight it."

"I didn't mean to scare you. I got overwhelmed and hot and —" James grabbed him and pressed his mouth over Kieran's. "No, don't —" He tried to squirm away. "I just threw up," he said, but James snickered.

"You've had water since then," he said, brushing his nose against Kieran's cheek. "Besides, it's true. You did scare me a little."

"I'm sorry. I'm fine, really," he reassured James. Just then, the door swung open, and James jerked away from him.

"Anything I can get for you, Mr. Jackson?"

"No, ma'am, thank you," he answered. The nurse nodded and left the room. "Why do you do that?"

"Do what?"

"Flinch away from me anytime someone comes in the room."

"Kieran, I —" James paused, his heart pounding. "We can't be out right now." The pain in Kieran's eyes seemed to intensify, and James added, his eyes dropping, "I can't be out right now. I've had a weird time...coming to terms...you know? I haven't been in a serious relationship with a man in a long time."

"You know, before you told me you were gay, I just figured you were like every other semi-straight guy I've ever been with."

"What's that supposed to mean?" James frowned, but didn't look up.

"Usually guys just fuck around with me for a while until they get bored."

James felt like he'd been struck. "You think I'm just fucking around with you?"

"James—" But James got up. The room felt hot and small, and the more Kieran talked, the more it hurt. "James." He looked over at Kieran in spite of the stinging in his eyes and throat.

"Kieran, I..." He faltered, swallowing hard. "I adore you." The words came out rough but strong and seemed to render Kieran momentarily speechless.

"Then act like it," Kieran bit out, looking even angrier than before. "Don't treat me like your dirty little secret."

"I'm trying!" James took a breath. "You have to be patient with me."

"James, this isn't like the other stuff. Past trauma, emotional baggage, I can work with that. But if you're ashamed of being gay, of being with me? I can't work around that."

James rubbed his forehead. "I'm not ashamed."

"No?"

"You don't understand. My ex *was* ashamed. He forbade public affection and berated me if I ever tried," he explained, exasperated into telling such a painful, embarrassing piece of the truth.

"I'm not him," Kieran said. "I'm not ashamed of who I am. And I'm not ashamed of loving you." James blinked at him. "Fuck—"

"You love me?"

Kieran's shoulders dropped, and he shook his head, clearly frustrated with himself. "Yeah, I do," he said irritably. "Sorry, I didn't mean for it to come out like that." He rubbed his eyes. James sat back down, feeling like he'd been hit by a bus. "You don't have to look so thrilled." James met his gaze, all frustration and irritation gone from his eyes. "Please say something."

"I…" He faltered, trying to find words. "I don't know what to say."

Kieran bit his lip. "Jamie, let me in. I do love you, but I can't properly do that from the outside."

"I'm just not ready, Kieran." Kieran's face fell. "I'm trying, please, I'm trying. Just give me time." He reached for Kieran's hand, lifting it to his cheek, holding it there.

"Jamie—"

"Please don't give up on me," James pleaded. "Please."

"I'm not," he said. "But you're going to have to let me in. You can't have a relationship like this. Both people have to know the truth."

"I know." James squeezed his eyes shut.

The doorknob turned, and James flinched away from him again. Kieran looked up at him in disbelief. James stood and made his way to the door. "Excuse me," he said, sliding past the doctor and out of the hospital room.

James walked out of the hospital, tears blurring his vision. He passed a hand over his eyes, frustrated with himself. He couldn't be in there, couldn't speak anymore without losing control. Because Kieran's words stung him.

He thinks I'm ashamed of him, of us. The thought tore at his chest. *And why wouldn't he?* And that's when it hit him for the first time. *Dear God, I'm in love.* He sat down in the rental car, slamming the door shut behind him. He punched the steering wheel a few times, hard enough to split a few knuckles, and then leaned forward, holding his head in his battered hands. He then gripped the steering wheel, trying to will the pain and tears away, and failing. *I'm in love with him, and he thinks I'm ashamed of him.* Tears ran down his face, and he hated himself for them, hated that he'd let anyone this close to him after last time.

Fourteen

James trudged upstairs to his apartment, his bags hanging across his weary frame. He let himself in, locking the door behind him. His apartment was cool and quiet. He dropped his bags behind the sofa and turned on the single lamp on the battered end table. He then came around the sofa and sat down hard. Even though he'd been sedentary most of the day, between his flight home and taking the cab to his apartment, he was exhausted. *Because you might as well have run away on foot.* He sighed, scrubbing his hands over his face, thankful that the tour was over.

"Fuck!" His voice felt strained. The thought of using the end of the tour as an excuse to run from Kieran, from his own hang-ups, from what was happening between them, made him want to flip the coffee table before him, to take satisfaction in physically expressing some of his frustration. But he wouldn't. Because the tears were so close to the surface that if he let himself feel too much, he'd end up sobbing in a pathetic ball on the floor.

He forced himself to his feet and headed for the bathroom, stripping on the way, leaving everything in a trail to the door before stepping into the shower. He turned on the water, cool at first, then as hot as he could stand it. He leaned against the wall, letting the water flow over him, willing it to calm him. *"I'm not ashamed of loving you,"* Kieran's voice echoed in his mind. He chewed his lip. *And if I wasn't so broken, I wouldn't act like I'm ashamed of loving you,* he thought. He closed his eyes and saw Kieran's blue eyes, long brown hair, his narrow frame. He felt his emotions bubble up, and sat down in the corner of the shower, folding into himself.

"Goddamn it," he whispered. He sat there for a long time, sometimes sobbing, sometimes silent. When he felt the water begin to cool, he stood and rinsed. He toweled off, not bothering with clothes before falling into bed, heartbroken and exhausted.

It wasn't until early the following afternoon that James woke up. Sleep had been a hard-won battle, but once he finally drifted off, his rest was dreamless and peaceful. He rolled onto his back, stretching, his muscles achy from having slept in the same position for so long. Out of habit, he reached over to the nightstand for his cell phone. He felt around for a moment before looking over, realizing it was still at the bottom of his bag in the living room. He sighed as he pushed himself up, sitting for a moment, letting everything from the previous day sink in. Kieran's episode, finding out Kieran has tinnitus, admitting they have feelings for each other, his own hang-ups making their presence known. *We have feelings for each other, and I'm too screwed up to give him what he needs.* He swung his legs over the edge of the bed and pulled on an old pair of gym shorts before going to find his phone.

Twenty minutes later, and while waiting for his phone to charge enough so he could check it, he'd brewed coffee and found cereal that wasn't completely stale. He sat down with a bowl and looked over the messages he'd avoided the night before.

First Phil's: *Hey, man, I don't know what happened, but please call/text so I know you got home okay.*

Then Ed's: *Great job on the festival tour! True North is doing as well as can be expected...but Theo's been in touch. I know you're probably going to shoot this down, but I think we should start considering a new Eden project. Call me when you get in!*

James felt the tightness in his jaw, the tension creeping into his neck and shoulders. *Every time I think I'm finally rid of him, he crops up.*

And finally, after some hesitation, he read Theo's message.

Hey, how've you been? Just talked to Ed about working on some new stuff. Call me.

James had to make himself breathe, had to restrain himself from throwing his phone across the room.

And the worst part? Not a word from Kieran.

James had just put on clothes when he heard knocking at his door.

"It's me," Phil called from the other side of the door. James unlocked it and let him in.

"I was just about to call you."

"You really need to learn how to respond to a text," Phil snapped.

James put his hands up. "In my defense, I was exhausted when I got in. I forgot to charge my phone."

Phil rolled his eyes. "Yeah, well, if I'd taken off the way you did, I'd probably be exhausted too." James averted his eyes. "What happened?"

"Nothing I didn't see coming," James said.

"Did you guys argue or something? You seemed pretty cozy when I left," Phil said, sitting down at the kitchen table.

"Coffee?"

"Sure." James poured the coffee and brought the mugs to the table, sitting across from Phil. "Thanks. So, are you going to answer my question?"

James took a drink. "I don't really want to talk about it."

Phil looked down at his mug. "Alright. How about we talk about this Eden thing?"

James sighed, scrubbing a hand over his face. "What about it?"

Phil gaped at him. "What do you mean, what about it? We shut that shit down quick and in a hurry."

James slowly rolled his mug back and forth in his hands. "What does David say?" He could feel Phil's wide-eyed stare.

"You're not actually considering this —"

"Maybe I am. I mean, with Kieran's hearing —"

"Kieran has more talent half-deaf than Theo ever had! James, look at me." James lifted his gaze, meeting Phil's. "What happened?"

"It's like you said. I shouldn't have gotten involved with another band member. It creates a conflict of interest —"

"Oh, give me a break," Phil said. "Twenty-four hours ago, you thought he hung the moon and stars for you."

"We admitted we have feelings for each other," James said.

"I'm sorry, bud, but I think you're out of practice. That's a good thing."

"I'm too screwed up to give him what he needs."

"And tell me, what is it you're too screwed up to give him? Because something tells me he'd wait on the...you know...sex stuff," Phil said.

"He wants to be out."

Phil shrugged. "So? Be out."

"You have no idea what you're talking about," he snapped. "You don't get to say that to me."

"I swear to you, no one would care."

"You can't know that," James said, exasperated. "We're members of Eden, for God's sake. Do you have any idea what those fans would do if they found out I'm gay?"

"Fuck them," Phil said. James stared at him with a mix of anger and disbelief. "I'm serious. Fuck them. And I'm ninety-nine point nine percent sure that Ed and David would back me up on that." James shook his head, leaning back in his chair. "Your happiness doesn't come in second. Neither does mine, or David's, or Kieran's. Do I want to keep making music and retain fans? Absolutely. But it doesn't matter if we're not happy. It's going to show in our music, and it's going to show onstage. You can cling to sobriety and therapy and all that, but eventually, it's going to eat you alive." James rubbed his forehead. "Look, I know I don't know shit about being gay. I know that. And it's probably super condescending of me to tell you to stop worrying about it and be out with him. But you're my brother, and I care about you. And I know for a fact that he makes you happier than I've seen you in a long time. Maybe ever. But even if it doesn't work out with him, I hate that you feel like you have to hide who you are."

"I don't know if I can, Phil. I wish I was that brave, but I don't think I am."

"You honestly don't believe you're brave? You weathered abuse, you survived an assault, and you walked away from your own suicide attempt. You're...what is it now? Two years sober? And I know that doctor doesn't go easy on you. I've seen you after some of your appointments."

James swallowed hard, his gaze faltering. "Jesus, what's wrong with me?"

Phil sighed. "Nothing. You're scared—"

"I'm not scared—"

"James, it's okay to be scared. I might not know what it's like to have to come out, but I understand that it's a scary thing. But, look at me." He paused until James met his eyes. "You've been scared before. And you've beat it, every single time."

James shook his head, trying not to fall apart again.

"But you're not too scared to work with Theo again?"

James looked at him hard. "Phil, what choice do I have? Tell me. If I blow him off, if I blow this Eden thing off, how do I explain myself?"

"You know I'd back you up. David too."

"You don't understand—"

"Then explain it to me, James."

James tried desperately to stop the tremor that had built in his gut as they spoke. "If I turn this down and run away, what does that make me? I can't spend my life being too afraid of him to make music. True North, that's the band I want to be known for, but I—we—can't deny that there would be no True North without Eden. I can't turn away from those fans, and I can't run away with my tail between my legs, too damn afraid to what? Maybe brush shoulders with him in the studio a few times?"

"We both know Ed is going to ask about a reunion

tour."

James scrubbed his hands over his face. "Then we cross that bridge when we come to it."

Later that afternoon, James, Phil, David, and Ed sat around the conference table at the studio, discussing the possibility of a new Eden album.

"So, what do we think?" Ed asked the three of them.

"I think it's a bad idea," David said. "Things were getting tense toward the end there. And things are so much easier with Kieran. Why bother?"

"Money. That's why we bother," Ed said evenly. "I know you guys get along with Kieran better, but we can't deny the money that Eden brings in."

Money, James thought. *It's going to come down to money.*

"What about you guys? Any thoughts?"

Phil looked over at James, but James kept his eyes trained on the table.

"I don't think it's a good idea either," Phil said. "Tensions were awful high before the breakup."

Ed sighed. "What about you?"

James gathered his strength and looked up at Ed, then at David and Phil. He wished he could just focus on the money, wished his feelings were simple enough to make the decision easily. But a little piece of him wanted to do it just to prove that he could, that he could be around Theo and not feel mortally afraid. "Eden does make a lot of money." Phil shook his head. "I mean" — James paused — "what are we talking? Just an album? A tour?"

"I hard veto a tour," Phil cut in.

"Me too," David said.

"That's fine. But, are we on board for an album?"

Just then, James heard the front door open and close. *Theo*, he thought, and his mouth went dry. He heard the footsteps and felt a cold sweat break out under his arms and at the small of his back. *So much for not feeling mortally afraid.* He managed to keep himself from flinching at the knock on the conference room door.

"Yep," Ed called out. Kieran entered the room, looking paler and more tired than usual. "Shouldn't you still be in the hospital?"

"They released me last night. I wanted to get back here so I could talk to you all." He took the seat beside David, adjacent to James, across from Phil. "I don't know if James and Phil already told you guys, but I told them something yesterday that...well." He paused. "I have tinnitus."

Ed eyed him.

"How bad?" David asked.

"Not that bad. It's manageable. But yesterday it set off a migraine, and that's why I freaked out."

"Don't you think you should've told us this up-front?" Ed asked, and James shot Ed a look. "What? It's what we're all thinking. Or should be, if you're not."

"He's light-years better than Theo on his worst day," James said with an edge, and Kieran looked at him in surprise.

"Look, I'm just saying, honesty is the best policy," Ed said, turning back to Kieran. "Especially for the new guy."

"But we'll ignore Theo's known drug problem?" David asked.

"He says he's sober," Ed said.

"Theo?" Kieran asked.

"We're just talking about doing an Eden album. True North is still fine," Phil said. Kieran nodded, and James watched him relax.

"So, what should I tell him?" Ed asked, clearly frustrated.

"What do you mean, what should you tell him?" Phil asked. "Whose idea was this?"

"I don't really see why that matters, but it was Theo's idea. He wants to do this, but he doesn't want it to be awkward, so he asked me to present the idea to you guys."

James felt his eyelid twitch. *Doesn't want it to be awkward.* He wanted to break something. He'd almost forgotten Kieran was in the room until their eyes met. He could sense Kieran trying to read him, and he forced a good-humored eye roll.

"Tell him we're in," James said, looking at Phil, then David.

Phil sighed, shaking his head. "Yeah, I guess so," he conceded.

Ed looked at David.

"Whatever, sure," David said.

Kieran looked around at all of them. "Boy, I wonder what you guys say about me when I'm not around," he joked.

"Apples and oranges, man," David said, clapping him on the shoulder.

"More like apples and goddamn bricks," Phil said.

After the meeting, James approached Kieran. "Can we talk?" James asked.

Kieran paused in the hallway, his phone in his hand. "I need to pack," Kieran said, and James felt pain lodge in his throat. "I'm going home, you know, while you guys do the Eden thing."

"When do you leave?"

"Tomorrow morning."

"Please, come back to my apartment. I need to talk to you."

Kieran sighed, shoving his phone back in his pocket. "Okay."

James opened the door to his apartment, letting Kieran and himself in. James sat on the sofa, hoping Kieran would sit next to him. He didn't, opting for the armchair instead.

"Can I get you something to drink?" Kieran shook his head, and James leaned forward, resting his elbows on his knees, looking down at his fidgeting hands.

"You wanted to talk?"

"I do," he said, rubbing his forehead. "I don't want to lose you, Kieran. I feel like I'm losing you." James fixed his eyes on him.

"Hard to lose something you never really had," Kieran said. The chill in his words hit James's veins like ice water. "James, I know you're younger than me, so maybe this is unfair, but I'm too old to go back in the closet."

James felt his temper surge. "You're right, that's not fair. You're the one who came on to me drunk and then pretended it never happened."

"Because I didn't think you were gay! Because you hide it behind this persona that's all muscle and guitar-hero tough guy!"

"Just because I'm not shouting about my sexuality from the rooftops doesn't mean I'm hiding it either."

"Oh no? Who all knows for a fact that you're gay? Phil? Your therapist? Me? This mysterious ex you've mentioned?" James felt the searing pain of each question, like lash marks endured from the inside. "How about your family? You never mention them. How about Ed? David? Theo?"

"If you're trying to make me feel even shittier about myself, you're doing a good job," James bit out.

"I've been with guys in the closet. I've done the dirty-little-secret bit, and I can tell you, it gets old fast. I get it. The long hair, small frame, it's easy for guys to fuck around with me and still believe they aren't queer."

Angry now, James lifted his gaze. "If you think I'm in denial about who I am, about who I want, then why are we even arguing?"

"Because I'm in love with you!" He heard the distinct emotional quiver in Kieran's raised voice. "And it kills me because it feels like I'm drawn to assholes who refuse to take me seriously."

James felt the tide of his own pain recede a little as he watched Kieran fight the tears welling in his tired eyes. He tried to hide them, leaning forward, trying to pull himself together. James moved to sit on the coffee table directly in front of him. He pulled a handful of tissues from the box on the table and began wiping Kieran's face.

"Sorry," Kieran said.

James leaned in close, smoothing Kieran's hair back, tucking it behind his ears. Kieran leaned into the tender touch, even though they'd been fighting. Even in anger, James refused to be cold or rough with him.

"I'm in love with you too," James said. "And I know I'm screwed up, but I do take you seriously."

"Every time you jerk away from me, it h-hurts,"

Kieran said, and James swallowed hard.

"I know," he said. "I know it does, and I'm sorry. But I'm…" He faltered, fighting to keep his voice steady. "I'm scared. But I want to do this for you. I don't want to lose you."

"No," Kieran said. "You have to do it for you. Coming out isn't about being with me. It's about being who you are."

James winced in despair, feeling each and every one of the five years that separated them. Kieran was right, his reasoning so much more mature than his own. He realized then that there was no way to be certain about their future.

The following morning, James followed Kieran to the car-rental office. Kieran could've done it himself and taken a cab to the airport, but James insisted. He'd parked the rental in front of the office just as James swung his Jeep in beside him and got out.

"I've got it, Jamie."

"Go on and close it out," James said. "I'll get your bags." He opened the trunk, pointedly avoiding Kieran's eyes as he began moving his bags over to his truck.

After dealing with the car return, Kieran stood for a moment watching James. He noticed the set of his jaw and shoulders, the obvious tension in him. He'd scarcely met Kieran's eyes, but when he did, all Kieran could read was sadness. He hated this, hated leaving, hated doing this to James, but what he'd said the day before was the truth. He badly wanted to be with him, but James needed to address certain things before he could be with anyone.

Kieran observed James as he finished and climbed back into his truck. He left the rental office and walked over to the car.

"All set?" James asked as Kieran opened the door and climbed in.

"Yep." Kieran buckled his seat belt, and they drove away.

James walked with him into the airport as far as Security would allow.

"Hey." James reached for his hand, and Kieran turned to him, dropping his duffel beside him.

"Hey yourself." Kieran watched James look around to see if anyone was staring before he stepped closer. *I guess that's progress.* Then he pulled Kieran into a kiss. Kieran stiffened in surprise. James broke the kiss, leaning his forehead against Kieran's.

"I'm gonna miss you," he said, his voice drawn tight.

"I'm coming back," Kieran said, trying to lighten the obvious goodbye happening between them. "Remember, True North is fine, right? You promised."

"I know." He pulled back enough to look down at Kieran, cupping his face in his hands. Kieran watched him start to say something before stopping himself.

"I love you, Jamie." Kieran watched it land on James's face like a strike.

"I love you too, Kieran." James leaned in, kissed him again, this time with a passionate need that Kieran hadn't felt before. He could sense James wanting this to work, wanting to be what Kieran needed in a partner. It made him ache because he could also sense the mental strain James was putting on himself to be affectionate in public.

I don't want to leave. Jesus Christ, I want him. Kieran broke the kiss, picked up his duffel bag, and slung it over his shoulder.

"Kieran—"

"I have to go," he said, digging out his wallet along with his ticket.

"Will you let me know when you make it home?"

Kieran felt the sting in the back of his throat. "Sure."

James shoved his hands in his pockets as Kieran turned and walked away.

Fifteen

James sat across from Dr. Evans.

"What's going on, James?"

"Kieran left."

She frowned. "I thought things were going well with him."

He laughed wryly, shaking his head. "This is me, remember? Things only go well for me for so long."

"I thought we agreed that that kind of thinking isn't helpful."

He sighed. "I need your help."

She softened. "You know I'm always here to help you."

"I need help coming out."

Her eyebrows lifted as she leaned back in her chair. "And why do you want to come out?"

He grimaced. "Shouldn't I want to be out?"

"You should want what feels right for you. Does coming out feel right?"

"I'm a twenty-eight-year-old gay man. Getting a little old for the closet, Dr. Evans."

"Have you talked about this with Kieran?"

"How do you know that?"

She gave a knowing smile that was probably charming if you weren't her patient. "You've never expressed a desire to come out before now. Frankly, I was fine with that given your public image. Plus, I firmly disagree with thinking there's any right or wrong time frame for 'coming out.' There has to be a reason for it."

"Kieran wants to be out about us."

"And what do you want?"

He chewed the inside of his lip. "I want him. I love him."

"I understand that. And I think it's good that you're open to pursuing relationships again. But I also think bowing to the desires of another person can be dangerous, especially when we're talking about something as potentially life-altering as coming out."

"Do you have any idea how life-altering it feels for me to be in love? I didn't think I would ever feel this way for anyone."

"I agree it's a good thing. I think you've come a long way to be able to fall in love again. But don't let it sideline all the progress you've made on yourself."

James huffed. "I want to be out for me too. Theo taught me to be ashamed of being gay. Before him, I was just reserved. Theo's the one who taught me to jump back every time we heard a door or footsteps. He's the one who taught me it was normal to pretend nothing was going on while in public. I don't want to be like that with Kieran." He paused. "Not that he would stand for it. He's so much stronger and braver than me."

"I don't know Kieran, but I think if he knew the whole story, he'd beg to differ. I don't mind telling you that you're easily one of the bravest, strongest people I know."

He looked up at her. "You could've fooled me."

"You can be stubborn. And you definitely do everything in your own time. But some of the strongest people are like that," she said. "Unfortunately." He smiled. "I highly doubt Kieran would ever compare you to Theo, even if he knew everything. I'm surprised you would compare yourself to him."

"You've never seen the look in his eyes when I flinch away from him because I think I hear someone coming."

"I'm sure that hurts him if his feelings for you come close to matching yours for him."

"He thinks I'm ashamed of him. That I treat him like my 'dirty little secret.'" The words echoed in Kieran's voice in his mind. "I don't feel that way about him. I certainly don't want him to think I do."

"And why is that?" He looked at her with contempt. "Humor me."

He thought for a moment. "Because that's the way Theo made me feel. Like he was ashamed of me, of what went on between us. I know how it feels, and"—he paused—"I never want to make anyone ever feel that way because of me. Especially not—" He scrubbed a hand over his face.

"And what about you? How does Kieran make you feel?"

"Like I'm not completely screwed up. Like I'm normal."

"Like you're lovable?"

"I didn't even think I liked being touched anymore. The idea of another person's—another man's—hands on me, it used to give me the creeps. I didn't think I'd ever want that again."

"I'm going to ask you a difficult question," she warned. "Did you feel that way about Theo prior to the rape? Like you didn't want to be touched by him?"

He thought back and was startled by what he found

in his memory. "I... I think I did."

"Do you remember why?"

He came to a realization, and closed his eyes against the pain. "Because he didn't want to touch me. He liked..." He faltered, took a deep breath. "He liked when I touched him. But it was pretty clear early on, he hated touching me. I could see it in his eyes. I could see it in how much coke he had to do before he'd even consider coming on to me."

"And you're afraid of making Kieran feel like that? Like how you felt because Theo was ashamed of being intimate with you?"

He nodded.

* * *

After a week of being on edge for if and when Theo would show up to begin working on the new Eden album, even James was tired of waiting.

"So are we doing this thing, or what?" David asked Ed.

"We are," he said. "Theo's just having some scheduling issues."

James suppressed the urge to rub his forehead.

"Funny, I don't remember hitting a time warp on the way in this morning," David continued. "And yet, here we are, two years ago."

Ed rolled his eyes.

"When is he going to make it out?" James managed to keep the edge out of his voice.

"He says he hopes to be here by the first of the month."

James gaped at him. "Christ, that's —"

"Two weeks out." Ed sighed. "I'm not happy about it either."

David threw his hands up. "Unbelievable."

"Not really, considering who we're talking about," Phil chimed in. James had hoped to get his parts of the album recorded quickly so he could go to Portland and surprise Kieran. Now he felt like a horse led around by the promise of a carrot dangling before its face just out of reach. The more he wanted it, the further away it seemed.

After their chat, James caught up with Phil outside.

"Hey," Phil said, searching his face. "How're you holding up?"

James shrugged. "I'd love to find my way out of limbo before I turn thirty," he joked. "We should've just turned him down in the first place."

"Much longer, and I think David will initiate it." James chuckled. "Come on. Let's go get dinner. I'm starving, and you look like you are too."

James rolled his eyes. "Yes, Mom."

"So how're you holding up, really?" Phil dunked a french fry into the sea of ketchup on his plate.

James swallowed a bite of his club sandwich. "Fine, I guess," he said. "Haven't had to face him yet, though. How bad could I be?" He sensed Phil taking stock of him.

"I can tell you've lost weight," he said, and James sighed.

"How bad do I look?"

Phil wiped his mouth before taking a drink of his beer. "Not bad. Just tired."

"If I look like shit, you can tell me," he said. "I won't go home and cry into my pillow."

"No, man, you don't look like shit. But you do look

like you've taken a hit. Heard from Kieran?"

James shook his head. "He let me know he made it back to Portland okay, but other than that..." James trailed off, shrugging.

"I'm sorry, brother."

James took a drink of his diet cola. "I actually wanted to run something by you."

"Shoot."

"I want to go to Portland and surprise him. But I don't want to go alone, in case it doesn't go well."

Phil eyed him with a smirk. "Aww, that's fucking adorable—"

"I'm serious. Will you go with me, in case it backfires?"

"How's it going to backfire? I bet he's sitting in some restaurant over there, pouting over a veggie burger with that same expression on his face."

James smiled through his nerves. *What if he doesn't want to see me?*

"Will you please come with me?"

"Of course. Anything to get that lost-puppy look off your face."

* * *

When Kieran arrived home, it'd felt just like last time. He hadn't wanted to look at a guitar, let alone pick one up and play it. But giving guitar lessons kept him sharp, soothed him. Seeing the light in kids' and teens' faces when they finally nailed a chord or song they'd been working on reinvigorated his love for music. He placed the guitar he'd been using in its stand and stood up, stretching his back and arms. He glanced down at his watch. 4:15. His workday was over, and he didn't have to work at the coffee shop until the next morning.

He went to the bathroom before heading for the front of the music store to leave. Jude stood behind the counter, counting down the cash register drawer. There was one downside to getting back into teaching.

"Hey there," Jude said, smiling at him.

"Hey, I'm out," Kieran said.

"Nope." Kieran frowned. "Check the schedule. You're down for a four-thirty lesson." Kieran came around the counter and looked. 4:30, along with a name written in Jude's illegible scrawl. "Sorry, darlin'," he said, closer than Kieran expected. He felt Jude's hand on his side, felt his breath on his cheek. He leaned in, nuzzling Kieran's throat. Kieran squirmed.

"You think you're so damn funny. There's no four thirty, is there?" Just then, he heard the front door bell, one of those little bells tied up just so that when the door opened, it rang. He looked up and thought he was seeing things. It'd happened a few times since he'd been back. He'd see James in a crowd, think he was in line at the coffee shop, only to realize it was some guy with a similar build or haircut. *He's not coming after you*, Kieran had had to remind himself more than he'd ever admit. Only this time, the initial impression didn't dissolve with a blink. And just a few seconds too late, he realized Jude's arm was still around him.

"Morgan?" Jude said, releasing him.

James had one of his guitars in a soft case on his back, and a drink carrier with two cups in his hand.

"James?" Kieran said his name just as James turned and walked out of the store. "James!" Kieran called after him, taking off around the counter. The door banged open as Kieran shot out onto the sidewalk, spotting James about half a block away tossing the cups into the trash. "James, wait!" He caught up to James, grabbing his shirtsleeve. James jerked away from him, but Kieran didn't give up. He managed to get in front of James, his hands up. "James, please, it's not—"

"Leave me alone," he said, backing up a step.

"What're you doing here?"

"I don't know," James said, his face bright red. Kieran couldn't tell if it was from the waning heat of the day or anger.

"It's not how it looked—" Kieran pulled him into a side alley, away from the bustle of people heading home. "Were you the four thirty?"

James met Kieran's eyes. "Pretty stupid, right? I guess I thought when you said you loved me and you'd be patient with me, that it meant something."

Kieran looked up at James, still not quite believing it. *He came. He came after me.*

"I do love you," he pleaded.

"I may not be very good at this, but I do seem to remember that loving one man doesn't mean another gets to..." He faltered. "Just forget it." He turned to walk away.

"James, please," he said, grabbing the front of his shirt. "Please." James reached up, and for a moment Kieran thought he'd gotten through. Instead, he took Kieran's hands and pushed them away. And before he could do anything more, James turned and was gone.

James shoved the guitar into the trunk of the rental car, wishing what he'd just done—attempted to do—could be as easily contained and concealed. He got in the car, slamming the door behind him. *I could use a drink.* It was a scary thought. Almost two years sober, and here he was, gripping the steering wheel tight so he wouldn't have to watch his hands shake with need. Sobriety was easy for him when there was no stress. Until recently, he'd had nothing for which he'd want to drink himself numb. It was this reasoning that had led him to decide — to his own detriment, he now understood — against Alcoholics Anonymous nearly two years ago.

"Come on, hold it together," he told himself, eyes shut tight. He tried to breathe through the sting. Kieran with another man's arm around him, another man's mouth nuzzling his throat. The way Kieran had smiled, slow, easy...

It's never going to be easy with me. As jealous as he was, he was more envious of the other man's ability to just do it, like kissing Kieran in public wasn't something he had to talk himself into. Like he was a normal, well-adjusted gay man who hadn't been taught to hide that part of him like some ugly thing to be ashamed of.

"Come on, man, quit," Theo said, pulling away from him, looking around.

"Relax. We're alone," James said, nuzzling behind Theo's ear, his hands on Theo's bare arms. Although he felt Theo tense, for a moment Theo let it happen, let James kiss him. Finally.

"Man, quit!" he said, tearing himself away from James. He turned, looking up at James with contempt. "What is wrong with you? Have you been drinking?"

"No." He shoved his hands in his pockets. "Sorry. I don't know what got into me," he said, trying to soften Theo a little. Because right then, Theo was staring daggers through him.

"Me neither," Theo said. "If you don't cut that shit out,

155

people are going to think you're a real faggot, James."

James felt the word hit him like ice water, taking his breath away. "Wha – " He hesitated. "What exactly do you think we are?"

"I still consider myself completely straight," he said. Cut-and-dried, no room for any question. He looked at James, waiting for him to agree.

James frowned. "But – "

"I'd think through very carefully whatever you're about to say, James," he warned.

James looked at him. "I don't know what you think, but I'm a man and you're a man. That's a gay relationship." Theo snorted, shaking his head. "Don't laugh at me."

"Why not? You're pathetic," he said. "You're so goddamned backward, you don't even know to be ashamed of it."

"Ashamed? Why – "

"Open your eyes!" Theo snapped. "We're in a band called Eden, one of the biggest bands around. And like it or not, our fans are a certain type of person. They aren't going to take well the news that their favorite guitarist is a queer – "

"Alright! I get it." He backed away, avoiding Theo's eyes. "It won't happen again."

James felt himself come out of the flashback. Oh yes, he knew a thing or two about shame. He turned on the car and pulled out of the parking spot, not quite sure where he was headed. All he knew was that he was going to have a drink.

Sixteen

Twenty minutes later, James found himself seated at a bar for the first time in almost two years. Though the bar was nearly empty—it was a weeknight, after all—it took longer than he'd expected to put in his drink order. He thought maybe that was fate giving him the opportunity to reconsider what he was about to do.

"What can I get you?" the woman behind the bar asked.

"Double bourbon, neat," he said.

"What kind of bourbon, handsome?" He looked at the rows of bottles behind her. He didn't see the expensive bourbon he'd had the night of the accident, so he settled for his old standby. She poured the tall double shot and placed it before him on a bar napkin.

"Care to open a tab?"

He hesitated. *How drunk am I looking to get?* He thought of Kieran's easy smile as the man at the music shop nuzzled at him. He pulled out his wallet and handed her a credit card.

"Please."

She opened the tab, watching him out of the corner of her eye. He stared at the drink before him intently, pain hiding behind his calm, good-natured mask. She handed him his card, and he put it back in his wallet, shoving it in his back pocket before turning back to his drink. He picked it up, inhaling its scent before tossing it back all at once.

"Oh, sweetie," she said. "How long have you been on the wagon?"

He smirked, the alcohol hitting him hard. "About ten seconds," he joked. "Another, please."

She looked at him hard. "You can stop now, and it's just a slip."

His smile faded. "Either serve me, or I'll go somewhere else," he said with a hint of desperation. She conceded, taking the glass and refilling it. He read her nametag. *Mary.* He laughed.

"Something funny? You hit your head falling off that wagon?"

"No, ma'am." He lifted the glass to her. "To you, Mary." She rolled her eyes as he downed the second drink.

Four hours, three beers, and one more double shot later, James stumbled out of the bar. Mary had tried to take his keys, and when he refused to give them to her, she threatened to call in his description as a drunk driver. He swore he wouldn't drive home and left her with an intense look of mingled doubt and pity. No words of wisdom imparted by this Mary, nor did she recognize him. Maybe that was for the best, although he couldn't help but wonder if that made him a has-been. *Because what's more has-been than falling off the wagon and drinking yourself stupid because your boyfriend found someone else?* He climbed into the rental car. He checked his pockets. Wallet, check. Keys, check. Phone, check.

Phone. Forcing his eyes to focus, he clicked the screen on to find several missed calls. Two from Kieran, five from Phil. He unlocked his phone to find several unopened text messages as well.

Phil: Are you okay?

Phil: Where are you?

Phil: Kieran called. He's worried about you. Call me.

Kieran: It's not what it looked like.

Kieran: Please pick up your phone.

Kieran: Please.

He clicked the screen off. Surprisingly, he could still feel the pain. The edge was gone, but the intense disappointment at seeing he was too late loomed over him.

Phil was pacing the room when he heard the key card in the door. He listened to James fumble, just a little too slow on the draw to open the door before the security feature turned back on.

"Shit."

He heard the muffled swear from the other side of the door. *I'm going to murder him. If he comes through that door drunk, I swear it.* He heard the key card again, and this time, James managed to turn the handle in time and let himself in.

Phil took him in — bloodshot eyes, his color off, pale except for the hectic flush in his cheeks and mouth; his movements slow, clumsy.

"You didn't have to wait up, Mom," James quipped. He walked over to the far bed and sat down, emptying his pockets. Phone, wallet, keys. *Keys?*

"Did you drive here?"

"Don't worry. Not a scratch on her," James said.

"You fucking idiot, you could've — " He stopped, but even drunk, James heard the end of his statement.

"Killed myself?"

"Do you think that's funny? You could have been hurt, you could have hit someone." James's face turned ashen, and Phil shook his head and took a deep breath. "What happened with Kieran?"

"What was always going to happen with Kieran. He found a guy who's not so messed up in the head that he can't touch him in public without worrying about who might be looking."

"Oh yeah? Because he called looking for you. He said he tried to explain himself and you wouldn't listen." Phil watched him, waiting for it to sink in, to show in his face. "He loves you, James. Please tell me you know that."

"No, he doesn't," James said. "He doesn't know me."

"And whose fault is that? He wants to know you. Jesus Christ, are you that blind?"

James shrugged like it didn't matter. Like he couldn't have cared less. Phil's fists clenched at his sides. "What, Phil? You gonna hit me?"

"What the hell is wrong with you?" Phil asked, his voice rising.

Though James stood a head taller than Phil and was decidedly more muscular, Phil didn't seem to care right then. He stalked over to James, hauled him up by the front of his shirt, and slammed him into the nearest wall. "Seriously, what the fuck is wrong with you?"

"Let me go," James said, squirming, trying to push Phil away from him. Phil's fist connected with James's jaw, hard enough that it drove his head back, knocking it against the wall behind him. James's hand came up to the spot where he'd been hit, cupping his jaw. But Phil grabbed him by the collar, shoving him back against the wall.

"You're going to explain this to me right now. I'm

tired of dancing around it."

"I'm fucked up, alright? Is that what you want to hear?"

Phil let go of James, standing back. "That's a cop-out and you know it." Phil looked at him, really took him in for the first time since he'd come in, maybe for the first time in a long time. James leaned against the wall, his color off from booze and anger, the place on his jaw where Phil had hit him red, already beginning to bruise, his shoulders slouched. "You know, sometimes I really miss my friend. The old James would kick your ass for being this way."

James glared at him. "Oh yeah? You miss him? Well, guess what, Phil? That fucking makes two of us. I'd give anything to be him again. I miss who I was before Theo. I miss not second-guessing everything I do, everything everyone says or does to me. I miss sleeping through the night without dreaming about what he did to me." Phil heard the tears in his voice, watched the ugly sobs bubbling up as James slid down the wall, covering his face with his hands.

"Get up," Phil said.

"Just leave me alone," James sobbed. "Jesus Christ, just leave me the fuck alone."

Phil grabbed him by the shirt, hauling him up once more. Drunk, bruised, sobbing like a child. Phil knew he wasn't going to get through to him tonight.

"One more thing before I let your pathetic ass pass out." James looked at him. "Don't you ever joke about suicide with me, you stubborn asshole," Phil snarled. "Do you have any idea how lucky you are to be here? That you're not paralyzed or seriously maimed? Or fucking dead!" Phil panted, red-faced and angry. "You walked away from a wreck that should've killed you, one that you" — he pointed in James's face for emphasis — "caused! When you got out of the hospital, all I wanted to do was shake the shit out of you for doing that to me!"

"It wasn't about you —"

"You let that asshole bully you into believing you weren't cared for, that you wouldn't have been missed. And it fucking kills me!" James shoved Phil off him, and Phil felt in his strength that his intoxication was wearing off.

"I didn't let him do anything to me —"

"Don't. Don't make it about the rape —"

James swung at Phil, landing a strike against Phil's eye, catching him by surprise. "It was about that! It's always about that for me, can't you understand that? I can't get away from it!" He paused. "I can't be normal, I can't think normal. Everything always leads back to it. You have no idea what that's like!"

Phil stood there panting, pressing his hand over his eye. "You know, for a drunk, you throw a pretty decent punch," he remarked.

"Fuck you, Phil."

Phil laughed, catching his breath. "I really hate you sometimes, you know that?"

"Seriously. Fuck you."

"You better get some sleep. Because tomorrow, you're going to go talk to your boyfriend."

James gaped at him. "Phil, I —"

"I didn't come all the way to Portland-fucking-Oregon — and got my eye blacked out — for you to chicken out of this. You're going to sober up, and then you're going to hear him out."

"I can't. I can't face him like this." James sat down on

the edge of his bed, head in his hands, elbows resting on his knees.

"You can," Phil said, sitting down on his own bed, facing James. "You know how I know?" James looked up at him. "Because you are the old James. The old James wouldn't have let me talk to him like that either. Although he might've blacked both of my eyes." James snorted. "The old James *never* would've let someone like Kieran slip through his fingers."

James woke the next morning around ten. He would've slept longer, but Phil threw open the curtains, letting in the overbright sunlight.

"Come on, Phil," James said, shielding his eyes from the light.

"Rise and shine, drinking beauty," Phil quipped.

"You know, some alcoholics might be offended at those kinds of jokes," James sneered.

"Good thing I don't know anyone like that," Phil shot back.

James shoved himself up and was immediately overcome with nausea. He ran for the bathroom and heaved the leftover alcohol into the toilet. He waited, making sure he was finished before slowly rising. He splashed cold water on his face, swishing some in his mouth to rinse the sour taste away. He looked at himself in the mirror. Along with the dark circles under his eyes, there was a slight but noticeable bruise on the left side of his jaw. *Oh yeah, you fell off the wagon alright. Right into Phil's fist.* He also noticed the weight loss again, evident in the way his cheekbones and brow were more pronounced. The thought of Kieran seeing him like this made his stomach flip again, and he had to brace himself against the sink and wait for the feeling to pass.

Kieran had just rung up the last customer in line when he saw Phil come through the door. He caught Kieran's eye just as James walked in behind him, in blue jeans, a black Henley, and sunglasses, with the morning sunlight behind him. Kieran had to force himself to breathe. And then James looked up, his head snapping over to Phil.

"Did anyone ever tell you guys you look like a couple of members of Eden?" Kieran joked.

Phil grinned up at him as they approached the counter. "Yeah, you know, I hear they have this new singer," Phil played along. "You kind of favor him."

Kieran chanced a look at James, which is when he noticed the bruises. One on James's jawline, the other over Phil's left eye. "What the hell happened to you two?"

"Lovers' quarrel," Phil quipped. James shook his head.

"What can I get for you?"

"Two black coffees and something greasy and carb-y for my hungover friend here," Phil said.

Kieran met James's eyes. "Breakfast sandwich? We have an egg, cheese, and bacon one that smells like a heart attack."

Kieran watched James fight the smile pulling at the corners of his mouth. James nodded. "Sure."

Phil held out his card as Kieran put the order in. "Nope, it's on me. Rock stars eat free."

Phil snorted. "Don't want to get you in trouble or anything," he said, putting his card back in his wallet.

"My sister's—" Kieran stopped, eyes widening. "Wait right here. I have someone I want you to meet."

Kieran disappeared around the corner and through the kitchen door.

James took his sunglasses off, squinting in the light.

"He's alive," Phil joked, nudging him.

"Why didn't you tell me he works here?"

"Because then it would've been like pulling teeth to get you here," Phil said.

Just then, Kieran reappeared through the kitchen door, this time with a woman trailing behind him.

"Phil Archer, James Morgan, this is my sister, Adrienne," he introduced them. Both James and Phil did a double take, looking back and forth between Kieran and Adrienne.

"Boy, if I had a dollar for every time," she joked.

"She even jokes like you," Phil said.

"We're twins."

"No shit," Phil said sarcastically.

"I thought men and women couldn't be identical twins," James said.

"We're not," she said.

"My ass," Phil said, and she laughed.

"Well, it was nice to meet you guys, finally put a couple of faces with names," she said.

Kieran snorted. "Don't let her fool you. She still has an Eden poster in her bedroom."

She flushed, shoving Kieran. "Asshole. Honestly, how do you put up with him?"

"Barely," Phil said, and she smiled, catching his eye.

Kieran saw it, saw the mutual interest pass between them and tried not to roll his eyes at it. He looked over at James then, wishing it could be that easy for them.

He watched James and Phil out of the corner of his eye as they found a table and sat down. James's color came back as he ate the sandwich. Kieran wondered how big a role he inadvertently played in James throwing away his sobriety. *Stop it. It's not your fault. He was a drunk when you met him, and it's not your responsibility to keep him on the wagon.* He cringed at himself.

"Hey, watch it!" Adrienne called out. He looked down, realizing he'd burned a bagel. A flush of embarrassment crept into his face. She came over, managing to pull the charred bread from the toaster oven before it could catch on fire. "Trying to burn the place down?" She hip-checked him.

"Sorry. I zoned out," he muttered. She looked over her shoulder at James and Phil.

"I don't think he noticed," she teased.

"I don't know what you're talking about," he said, avoiding her eyes.

"Just go. Be off," she said. "Go talk to him."

"He made it very clear last night that he doesn't want to talk to me."

"Sure, that's why he came all the way out here. To not talk to you," she said. He lifted his gaze, meeting another pair of eyes so much like his own.

"Yeah, and I ruined it."

"No, Jude ruined it," she said. "Just like everything else he touches."

"Yeah, and if I wasn't such a desperate—"

"Just go!" She shooed him with her hands. "I'm serious, go—"

"Addy, it's not going to—"

"Then make it work," she said sternly. "You're never this easily defeated, Kieran." He sighed, untying his black apron. She smiled as Phil approached the counter. "Refill?"

"Yes, please," Phil said, eyeing Kieran as she turned away to do so. "Don't even think about trying to slip out the back door. I will chase you down."

Kieran looked over at James, who was facing away from them. "How upset was he?"

"He took his first drink in two years," Phil said. Kieran couldn't help the guilty look on his face. "It's not your fault."

"Will he even hear me? Is it worth trying?"

Phil looked at him hard. "If that's an actual question—"

"I'm not asking if it's worth it for me," Kieran cut him off. "I'm asking if you think it's worth trying to get through to him. You know him better than me." He looked over at James.

"It's going to be like talking to a wall, but if you're serious about him, push," Phil said. "Hard." His expression lightened as Adrienne reappeared next to Kieran, handing Phil his cup. "Thank you."

"I was thinking," Adrienne began. "The four of us should have dinner tonight." Kieran turned to her, eyes wide.

"Hey, you know, that sounds great," Phil said before Kieran could protest. "Wait. Unless—" He stopped, regarding both of them. "Are you vegan too?"

She smiled sheepishly. "Most of the time," she joked, and Kieran rolled his eyes.

"She sneaks cheese all the time, so no, she's not," Kieran said.

"My kind of vegan," Phil said. Kieran caught the warmth and charm in his tone and narrowed his eyes.

"How about seven-ish?" She looked at her brother. "My place."

James felt the food settle his stomach, making him feel more human than he had since sometime the day before. The effect lasted about a minute and a half before Kieran sat down in Phil's place across from him.

"Hey," he said, wondering how bad he looked.

"Hey," Kieran said, completely devoid of his normal, playful sarcasm. "I want to talk to you."

James sighed. "I'm sorry about yesterday."

Kieran frowned. "What are you sorry for?"

James rolled his eyes. "For being a dramatic jerk."

Kieran scrubbed a hand over his face, looking frustrated. "Can we go somewhere alone?"

James looked back down at his coffee. "I'd prefer if you wouldn't do the whole take-him-out-back-to-shoot-him bit."

"James—"

"Look, I'm embarrassed enough," James cut him off.

Kieran reached out across the table and took one of his hands, and James tensed at the contact. "Please, Jamie," he said. "Please."

James thought it over for a moment, then squeezed Kieran's hand in his. "Okay."

Seventeen

James folded himself into Kieran's subcompact car. Old coffee cups and CDs littered the interior.

"Sorry," Kieran said, gathering the empty cups and tossing them into a nearby trash can. James couldn't help but chuckle. "What?"

"Nothing," he said. "You're just…" He paused, looking over at him, his smile warm. "You're exactly how I imagined you at home."

Kieran smiled. "Like a fucking mess?"

The choice of words caught James in the chest. "No." He shook his head. "Forget it."

He looked away, once again aware of how much distance the day before had forced between them.

Kieran let them into his apartment. It was small, but neater than his car had been. James observed the basic, self-assembled furniture, the multitude of CDs and books, and the distinct lack of a television as he sat down on the couch.

"Can I get you something to drink?"

"Do you have aspirin?"

Kieran nodded. He returned with two bottles of water from his refrigerator. He gave the tablets and one bottle to James. James popped them in his mouth, cracking open the water and washing them down.

"Is it bad?" James looked up at him. "Your hangover?"

James shrugged. "I've had worse."

"You really hadn't had a drink in two years?"

James sighed, making himself look Kieran in the eyes. "No, I hadn't." He watched Kieran study him. He wondered what was more apparent—the weight loss, the bruises, or the shadows beneath his eyes. "I know how I look."

"How do you look?"

James looked down at his hands. "Like a drunk who fell hard off the wagon and landed on his face."

"It's my fault," Kieran said.

James looked up at him. "No, it isn't." Kieran looked doubtful. "It isn't, Kieran. I'm…" He sighed heavily. "I'm an alcoholic. No one has to make me want a drink when I'm under stress."

"I didn't help, then," Kieran persisted.

"I don't know what I expected," James said.

"I do," Kieran said. "You expected me to act like I love you. Like I said I did. I fucked up."

James watched him, observing how he flushed, how he ground his teeth with frustration. "Who was he?"

"My ex."

James recalled the man—long black hair, taller than Kieran, not quite as attractive—at least in his opinion. "Are you back together?"

Kieran looked up at him. "I wouldn't call him my ex if we were."

"But you'd let him kiss you?" Kieran winced. "I'm sorry—"

"No, I deserve that," Kieran said. "I never thought you'd come after me."

James brushed Kieran's hair back, tucking a lock behind his ear. "I adore you," James said. "I love you. Why on earth wouldn't I come after you?" James watched Kieran's eyes then, first stunned, then something bittersweet he couldn't quite name. Maybe Kieran didn't have bruises or the physical signs of emotional strain, but there was something there, something begging to be soothed. "Just say it, Kieran."

"What?"

"Whatever you're thinking in there. I can see it all over your face, but I can't quite read it."

Kieran took a deep breath. "I was a wreck when I got back here. I was heartbroken, hurting." James braced himself. "And being the asshole he is, Jude pushed at my boundaries. But nothing happened, I promise." James relaxed.

"I believe you, Kieran. You don't have to take an oath," he said, lighthearted.

"You're not upset?"

"I was only upset because I thought I'd lost you," James said. "I thought I came out here and put my heart on the line for nothing."

Kieran shook his head. "You didn't lose me."

"Don't speak so soon." He leaned forward, resting his elbows on his thighs, running both hands over his short hair. "I want to tell you the truth about my past. You said you needed the truth before we could be serious?" Kieran nodded. "Well." He laughed nervously. "After the truth, you may not want to be serious with me. But, here goes." James felt the adrenaline. *Just do it. Just get it out.* "The last relationship I was in was an abusive one." He paused, choosing his words carefully.

"Physically?"

"No. Well, not at first," James said. "At first, it was just, you know, belittling me. Encouraging me to drink. Refusing to show any affection unless we were alone." He took another intentional breath. "One night, I-I did or said something that really set him off, and he, uh, he f-forced himself on me."

"He raped you?"

James couldn't bring himself to look at him. He knew if he did, he'd have to face the horror in Kieran's eyes. He nodded.

"We'd never, you know, gone all the way." He shook his head, like it was funny. *Or sad.* "Pathetic, I know."

"Jamie." James felt his throat tighten, but made himself look at Kieran then. "It's not pathetic. No one has the right to do that, and you shouldn't make light of it." James looked back down at his hands.

"After that, I was very depressed. I had these PTSD episodes, nightmares. I was drinking heavily pretty much all the time," he explained. "One night, I was driving home from the bar, feeling sorry for myself, and I, uh..." He faltered. "I got into a car accident. On purpose. I... I caused the accident."

"You tried to kill yourself?"

James nodded.

It hit Kieran in waves. Anger, horror, sorrow. Abused, raped, attempted suicide. *How is he still here? How is he the same man who drives this band? Who is so full of love and life that I'm falling harder than I ever have.*

"I'm sorry. I know it's a lot," James said. "Believe me."

Kieran absorbed it. Someone had belittled him, hit him, raped him, and it all had driven him to attempt

172

suicide. The same man who came through the door at the music shop, guitar on his back, coffee in hand, ready to surprise him. The same man who'd kissed him at the airport, trying to prove he was brave enough to do so. The same man who'd helped him off stage, carrying most of his weight because he was too ill to stand on his own. The same man who'd found vegan cake for *him* on his own birthday.

"Please say something." James's voice pulled him out of his head.

"I just... I...I can't...you...you're..." Kieran faltered. He felt the tears, the sobs bubbling up inside him. *Jesus, hold it together,* he berated himself. *Can you imagine how he feels, finally telling you all that? The least you could do is be strong for him.* "I'm sorry. I think I n-need a minute." He sat forward, covering his face with his hands. *Get a grip, Kieran.* But he couldn't. His self-control slipped, until he was actually crying, his body quivering, trying to hold in his sobs. He felt James put an arm around his shoulders, the other wrapping around his folded arms.

"It's alright," James murmured in his ear. "I'm sorry, Kieran. I should've told you a long time ago." Kieran felt horrible as James comforted him, stroking his hair. *He's comforting me.* Kieran let him for a few minutes before he pulled back, wiping his face.

"I was so hard on you," Kieran hiccupped.

James held one of Kieran's hands. "Hey, look at me," he said. "Look at me." Kieran looked up at him through teary eyes. "You make me want to be better. This relationship isn't all about me. You should have what you want too."

"How can you be like this after what you've been through?"

"I got a real good look at how I don't want it to be ever again." Kieran tried to fathom it, tried to find a place for all of it in his mind. "I love you, Kieran. I didn't even think that was possible for me." Kieran tried to avert his eyes as fresh tears welled. "Come here," James said, reaching for him. Kieran let himself be pulled to sit sideways in James's lap. He wrapped his arms around James's shoulders, James's arms snaking around his waist.

"I l-love you too, Jamie," he said, his voice ragged with emotion. "I'm sorry. I swear I'm trying to pull it together." He sniffled, and James kissed his temple.

"It's okay," he said softly. "I prefer tears over the nightmare I'd cooked up in my head." Kieran searched his warm green eyes. "It's a lot of baggage for one person. I just thought when I told you, you might bolt on me." Kieran shook his head, his eyes never leaving James's.

James's cell phone buzzed on the coffee table, and Kieran handed it to him.

"Phil. Probably checking to make sure I didn't lose the nerve," James joked.

"Phil knows?"

James looked over at him. "Yes. He's the one who got me through it." Kieran nodded. "Sorry."

"Don't be. He's your best friend. He's been around a lot longer than I have," Kieran said. He scrubbed a hand over his face. "God, I could use a—" He stopped short, flushing with embarrassment. James snorted. "I'm so sorry. Excuse me while I choke on my foot."

"Don't sweat it," James said. "Last night I slipped. But joking about booze isn't going to drive me back to the bottle."

"You really are something else."

"What else do you have to do today?" James asked him.

"Nothing. Why? Got something in mind?"

James smiled. "Well, I did pay for a guitar lesson."

Thankfully, another man Kieran worked with, Andy, was managing the store that day. James and Kieran walked in, James with his guitar in a case on his back.

"Hey, Kieran," Andy said. "I don't have you scheduled today."

"I know," Kieran said.

Andy's eyes widened as James came to stand beside Kieran. "Holy shit. You're James Morgan."

James smiled, extending his hand. "Nice to meet you…?"

"Andy," he finished for him, shaking his hand. "Andy Barnes. I've worked with Kieran for years. Couldn't believe it when he went out to work with you guys."

"He's not so bad," James joked, and Kieran gaped at him.

"Nice." Andy laughed.

"Ha-ha," Kieran said to both of them. "We'll be in my office."

James followed Kieran back to his office. There was a small desk crammed in the corner, piled with papers and folders. A few empty coffee cups littered the desk as well, along with some pens and guitar picks. James leaned his guitar pack against the wall.

"Yeah, yeah, I'm a slob," Kieran said with a smirk. "I wasn't expecting company, you know."

"I'm not laughing at you," James said. "I feel like I'm getting to see more of who you are. It's nice."

Kieran pushed the door closed. "Well, Mr. Morgan, what did you have in mind for this lesson?"

James smiled, reaching for Kieran. "Are you supposed to call me Mr. Morgan? Or am I supposed to call you Mr. Jackson?"

Kieran bit his lip. "I like the sound of that." He brushed his lips over James's as James pulled him closer. Kieran realized they hadn't actually kissed since James arrived.

"Well, you see, Mr. Jackson," James began, backing Kieran against the wall behind him. "I know this guy, a guitarist. And he makes some of the prettiest sounds I've ever heard."

"The guitar or the guitarist?" James nuzzled his throat, then nipped at his earlobe. Kieran gasped.

"Funny you'd ask," James breathed, and Kieran snickered.

"You know, this is one of the things I love about you, James," he said, leaning into his kisses.

"What's that?" James asked, looking down at him.

"You're an excellent kisser," Kieran said, and James smiled before seizing his mouth again.

"You're just so kissable," James murmured. A knock at the door startled them both.

"Fuck me," Kieran muttered. He disengaged from James and straightened himself before opening the door.

"Andy, look —"

"Sorry, wrong number," Jude quipped. He noticed James seconds before he recognized him. "I thought you looked familiar yesterday!"

James felt his jealousy surge but managed to keep calm.

176

"Why didn't you say Morgan was James Morgan? I wouldn't have dumped you in the four-thirty time slot."

James shrugged. "I wanted to surprise Kieran."

"What?" Jude looked back and forth between them.

"Get a life, Jude."

"No, wait, this is interesting." He leaned against the doorframe. "Is that why you came back with that stick up your ass?"

James knew it was just a trick of his mind, but Kieran seemed smaller when Jude talked to him like that.

"Probably," James interjected. "I was kind of a moody jerk toward the end of the festival tour. Homesick, you know?"

Jude smiled knowingly.

"Why don't you fellas join me for lunch?" Jude proposed. "I'd love to hear about this tour. Kieran would hardly talk about it."

"Sure," James said. Kieran whirled around, eyes wide.

"Great. Let me just get my shit situated for later," Jude said, departing.

"What the fuck, James?"

"I don't like the way he talks to you," James said.

"So we're going to have lunch together? Are you like, marking your territory or something?"

"No," James said innocently, then winked. Kieran narrowed his eyes but seemed unable to help the smile pulling at the corners of his mouth.

Jude led them to a pub and grill down the street. "Lunch is on me," Jude said.

"Thanks," James said as they took their seats at one of the high-top tables.

James knew Kieran was watching them size each other up.

"I'll have a pale ale," Jude ordered once the waitress appeared.

"Just water," Kieran said.

"Diet cola, please," James finished.

"Oh, come on, let me buy you a drink," Jude said, more to James than to Kieran.

"I don't drink. But thank you," James said. The waitress took their drink order back to the kitchen.

Kieran squirmed out of his barstool. "I'll be right back." Both men watched him walk to the restroom.

Jude wasted no time. "So, are you into him?"

James looked over at him. "I am, actually." He watched Jude slip at his honesty.

"My apologies for yesterday, then," Jude said. "He never mentioned you."

"That's my fault," James admitted. Jude looked curious, but didn't press.

"Aren't you from Georgia or something?"

"Florida."

"And you came all the way to Portland, Oregon, for him?" James looked across the table at Jude, frowning at the undertone of his question. Jude added, "No offense, but Kieran's not the type of guy you come cross-country for."

James shook his head, raising his eyebrows. *Charming.*

"Come to think of it, I never figured you for a queer either," Jude remarked.

"Sorry to disappoint you," James said. The waitress brought their drinks and, noting Kieran's absence, said she'd come back around for their order in a few minutes.

"I mean, don't get me wrong, he's a great fuck, but—"

James set his drink down harder than he meant to. "That's enough."

Jude put his hands up. "Jesus, chill out."

"Why did you invite us to lunch if you just wanted to tell me that Kieran is a shitty boyfriend?"

"He's your boyfriend?"

James didn't hesitate this time. "Yeah, he is." Jude snorted, and James felt his temper surge.

"Good luck with that."

"Alright, you know what? Get lost, asshole."

Jude gaped at him. "Wha—"

"What'd I miss?" Kieran interjected, looking back and forth between them knowingly. James was already on his feet, reaching for his wallet. He pulled out a couple of dollars and put them on the table.

"Nothing. Just suddenly not very hungry," James said.

Kieran didn't even feign ignorance. "Me neither," he agreed.

James turned back to Jude. "Always nice to meet a fan." He beamed with his best fake smile. Jude sat stunned into silence. James grabbed Kieran's hand, and they left.

Later that afternoon, after they'd retrieved James's guitar from the shop and his duffel bag from the hotel, they both readied themselves for dinner. James showered again, aware of the alcohol he was still sweating out.

He'd pulled his jeans on and was reaching into his bag for a shirt when Kieran came into the bedroom. James stood up, T-shirt tossed over one shoulder, cleaning his ear with a cotton swab. He noticed Kieran staring at him.

"What?"

Kieran flushed. "Sorry, but...you're kind of hot." James looked down at himself, then back at Kieran, shrugging. "Oh, fuck you. You know you're hot."

James snorted. "Yeah, here, let me finish digging the ear wax out of my ears," he joked, tossing the cotton swab in the trash can.

"You have ears?" Kieran asked, looking from his chest to his face, winking. James shook his head. "May I?" James nodded, and Kieran came to him and wrapped his arms around James's waist. James felt Kieran's hands on his back—smooth, apart from the calluses on his fingertips—so much like his own. "I heard everything you said to him." James placed his arms around Kieran, resting his forehead against his.

"Which means you heard everything he said too," James said regretfully.

"Nothing he hasn't said to me—or about me—before," Kieran admitted. Somehow, that was worse. For all the brutality James had been through, he wanted nothing but warmth and comfort and pleasure for Kieran. "So, we're boyfriends?" Kieran lifted his head, and James smiled down at him.

"Yep," James said, brushing Kieran's long hair back from his face. "If you'll have me."

Kieran snorted. "You're such a sap. So, are you properly courting me, then?" Kieran batted his eyelashes.

"Excuse me if I turn into a sap looking into those blue eyes," James said.

"Stop," he said, wrinkling his nose.

"Nope." He cupped Kieran's face in his hands. "Now you have to listen to me tell you how gorgeous I think *you* are." He felt Kieran squirm, saw the pink on his throat and cheeks. "All pretty long hair and blue eyes and sexy little frame," he continued. "Should I go on? Because that flush looks good on you too."

"Are you this goddamn sweet to all your boyfriends?"

I've never had the chance. James's smile slipped, and Kieran seemed to cringe at his own words.

"I can honestly say that you are the best-looking guy I've ever been with," James said.

"Same," Kieran said, making James laugh. He couldn't help but adore Kieran's playfulness and sense of humor.

"I don't know about all that," James said.

"I fucking do. Flexing all over the place, smiling that stupid smile, hung like a fucking horse," Kieran said, and James laughed at that, a real, uninhibited laugh just before Kieran stole another kiss.

Eighteen

James and Kieran walked downstairs to Adrienne's apartment. Kieran knocked on the door.

"Door's open!" Adrienne called from inside.

Phil was already sitting at the kitchen table.

"Oh, good. Kieran, help me with this," Adrienne said as James sat down next to Phil.

"You told him?" Phil asked, and James nodded. "Everything?"

James leaned in. "Not that it was Theo."

Phil drew back, looking at him in disbelief. "James—"

"I can't tell him yet. How would I explain about the new album?"

"The new album is a dumb idea. Like I've been saying this whole time."

James shrugged. "We're committed now. Please don't say anything. I promise I'll tell him eventually."

Phil sighed, conceding.

"So, you just got here early or—"

"Shut up," Phil said.

"I thought skinny little frames and dark hair weren't your thing," he teased.

Phil laughed. "Fuck you, asshole."

"She is cute," James remarked.

"She's like, a solid ten."

"I hate when you talk about people in numbers."

"Said the solid ten," Phil shot back.

"I'm touched," James deadpanned.

"Not by me, you're not."

James snorted.

"So, James, Phil," Adrienne began. "Not to be a nosy fan girl, but when is the new Eden album coming out?"

"We're not really sure," James said. "We haven't had much luck getting into the studio together."

"It's Theo, isn't it?"

"What makes you say that?" James tried to sound casual in spite of the adrenaline rush at the mention of Theo.

"Come on, guys. We all have Facebook," she said. "I'm already sworn to secrecy on everything."

"It is Theo," Phil said. "He's not exactly the easiest guy to work with."

"Do you like the True North stuff?" James asked.

She regarded him, making him wonder what she was looking for. "I do," she said.

"But?" Phil asked.

"But it's kind of hard to get all hot and bothered over a band your brother's in," Kieran said.

"Pretty much," she admitted, blushing. They all laughed.

James helped clear the dishes away while Phil and Kieran chatted in the living room. He sensed Adrienne sizing him up, trying to get him alone so she could talk to him.

"James?" He turned to her. "You wash, I'll dry?" He nodded, and they began working through the dishes together. "So how long are you and Phil in town for?"

"I'm not exactly sure," James answered. "I hadn't really thought that far."

"Look, I'm just going to ask it," she said. He looked over at her, leaning his wet, soapy hands on the edge of the sink. "Are you serious about Kieran?"

"I am."

"Because he was pretty broken up when he came home," she persisted.

"I know. I'm sorry for that. I'm...kind of new at this. I've never been with anyone like Kieran."

"A man?"

"A man who's not afraid to be out," he gently corrected.

"I just don't want to see him get hurt," she said, and in the silence that followed, he heard the "again" she didn't say.

"I won't hurt him," James said. She looked at him skeptically. "I'll do my best not to. I promise, Adrienne." He could feel her resisting his reassurances, so he reached for her hand. "I love him. I wouldn't have come out here if I didn't."

"I don't trust you yet, but you seem like a nice guy," she said. "And he's over the moon, so..." She sighed, trailing off.

"I'm not Jude," James said.

She looked up at him. "You've had the pleasure?"

He released her hand, turning back to the dishes. "He's like that with everyone, then?"

"I hated him," she admitted.

"I can understand why."

That evening, James lay in Kieran's bed, reading the

book he'd brought with him, *Black House* by Stephen King and Peter Straub. Anything to distract himself from the sound of the shower, from the thought of Kieran under the spray, naked and wet. He'd read the same paragraph three times before absorbing it.

Kieran came into the bedroom a few minutes later, toweling his wet hair. He wore a threadbare T-shirt and boxers.

"Aww, my little bookworm," Kieran teased, and James shook his head. "Those glasses are kind of sexy, though." He crawled onto the bed, coming to rest beside James. James drew Kieran into the crook between his arm and his chest. Kieran took his glasses and put them on, looking around. "Jesus, are you blind?" He squinted around comically, making James laugh.

"Only when I read," James said. Kieran snickered, handing them back. James closed his book, laying it and his glasses on Kieran's nightstand. He wrapped his arms around Kieran, hugging him tightly, pressing a kiss to his hairline.

"You didn't have to wait up," Kieran said. "You've got to be exhausted."

"I'm always tired," he joked.

"Would it have been easier for you to sleep at the hotel?" James tensed, and Kieran lifted up to look James in the eyes. "Oh Jesus," he said, his voice a somber whisper. "Is that why—" He stopped himself. James blinked heavily, nodding. Kieran reached for his face, his warm, clean-smelling fingers brushing James's cheek. "You're made of steel, you know that?" James leaned into his touch.

"Your bed is more comfortable anyway," James said, and Kieran smirked.

"Oh yeah?"

James ran his fingers through Kieran's damp hair. "Company's better too."

"I'm telling Phil you said that."

"Something tells me, given the circumstances, Phil wouldn't mind," James said, leaning in to kiss him for emphasis.

"True," Kieran murmured against his lips. "So, do I have to worry about you getting handsy in the middle of the night?" He waggled his eyebrows suggestively.

James chuckled. "No. I'm too tired to be horny," he said, and Kieran snorted.

James reached over and turned the lamp off. Kieran turned, facing away from James. Not even a minute had passed before James was pulling Kieran back against him. He wrapped his arms around Kieran's waist, nuzzling his damp hair.

"Jamie?"

"Hmm?"

"I love you. I love you so fucking much."

James hugged Kieran to him. "I love you too," he said, low and soft in Kieran's ear.

The sun shining through Kieran's window woke James first. For a moment, he forgot where he was. But then he felt the little puffs of breath against his side and looked down.

At some point during the night, he had shifted onto his back, and Kieran had curled into the crook between James's chest and arm again. His head lay on the soft, fleshy place just beneath the hard curve of James's shoulder, both arms folded between their chests. James leaned in, intending to press a kiss to the top of his head when a sudden ringing blared in his ears, making him jump. "Jesus!"

Kieran leaned up on one elbow, looking around sleepily before reaching across James. James lay there, startled, heart pounding, as Kieran found and silenced the alarm on his cell phone. He dropped the phone on the nightstand, shifting over, not quite moving off James's chest.

"Mmm, hey," Kieran said, and James laughed, shaking his head.

"Hey yourself," he retorted.

"This is nice," he said, leaning in to kiss James.

"It is," James said, pushing Kieran's long, messy hair back from his face. But Kieran immediately hugged himself to James's chest, and James chuckled. "Not a morning person?"

He felt Kieran smile against his bare skin. "I am, but you're warm."

"I know," James teased him. "Heat thief."

Kieran snickered. "You better get used to it. I'm also a blanket thief." James snorted. "I haven't slept this well in weeks."

"Me neither," James said, running his hands over Kieran's bare arms. Kieran shifted onto his elbows, looking down at him. James tried to push a lock of his long hair behind his ear, but Kieran resisted. "Sorry, I just like playing with it."

"No, it's just…" Kieran paused. "My ears are kind of huge. I'm sure you've noticed."

"I happen to love your ears," James murmured, shifting to nuzzle one of them. "You're pretty cute for an elf."

Kieran pushed at James playfully. "I bet that's a

fantasy of yours, you big nerd."

James pulled Kieran into a kiss. The kiss deepened as James pulled Kieran on top of him, running his hands through his hair, smoothing up and down his back, pushing up his shirt. He felt Kieran shiver and break out in goose bumps as James touched him directly.

"Sorry," James murmured against Kieran's lips.

"Don't be," Kieran said. "Feels good." He rose up, and James helped him out of the battered T-shirt. "'M a bit scrawnier than you," he said, squirming with self-consciousness under James's gaze. James shook his head, one hand remaining at Kieran's waist, the other reaching for his face.

"You're beautiful, Kieran," he said, watching the flush creep up from Kieran's chest onto his neck and cheeks. He suddenly became aware of how aroused they both were. "Come here," he murmured, pulling Kieran back down against him. "You got anywhere to be, pretty thing?" Kieran bit his lip, shaking his head. "Good." James shifted, turning Kieran over on his back. James rose up, stripping off his shirt and tossing it away. And suddenly, he was back down with him, skin against skin, mouth against mouth. James slid his hand down Kieran's trim stomach, inside his boxers, wrapping his fingers around Kieran's cock. He gripped him and stroked him once, causing him to groan into James's mouth.

"Jamie," Kieran breathed as James stroked him again, slow and firm. He reached for James, his hands on his arms, his waist. "Jamie," he said, this time with more coherence. James looked down at him. "May I touch you?"

James choked back his gratitude, trying desperately not to ruin the mood. "Please." Kieran reached up, stroked the back of James's neck, fingers brushing through the short hair at his nape.

"I love you, James." James frowned at the tender affection.

"I love you too," he rasped. Kieran leaned up on one elbow and kissed him, his cheek, his jaw, his throat. James shivered, feeling the goose bumps rise on his own skin. He pressed his forehead against Kieran's as Kieran slid one hand inside James's boxers. James hissed at the contact.

"Look at me," Kieran said. James opened his eyes, and Kieran stroked him. James murmured in pleasure, fighting to keep his eyes on Kieran's. "Stay with me."

James swallowed. "'M trying."

"I want you naked," Kieran murmured against his ear. "I want to be naked with you."

James recalled himself enough to nod, to be able to stand up and remove his boxers. Kieran shucked his own, tossing them aside just as James crawled back onto the bed with him. Kieran turned onto his side, and James followed suit so they faced each other. *I have no idea what I'm doing. Months with that jerk, and I have no idea how to be intimate with another man.* James watched as Kieran's eyes moved down, then back up the length of his body. Kieran smirked, and James couldn't help but smile.

"Well, I know you like it when I stroke the back of your neck. I know you're an excellent kisser, which probably means you like to be kissed. But I'm afraid you're far more acquainted with what I like than I am with you." James flushed as Kieran slid closer. "Tell me what you like, James."

James chewed the inside of his lip. "I like the way you touch me."

Kieran reached down, taking him once again in his hand, stroking him. "This?"

"Mmm-hmm," he murmured.

"All men like this," Kieran said. "Tell me more."

"W-would you believe me if I said I didn't know?"

Kieran's hand stopped, releasing him. James's eyes opened, and the shock in Kieran's face startled him. Kieran leaned up on one elbow.

"What do you mean you don't know?" The way he asked made James flush with embarrassment, which did nothing to soften the way Kieran was looking at him. "Have you—" He stopped. James felt more and more mortified by the second. "Y-you…you're twenty-eight." James threw his legs over the side of the bed and sat up, rubbing the back of his neck. "You're a v—"

"I'd think very carefully about the way you want to word that," James warned.

"James, look at me."

James turned, peering at Kieran over his shoulder. "Kieran, aside from my ex, I h-haven't been with anyone else. And like I said, we…we didn't, not until…" James faltered. "Jesus, stop looking at me like that." James shoved himself up from the bed.

"I'm sorry," Kieran said. "I'm sorry. I didn't realize—"

"Didn't realize what? I've told you all of it. We were together for months, and all it ever came to were fumbling handjobs and me blowing him. That's it. It's like he couldn't stand to touch me, and it got to the point where I didn't even want him to." Without realizing it, James began rubbing his forehead, his gaze turning inward.

"No." Kieran came to him. "Jamie, look at me." Kieran wrapped his arms around him, cupping his cheek in one hand. "Stay with me." James looked down at him. "That's it." He held his face with both hands. "Eyes on me, handsome." James felt Kieran's erection flagging against his thigh and stifled a cringe.

James's phone dinged. He turned to the nightstand where it lay plugged in next to Kieran's. James pulled away, went to the table, and picked it up, grateful for the distraction.

"Who is it?" Kieran asked, clearly frustrated that James would even be concerned with a text message in that moment.

"Phil," James said. Kieran rolled his eyes.

"Can't it wait for—"

James sat down next to him, only he didn't really sit. He practically fell, unable to look away from his cell-phone screen.

"What's wrong?"

"I, uh, I guess, I…" James faltered. "I guess I'm…I'm out."

"What do you mean?"

"Out, like, *out*. Like, the world kn-knows I'm—" He stopped, looking up at Kieran, his hands shaking. "I'm going to be sick." He stood then, hurriedly making for the bathroom.

Nineteen

Twenty minutes later, Phil, Kieran, and James sat around Kieran's kitchen table. Kieran had made James breakfast — oatmeal, bland, easy on the stomach — but so far, he'd only picked at it.

"It wasn't me," Phil said. James nodded. Phil looked up at Kieran. Kieran's eyes darted between Phil and James.

"I would never do that to you. You know that," Kieran said.

"Who else knows?" Phil asked.

"My therapist, but she wouldn't. She can't."

"Adrienne wouldn't either," Kieran said. "I can check, but I promise, it wasn't her."

"No, I don't think she would either," James agreed.

"What about your ex?"

James felt his stomach lurch and pushed away the oatmeal. "I doubt it," he said. "He'd have to admit he's gay too. And" — James shook his head — "he would never be okay with that."

"Then I don't understand how it got out. Ed probably suspects, but he doesn't know. David doesn't know." Phil worked through the possibilities, coming up with no viable explanation.

"You kissed me at the airport," Kieran said. "Maybe someone saw, realized who you are."

"And waited a week to say anything?" James countered.

Suddenly, Kieran's eyes went wide with shock and guilt. "Jude."

James frowned, running it through his mind.

"Who's Jude?" Phil asked.

"My ex," Kieran said. Phil looked at James.

"We had kind of a...run-in yesterday." James swallowed, looking over at Kieran, who could scarcely meet his eyes.

"What kind of run-in?"

"He invited Kieran and me to lunch and..." James hesitated, almost smiled. "It didn't go well."

"Why would your ex invite you and James to lunch?"

"Because he's a shithead," Kieran said.

"Takes more than a shithead to out someone," Phil shot back.

Kieran winced. "You're right, you're right. He's not exactly a good guy. But I didn't think he'd do something like this."

"You didn't think," Phil said. "Do you have any idea what he's been through? And he gets outed by some asshole because you didn't think—"

"Guys, stop," James said.

"If you're suggesting that I don't look out for him, that I don't care—"

"Oh, sure, because you damn near broke his heart when you left him in Florida—"

"Enough!" James shouted. Phil and Kieran both stopped, looking over at him. He shoved himself up from the table, turning away, scrubbing a hand over his face. "I'm twenty-eight years old. No one has to look out for me."

"I'm not saying you need looking after," Phil said. He turned his gaze to Kieran. "I'm saying that someone who loves you should look out for you, whether you need it or not."

"Okay, then, with respect to that, where were you the night I was assaulted?" Phil's eyes went wide. "You feel that? That's how you just made him feel."

"Point taken," Phil said, hands up. "I'm sorry." He looked between James and Kieran. "I'm sorry." James leaned against the wall. "What do you want to do? Ed wants to talk."

"What exactly is out there? Just that I'm gay?"

"They know about you and Kieran," Phil said, and James sighed.

"It's fine, really," Kieran said. "Most people know about me anyway."

"I guess we should go home," James said to Phil. "Talk to Ed and David."

"When?" Phil asked.

"Let's see if there are any flights out tomorrow," James said.

Phil scheduled their return flight for the next morning and left to pack, leaving James and Kieran alone once more.

Kieran made two mugs of chamomile tea and was bringing them to the bedroom when he saw James sitting hunched over on the edge of the bed, the set of his shoulders suggesting the weight of the world.

"Jamie?" James turned, and Kieran handed him one of the mugs. "Chamomile."

"Thanks."

Kieran sat down next to him. "How're you feeling?"

James sipped his tea. "Anxious," he admitted. "Maybe a little nauseous."

"You do look a bit green," Kieran said.

James looked over at him. "Gee, thanks."

"That's for the elf comment." James smiled, but the smile didn't last near long enough. "I'm so sorry, James."

James shrugged as he took another drink of tea. "I was getting ready to do it anyway," he said. "I just thought I'd get to do it my way." He shook his head, looking down at the mug. "I can never do it in my own time, you know?" He swallowed hard. Kieran sensed what James wouldn't say. *It's like being raped all over again.* He heard it in James's voice, saw it in his eyes. Kieran stroked James's nape with his fingers. "Please don't give up on me."

Kieran set his mug on the nightstand along with James's. "Look at me," he said, taking James's face in his hands. "What on earth makes you think I'd give up on you?"

"I saw the way you looked at me when you realized I'm...that I'm technically a virgin."

"I'm sorry for that. I wish I handled it better," Kieran said. "But I'm not giving up on you. Not even close." He rested his forehead against James's.

"I need you," James said. "I don't know how to do this."

"I'm right here." Kieran leaned in, kissing his cheek. James pushed into the kiss, turning his head, seizing Kieran's mouth with his.

"Come back to Florida with me," James said.

Kieran pulled back. "James —"

James winced. He pushed himself to his feet and walked over to the window. "Forget it. Forget I said it."

Kieran could hear it all in his voice, could read it in the set of his shoulders, still bearing far more than his fair share. Kieran looked around his bedroom in his generic little apartment. When James left, he knew how empty it would feel again, how empty he would feel. He stood, then came up behind him. He touched James's back so as not to startle him before wrapping his arms around his waist, nuzzling at the dip between his shoulder blades.

"I don't want to forget it," he murmured, pressing kisses against his back and shoulders, breathing him in. "I want to come with you."

James turned, looking down at him. "You do?"

"I can't tomorrow. You..." He faltered, seeing the mixed nerves and excitement in James's face. "You're going to have to give me a couple of weeks. I can't just drop everything and move."

"Of course," he said. "As long as you need."

"Are you sure this is what you want?"

James looked at Kieran, cupping his face in his big, warm hands. He nodded. "I love you." His tone lacked the typical fervor of other professions of love. And yet, the simple sweetness, the uncomplicated, direct way he said it, all big green eyes and warm hands and hope, knocked the wind out of Kieran. He shivered at the beauty of love that pure.

"I love you too," Kieran said. "Now kiss me, damn it." James laughed and did as he was told.

That evening, in light of James and Phil's impending departure, the four of them met for dinner. They'd all agreed on a restaurant with mixed vegan, vegetarian, and omnivore fare.

Kieran sat next to Adrienne, across from James, while

Phil sat next to James, across from Adrienne. Thankfully, no one seemed to recognize them. James knew he'd be nervous in public for a while, at least until he settled into his newly outed status.

After placing their drink orders—wine for Kieran and Adrienne, beer for Phil, and diet cola for James— Adrienne turned to James.

"So, I know Kieran has probably already pled my case, but I promise you, I never said a word to anyone."

James smiled. "He did, but he didn't have to. I know you wouldn't have done that."

"Will this affect the Eden stuff, you think?"

"We can only hope," Phil quipped, drawing laughter from the whole table. Adrienne smiled ruefully. "Sorry, darlin'. I keep forgetting you're a fan."

James watched Kieran's eyes narrow at Phil. Everyone was always "brother" or "man" to Phil, even women. Maybe "sister," once in a while. James caught Kieran's eye, and Kieran shook his head, looking back down at his menu. James looked at his as well. He hadn't eaten much all day, and suddenly, in the comfortable company of his friends, knowing that he no longer had to worry about being closeted, knowing Kieran was a permanent part of his future, he felt his appetite come back with a vengeance.

"Is it going to bother you guys if I have a steak?" James asked.

Phil snorted. "Such a gentleman."

"I don't care what you have as long as you eat something," Kieran said. James looked over at Adrienne, who shrugged. "She doesn't care as long as you sneak her a bite."

She nudged her brother. "Shut up."

James closed his menu. He watched Kieran, still scanning over his, his hand lying idly on the table. James considered it, considered the man before him. *You're not going to see him again for a few weeks. And those few weeks may be rough.* He took a breath and reached across the table, sliding his fingers over Kieran's. Kieran's eyes went to their hands joined on the table for everyone to see, then flicked to James's. Kieran made no face, no wink, said nothing. His eyes returned to the menu, a smile pulling at the corners of his mouth. James stroked his thumb once over Kieran's knuckles, noting the slight flush spreading across his nose and cheeks. He felt Kieran squeeze his fingers gently, and he couldn't remember ever feeling so sure of anything in his life.

The waiter came back with their drinks and took their orders. James felt his own hand go clammy, but he didn't let go.

Once the waiter was gone again, Adrienne lifted her glass. "A toast."

James let go of Kieran's hand then so they could be part of it. Kieran lifted his wine, Phil his beer, and James his diet cola.

"To being exactly who you are, regardless of what the world may or may not think. Happy coming out, James." James smiled, and they all clinked glasses.

"Hear fucking hear," Phil said.

"I'm only sorry that the consolation prize is my brother," she teased, and Phil snorted.

"Ha-ha," Kieran said.

James let them all go in for a drink before, "Sweetest prize I've ever won."

Phil rolled his eyes. "Great. And I have to ride home with him."

"We, um, we actually do have some news," Kieran began.

"You're pregnant?" Phil joked.

"No. He is," Kieran quipped back, pointing to James. Adrienne laughed, shaking her head.

"The amount of smartass at this table is staggering," James said.

"No, but seriously," Kieran restarted. "In a few weeks, I'm going to move to Florida." Adrienne smiled in a way that reminded James of Dr. Evans, and it was charming coming from someone who didn't have an all-access pass into his mind.

"I figured that was coming," she said.

"Me too, actually," Phil said. "He was a complete drag when you left."

Kieran eyed his sister, clearly trying to gauge her reaction.

"Don't worry, little brother, I'll be fine."

James frowned.

"I thought you were twins," Phil said.

"We are, but she was born first," Kieran explained with a hint of irritation.

"He got all the talent and charm. I had to have something to hold over him."

Kieran shook his head. "And she has for thirty-three years."

"Charm?" Phil frowned.

"Says Prince Charming himself," Kieran tossed back.

After dinner, James and Kieran returned to Kieran's apartment. They took turns showering, first Kieran, then James. James wrapped a towel around his waist, heading for his duffel to dig out clean underwear when he saw

Kieran on the bed, naked. He stopped short, eyes wide.

"Hey there, handsome," Kieran said playfully. James flushed. "Why don't you pick your jaw up off the floor and come lie with me?" James reached back, shutting the bathroom light before coming to the bed. "Lose the towel," Kieran said. James removed the towel and tossed it over the back of a chair. He lay down on the bed next to Kieran, facing him, in the same position they'd been in that morning before it all went south. Kieran scooted closer. "We're going to get it right this time."

"Kieran—"

"Do you trust me?"

James swallowed hard. "You know I do."

"May I touch you?"

"Yes." He'd expected Kieran to reach for his member, but instead, he touched James's face. He ran the backs of his fingers over one cheek, ran the pad of his thumb over James's lips. James's eyes fluttered as goose bumps rose on his chest and arms.

"I want you to tell me if you want to stop," Kieran said, holding his gaze. "Or if you don't like something I do. Okay?"

"Okay."

"Promise?"

To someone else, it might've seemed excessive, or like stalling. Not to James. "I promise."

"Okay." Kieran smiled. "Now, we know your neck. We know you love to be kissed." Kieran looked the length of his body again. He scooted even closer, drawing James's body against his own until they were chest to chest, hip to hip, cock to cock. Kieran leaned in, nuzzling James's neck, pressing kisses along the smooth, freshly shaven column of his throat.

"Mmm," James murmured, nudging his hips against Kieran's. Kieran continued down his chest. He paused, peering up at James, who felt the pause and looked down just in time to see Kieran run his sweet, pink tongue over James's nipple. He gasped, unprepared for how sensitive it would be. Kieran did it again. James groaned, and Kieran closed his lips around the dark-brown point, grazing it with his teeth. James's hand slid into Kieran's hair, and he arched against him. Kieran switched sides a few times, seemingly enjoying the little noises of pleasure James made. When Kieran stopped, sliding back up, James felt almost disappointed.

"So sensitive," Kieran remarked, leaning in to kiss him. James kissed back, more passionately than before. "Did you like it?" James nodded, whimpering as Kieran teased James's nipples with his fingers. "Noted."

"Are yours like that?" James blurted out, cringing at how juvenile he sounded to his own ears.

But Kieran smiled and answered, "Not like yours."

"Is that weird?"

"Nope." He nuzzled James's throat, trailing kisses to his ear. "I want to taste you," he said, his lips brushing James's ear as he spoke. "All of you."

"Yes." He turned onto his back, watching Kieran kneel between his legs and take James's cock in his hands, wrapping his long fingers around the base. He let the tip brush over his lips, swollen and flushed from kissing.

"We meet again," Kieran murmured, winking at James. James shook his head, unable to stifle his brief laughter. Kieran leaned in, took the tip into his mouth. James's laughter dissolved into a soft groan as Kieran dragged his mouth back, giving a faint *pop* as he released him. He continued mouthing the sides of his cock as

James relished his plush lips, the warm wetness of his tongue. Once James's cock was sufficiently lubricated, Kieran gave him one slow, firm up-stroke with his hand, pausing to draw the edge of his thumb along the slit.

"*Ahh,*" James moaned, falling back against the bed.

"Oh, we like that, don't we?" Kieran teased, continuing to draw back and forth with his thumb.

"Mmm," James groaned, eyes closed, brows drawn into a deep frown. "Mmm-hmm."

"How about if I…" James's eyes fluttered open as the overwhelming pressure stopped. He looked down in time to see Kieran press the tip of his tongue against the slit. Where his thumb had been firm and sure, his tongue was soft and wet, delivering pleasure in mild, rolling waves instead of sharp, crashing surges. Kieran pulled back, running his tongue along the sensitive underside of James's cock, tracing the thick ridge there. James groaned and panted, his thighs tensing to stop himself from thrusting up into the pleasure. Kieran paused, and James lifted up on one arm, watching him reposition himself. "Might take me a few tries to work up to" — Kieran eyed James's erection — "that." James huffed a laugh, reaching down to push Kieran's hair back. "Bear with me." He wrapped his hand around the base again and took him into his mouth. James dropped back to the bed, falling once again to the onslaught of pleasure Kieran rained down on him. He felt Kieran take him down his throat as far as he could.

"Sh-shit," James swore as Kieran began to move. He drew back, taking a breath before doing it again, taking him farther. And again. And again, finally managing to take all of him. "Kieran, oh, Kieran, oh my God," he babbled. Kieran cupped James's balls, giving them a gentle squeeze as he continued to suck him. Carried away by the skilled pleasure Kieran was giving him, James was completely lost to it until he felt Kieran brush one finger over his hole. James flinched. "No!" Kieran stopped, sitting back. "Not, not there. Sorry." James sat up. "Not there."

"Okay," Kieran said. "I'm sorry. I won't do it again." James nodded, trying to calm down, trying to slow down his breathing and heartbeat.

"I didn't mean to panic." He saw the concern in Kieran's eyes and hated himself. *It shouldn't be like this.*

"No, it's okay, hey." He crawled up next to James, wrapping his arms around him. "It's not your fault. I asked you to tell me, and you told me." He tilted James's face up, looking him in the eyes. "I want you to always do that. Whether it's with me or not."

James winced. "I want it to always be with you."

"Me too," Kieran said. "But even if it's not—" James seized his mouth, cutting him off. He kissed Kieran deeply, pressing his tongue into his mouth. "You like tasting yourself on me too?"

James broke the kiss, but didn't pull away. "It's strange."

"It's an acquired taste," Kieran joked. James snickered, continuing to press soft kisses to his lips, his cheeks, even the tip of his nose.

"I want to make love," James murmured.

"There's lube and condoms in my nightstand," he said as he lay back on the bed. James found them and handed Kieran the lubricant, opening the condom and applying it to himself. *Thank God I know how to do that at least.* He watched as Kieran opened the tube and took some of the lubricant on his fingers, then reached down between his legs, bent at the knees and spread, and touched himself. He stroked his already leaking cock with his dry hand while applying the lubricant to his ass. "You like watching me touch myself?" James looked up at him, startled to find Kieran watching him too.

"I like watching you do anything," he said.

Kieran pressed a finger into his ass, and James took a shuddering breath as he continued to observe.

"Can I help?" Kieran handed James the lube. James took some on his fingers, then passed them over Kieran's already slick hole. He pressed one finger into him, observing Kieran bite his lip. "Does it hurt?"

Kieran shook his head. "Deeper," he breathed. James pressed his finger in farther, turning it carefully, spreading the lubricant inside him. Kieran squirmed encouragingly. James pushed a second finger into him with as much care as the first. "Good," Kieran said. James felt Kieran's body relax, opening for him. He moved his fingers, sliding them back and forth, around, doing his best to prepare him. He was so focused on being gentle that when he looked up and saw how flushed and breathless Kieran was, it knocked the wind out of him.

"Hey," he said, pausing. Kieran opened his eyes, heavy with arousal. "You alright?"

Kieran nodded. "Add one more. Because you're fucking big."

James chuckled. "Above average," he joked, pressing three fingers into him.

"My ass," Kieran quipped.

"Mmm-hmm," James murmured. "Cutest I ever saw." Kieran shook his head. James leaned down next to him, continuing to move his fingers. He watched Kieran's face, his eyes falling closed again. The flush creeping up

Kieran's neck, blooming in his cheeks, so beautiful, James couldn't look away. He listened to the noises Kieran made, everything so much better than he'd imagined.

"Alright, I'm good," Kieran said, opening his eyes and reaching for James. James lifted up, applied some of the lubricant to his sheathed cock, then positioned himself between Kieran's legs. He took his cock in his hand, placing himself at Kieran's entrance. Kieran opened his legs wider, bracing himself. James pressed just inside, letting Kieran adjust. He moaned, wriggling his hips. "More," Kieran pleaded. Every muscle in James's body tensed from the self-control he was using not to bury himself in Kieran all at once. "More, please more." James pressed farther, Kieran reaching for him. James placed his hands under Kieran's knees and pushed his legs up, allowing him to lean more completely on top of him, needing the closeness. He needed to be able to touch Kieran, to kiss him, to look at him and ground himself in this beautiful reality. Finally buried, he held still.

"Kieran?" He opened his eyes, looking up at James. "You okay?"

"Absolutely. Fuck me," Kieran said, leaning up to kiss him. James drew back and then pressed forward, slowly, letting them both feel the intense friction between them. Kieran arched his back, groaning as James moved within him.

"That good, beautiful?" James reached down between them, taking Kieran's cock in his hand, stroking him in time with his thrusts. Kieran reached for James's hand, stilling it.

"Easy," he panted. James let go, embarrassed. "Hey." Kieran reached for his face. "Look at me." James made himself meet his eyes. "You're doing fine." Kieran's hands slid down his back, down over his ass, pulling him closer. Following his lead, James drew back again and then pressed forward. "F-fuck, that's it." With Kieran's guidance, James found a rhythm that suited them both. Kieran whimpered, his hands reaching for James's shoulders. "Jamie," he breathed. James opened his eyes and looked down at him. "Feels so good it hurts, doesn't it?"

James nodded. "You feel s-so good," he slurred, turning to stifle a groan against his own shoulder.

"Don't hold it in," Kieran panted. "I want to hear the sounds you make when you make love."

James huffed with laughter. "Don't you have neighbors?"

"Yeah, and they'll all be relieved to know the grumpy asshole next door is finally getting laid," Kieran retorted. James laughed, falling out of rhythm, unable to help himself. *Is this what it's supposed to be like?* he wondered. Kieran grabbed his face. "Come on, focus, Morgan." James wrapped an arm around Kieran's back, lifting him up onto his lap.

"Is it too much like this?" James asked.

"No." Kieran gripped his shoulders, and James watched as he began sliding up and down, fucking himself on James's cock. He ran a hand through James's short hair. "I love you." James's eyes focused for a moment, noting the heavy flush in Kieran's cheeks, the swollen pout of his lips.

"I love you too," James panted. Kieran wrapped one of James's hands around his cock.

"Now touch me," Kieran said, and James stroked him, nuzzling at his throat as he did, lips dragging across his skin, tongue darting out, teeth grazing. "Close, I'm close," he panted. James pulled back, looking up at him.

"Come." He leaned back a bit. "Come for me, Kieran." Kieran came, erupting all over James's hand and chest. He stifled a cry in his throat, muffling it into a quivering whine, which James regarded as one of the prettiest sounds he'd ever heard.

"Come, come with me," Kieran breathed as he continued to rock in James's lap. James came, half panting, half grunting, his body jerking with the power of it. "You are so damn sexy," Kieran remarked. James rolled his eyes, smiling.

They disengaged, and Kieran guided him down beside him. James pulled Kieran to him, still panting, and kissed him. Kieran rested his head against James's shoulder, tossing an arm over his chest, a leg over his legs. "So?" Kieran asked, and James snorted.

"Is it always like that?"

Kieran chuckled. "No, it isn't. Not in my experience, anyway."

James frowned. "That bad?"

Kieran lifted up on one elbow. "Didn't we just have the same experience? I fell apart in your arms."

"Beginner's luck?" James said with a smirk.

Kieran eyed him. "I like post-fuck-James. He's more of a smartass than regular-James."

"There's only room for one smartass in this relationship," James quipped.

"What did *you* think?"

James let out a breath. "Not that it means much, but it blew everything I've ever had out of the water."

Kieran smiled, seemingly pleased with himself.

Twenty

After returning the rental car, Adrienne and Kieran walked with Phil and James into the airport. James turned to Kieran, and Kieran had time to note how much younger and more uncertain James looked during goodbyes. The first time, he'd looked desperate. This time, he only looked slightly forlorn. Kieran pulled him into a loose embrace.

"I'll be right behind you," he said.

"I know," James said. His hands touched Kieran's shoulders, then gripped them.

"It'll give me time to recover," Kieran said, leaning his forehead against James's.

James snickered. "That bad?"

Kieran pulled back to look up at him again, smiling. "That good."

James cupped his face, his fingers lacing through Kieran's hair. He drew him in, brushing his lips over his.

Phil caught Adrienne's eye. "Ever feel painfully like the third wheel?"

"Not so often, usually," she said, looking at them, and Phil registered the wariness in her eyes, the apprehension.

"He's a good guy," Phil said. She returned her gaze to him. "I promise."

"I hope so. I might have to kick his ass if he's not," she joked, and he laughed.

"All five feet six and a hundred and twenty pounds of you?"

She smirked. "Five feet, seven inches. And a lady never reveals her weight," she quipped.

"I thought it was her age." Phil turned back to Kieran and James. "Alright, break it up. We have a flight to catch," he called out. James and Kieran broke their kiss, looking over at Phil and Adrienne. "I'm pretty sure your sister has had enough of my bad jokes for one trip." He turned to her and winked.

"Your words, not mine," she said.

"Alright," Kieran said. "Let me know when you make it home." James nodded. "And let me know what Ed says."

"I will." He leaned down and kissed Kieran's cheek. "I love you."

Kieran squeezed his arms around James once more, closing his eyes. "I love you too, Jamie."

James released him, slung his duffel bag over his shoulder, and took his boarding pass and ID from his back pocket.

"Right behind you," Kieran said.

"Oh, great, he's got that droopy look already," Phil needled. He looked at Kieran. "See you in a few weeks, brother."

Once seated on the plane, Phil looked his friend over. James leaned back into his own seat, book and reading glasses in hand. And that's when Phil noticed it.

"What the hell is on your neck?"

James frowned, brushing at his neck with his hand.

"What? Is it a bug?"

When it didn't move, Phil gave him a look of disbelief. "Is that a hickey?"

"I...maybe, I don't know, I can't see it."

"What are you, in high school?" James laughed, settling back into his seat, and Phil registered embarrassment mingled with pride on his friend's face.

"There might be some whisker-burn there too, if you look hard enough," James joked. Phil shook his head, chuckling.

"You know you're meeting with Ed later, right? Like later today."

James shrugged. "It's not like it's not all over social media anyway."

"You're right," Phil said. "Wait, does this mean you finally got laid?" James smiled, looking over at him. "Ho-ly shit." He clapped James on the chest. "Good job, buddy. Proud of you. At least one of us got laid on this trip."

"What, you mean you and Adrienne didn't sneak away?"

"Ha-ha, very funny."

"I saw you making eyes at her," James said as he slipped on his reading glasses.

"Did you see her?"

"She's pretty."

"She's pre— You know what? Never mind. Look who I'm talking to," Phil said, and James chuckled as they settled in for the ride home.

* * *

Back home, James had just enough time to drop his

luggage off at his apartment before he had to meet with Ed. On the plane, he'd felt subdued, resigned to his possible fate. If Ed was supportive, that would be amazing. But if he took a hard line with James, it was an easy out of the Eden album.

James pulled behind the studio, leaving a space between his vehicle and an SUV he didn't recognize. Distracted, he locked his car and walked in through the back door. He found Ed alone in the conference room.

"James! That was quick! Come in."

James closed the door behind him, not wanting anyone to overhear this conversation, out or not. "Hey, Ed." He sat in one of the conference room chairs.

"How was Kieran?" Ed leaned back in his chair.

"He was good."

Ed regarded him, and James felt the awkward tension spike. "Look, just say it. You wanted this meeting because I…" He looked down at his hands. "It came out about me being gay."

Ed sat forward. "James, if you think I didn't already know that, you must think I'm an idiot. We've been working together for what, five years now?"

He looked up at Ed, alarmed. "Jesus, how obvious is it?" *And what else of what I've hidden is that obvious?*

"It's not. Not for someone who doesn't know you. But come on, man, all those years with Eden riding high. All the girls hanging all over you guys, and not once did you take advantage."

"Maybe I'm just not into 'taking advantage' of my fame like that," James said, and Ed gave him a sardonic frown.

"Maybe. Or maybe they just weren't the right kind of groupies," Ed countered.

"So then what's the point of this sit-down?"

"Kieran."

James pinned him with an intense stare. "What about him?"

"I just wanted to say that I don't want this to affect True North. If it doesn't work out between you two, I mean. We got incredibly lucky when we hired him."

"We both know I can't promise that. I mean, I hope that if it doesn't work out, we'll be able to continue to make music together. I think we would. But I can't predict the future."

Ed looked him over. "You've changed," he remarked.

"What do you mean?"

"The old James wouldn't be so honest with me." Ed smiled. "I like it." Ed stood up, and James followed. "Well, I hope you enjoyed your vacation, because I think we're finally ready to work on the Eden album. Theo's here."

James left Ed's office and found David and Phil leaning against the front desk, chatting.

"Hey, there he is!" David beamed.

"Hey, David."

"So Kieran, huh?"

"Yeah," James said. "Kieran."

"Hey, he's a handsome guy," David said.

"Speak for yourself," Phil joked.

"Oh, shut up," James said. "He could barely take his eyes off Kieran's sister."

"Kieran has a sister?" David asked, wide-eyed.

"A twin sister," Phil said.

"Oh, damn," David said. "You mean there's a lady-

Kieran walking around out there somewhere?"

"A lady-Kieran." Phil snorted.

"I haven't even seen her and I think I'm in love," David said.

James laughed. "I had no idea you found my boyfriend so attractive."

"I'm secure enough to appreciate a handsome man," David said.

James looked at Phil.

"He's not my type," Phil said, eliciting another round of laughs from James and David.

"And yet, Adrienne," James quipped.

"Adrienne," David sighed, hand over his heart.

"You're such an idiot," Phil said.

James felt at least part of the weight lift from his shoulders. Being out would've been much harder if he hadn't had the support of his bandmates and management. He turned into the sound booth and leaned against the mixing table. He reached into his pocket and pulled out his cell phone to text Kieran.

*Made it home. Everything's okay. Ed and David don't care. Love you. :**

He'd hesitated over the kiss emoji but decided to send it anyway. If Kieran thought it was dorky, he could tease him about it next time they saw each other.

Happy to hear that! Love you too, babe. : :* :**

James couldn't help the smile beaming on his face and was still relishing the moment when movement in the doorway caught his eye.

Theo.

Suddenly James realized whose SUV he'd parked next to and was astounded that it hadn't occurred to him right away.

Theo's eyebrows rose, and James read something between thinly veiled disgust and manufactured indifference in his face. He wondered what his own face gave away.

For a moment, he thought Theo was going to continue walking by, but after seeming to consider it, he turned toward the door. James stood to his full height, shoving his phone back in his pocket.

"Been trying to get a hold of you," Theo said.

James felt overwhelmed with the weight of every memory, every flashback, every nightmare. All of it led back to this man. Theo grinned at him, holding out his arms, intending to hug James. James took a step back. "Don't touch me."

"Come on, Jamie. I just wanted to congratulate you," he said, his arms dropping. "Heard you were a big, proud queer now." James winced. *Queer.* The word echoed in his head. *Mess. You're such a fuckin' mess.*

"Just leave me alone," James said, hating the pleading quality of his voice.

"We both know I can't do that," Theo said, and James grimaced.

"Why?"

"Because you decided it was a good idea to fly your rainbow flag while we record this album," Theo said. "If I pull out now, either I look like an asshole, or—" He stopped, looking up at James.

James narrowed his eyes. "Or what?" Theo shook his head, and James frowned. *Or what?* He turned it over in his mind and managed to relax enough for it to come to him. "Or they think you might be in the closet too?" James watched the rage flare in Theo's eyes, and for the first time in his life, he felt neither fear nor the obligation to calm that fire.

"Shut up," Theo snarled under his breath, through his teeth, and suddenly James could look him right in the eyes. He really looked at Theo and was taken aback by how small he seemed, how wiry. He and Kieran were roughly the same size, but he lacked Kieran's grace, his awareness of and comfort in his body. James felt the ghost of a smile tugging at the corners of his mouth.

"Is that what you're so afraid of, Theo? That the world might suspect you were in the closet right next to me?"

"You say a fucking word, and I will walk away from this album."

James chuckled. "Don't tempt me."

"I'm not afraid of you, you fucking faggot."

"Oh, I think you might be. I think you're terrified." James took a step forward, almost surprised when Theo took the same step back. "Hurl every slur you can think of at me, but it won't change the past." He took another step, and again, Theo mirrored it in reverse. "Our past. Couple of *faggots* that we are." Theo surged forward, fist raised. James anticipated it and didn't move, causing Theo to hesitate. "Do it." He held Theo's eyes. "But if you hit me, you better pray I don't get back up. Because if you put your hands on me now, I won't hide it. I won't be quiet. I'll tell the world what you did to me." Theo's fist dropped a little.

"Alright, look—"

"No," James interrupted. "This is what you're going to do. You're going to come here in the mornings. You're going to record your vocals, and you're going to stay away from me. If you see me coming, you turn around and start walking the other way. And when this album is over, no more Eden. I don't care what you do, I never want to see you again. I don't want you to text me, I don't want you to call. I don't want to hear from Ed that you're even thinking of coming down here and trying this again. Do you understand?"

Theo glared at him with resentment. "You think because the world is all warm and fuzzy for queers these days that you get to call the shots?"

James grabbed Theo by his shirt and slammed him against the wall behind him. "No. I think I get to call the shots because what I should do is tell the world exactly what you did to me," James growled. He shoved him again, then backed away. "You're getting off easy." Theo stood there, looking at James with what he first took for utter disbelief before it registered as despair. And for a moment, James thought he might try to argue with him further, but he turned and stalked out of the room.

Phil overheard the whole conversation. He'd been waiting outside the door, listening for any indication that he should intervene. When Theo left the room, he immediately came face-to-face with Phil. They locked eyes, but to Phil's surprise, Theo just shook his head and stalked down the hallway, slamming the back door as he left.

Phil turned into the sound booth. James was leaning over the table, facing away from the door.

"James?" James didn't turn. "You want me to buzz off?"

"Close the door." Phil did, locking it as well. James slumped into the nearest chair as if exhausted. Phil observed the way his hands shook.

"That was amazing," Phil said, sitting down across from James. "I'm so damn proud of you."

"I feel like I'm going to throw up," James said, his voice quivering.

"You look like you might throw up," Phil said. "But that doesn't mean that wasn't amazing." James rubbed his forehead, chewing the inside of his lip. "Are you okay?" James shook his head. "What can I do? Do you need anything? Tell me how to help."

"Just…stand by me," he said. "If I need it. If I have to put him in his place again."

"Of course. Every time. You know that." Phil paused. "I know Kieran doesn't know, but I wish he could've heard that."

"Phil—"

"I'm not suggesting you tell him. But, man, if you could've heard yourself just now."

"You mean, I didn't sound like I wanted to crawl into the corner and start rocking?" James joked.

"Not even a little bit," Phil confirmed. "You sounded pissed."

James frowned. "I am pissed."

"You should've seen his face. He was terrified."

"H-he came in here to push me around," James said. "Again. And he expected me to just take it. And I… I almost…" He stopped. Phil watched the weight of the last forty-eight hours catch up with him. Being outed, making plans for the future with Kieran, making love for the first time, confronting Theo. It all couldn't have gone better, but it didn't change the fact that it'd taken a lot out of him.

"It's alright, man." Phil scooted closer, put his hand on James's shoulder.

"I just want this to be over," James said, wiping his

eyes. "I just want to start over with Kieran and True North and put all this behind me."

"I know you do," Phil said. "You're so close. We just have to finish this piece of shit, and then we're done." He looked his best friend in the eyes. "Then you're done."

Twenty-One

Usually a light sleeper when he slept at all, James wasn't surprised to find himself awake in the middle of the night. He rolled over onto his side, finding that familiar back to him.

"Kieran," he murmured. He didn't move. Still drowsy, James scooted a little closer. "Kieran," he said again. Though they'd only ever slept in the same bed twice, both times Kieran ended up curled into the crook of his arm. It was strange that he remained on the other side of James's bed...

My bed? James started. Kieran was still in Portland, getting his affairs together before he moved in with James. But that was him...

Only, maybe it wasn't. He studied the back of the man lying next to him as a sense of dread crept into James's chest.

"K-Kieran?" James closed his eyes. Please, just be Kieran. Please...

He opened his eyes again...and it definitely wasn't Kieran. Not Kieran's thin, lithe frame, nor his long, pretty hair. This man, though of similar build, was fuller in the arms and shoulders, his hair slightly darker than Kieran's.

"No," James whispered, closing his eyes again, trying to will it away. Wake up. Just wake up. *James watched him turn over onto his back.*

"Jamie?" Not Kieran's soothing whisper. This voice was deeper, edged with a self-righteousness that never went away. Not when he sang, not when he spoke, never. "Open your eyes,

Jamie."

"You're not real," James said.

"Of course I am," said Theo. "I'm more real in here than I ever am out there. Because in here, I'm not afraid of you. And you can't fool me into believing you're not afraid of me."

James kept his eyes shut tight. Come on, James, just wake up.

"You let him see you like this? No, of course you don't. He's a queer too, after all, and if he sees what a pussy you are —"

"You're not real!"

"Look at me!"

James opened his eyes then, and there was Theo, lying in his bed, facing him. James jerked backward and was overcome by the sensation of falling...

James sat straight up in bed, panting, covered in sweat. His eyes darted to the right side of his bed, finding it empty. He put his hand on his chest, feeling his heart galloping away inside. He reached over and turned on the lamp. *Because screw being in the dark right now. I don't care what that makes me.* He swung his legs over the edge of the bed and sat for a moment, catching his breath. He looked over at his cell phone. *Don't call him.* But he wanted to, if only to hear a comforting voice. He picked up his phone and clicked the screen on. *11:48 p.m., 8:48 there.*

You up?

Less than two minutes later, his phone rang. James picked it up.

"What're you wearing?"

James snorted. "Sorry, I know it's late."

"It's late there. Can't sleep?"

"No, see, I kind of enjoyed sleeping next to this guy."

"Oh yeah? Anyone I know?"

"Maybe. Wiry little guy, attitude, elf ears," James said.

"Shut up," Kieran said with a chuckle.

"He's a little heat-thief too."

"And a blanket-stealer," Kieran added. "So it went well with Ed?"

"Yeah. Said he'd already figured me out," James said. "He just doesn't want it to affect the band if, you know, we don't work out."

"What'd David have to say?"

"I think David was more interested to find out you have a twin sister," James said.

"Great. Like it wasn't bad enough with Phil drooling all over her."

"I seem to recall eyes going both ways," James countered.

"Don't remind me."

"She's a pretty woman."

"Not you too!"

"I prefer the male model. But I know a pretty woman when I see one."

"The male model." Kieran snickered. He could practically see Kieran's expression, head shaking, blue eyes rolling, crooked smile pulling to one side. After a pause, "So, can't sleep?"

"I never sleep," James said with a sigh.

"You slept with me," Kieran said.

"Ha-ha."

"No, really, you did."

"If I did, it was because you wore me out."

"Noted. Must fuck James into oblivion so he can sleep. I think I can manage that. So, what kind of guy uses kiss emojis?"

"I don't know. What kind of guy uses three?"

"The kind of guy who thought it was so fucking sweet that you used one that he couldn't help himself."

"That's right, I almost forgot; kissing is your weakness," James said. "Sap."

"That's fair." Another pause. "I miss you, Jamie. I wish I was there already." James felt the sincerity of his statement, his tone, lodge in the back of his throat, stinging his eyes.

"I miss you too," James said. "I wish you were right here with me."

"So I could fuck you into oblivion?"

"So I could kiss that smart mouth," James shot back.

"It is the only surefire way to shut me up," Kieran remarked.

"I've noticed." He laughed. "Alright, I'll let you go. Thanks for being up."

"I'll see you soon, okay? I love you."

"I love you too." They disconnected. James placed his phone on the nightstand, relaxing back into his bed. He looked over at the empty expanse of his bed and imagined Kieran lying there in mismatched sleep clothes, or maybe no clothes, hair mussed or wet from a recent shower. After a time, he managed to fall asleep.

Kieran hung up. He looked at Adrienne over the half-packed boxes in his living room. She narrowed her eyes in playful suspicion.

"What?"

"Kiss emojis, huh?"

"Shut up," Kieran said, a smile tugging at his lips.

"Does he suspect?"

"I don't think so." He looked around at the boxes. Another day or so and he would be packed. After that, all he had to do was finish his shifts at the coffee shop — he'd already quit the music shop — and he was free to go.

"Are you sure this isn't too fast?"

He looked back at her. "No, I'm not," he admitted. "But, Addy, here's the thing. Even if it is too fast, even if it doesn't work out, it'll put me closer to them. It'll make it easier to be part of the band."

"Do you think they'd keep you on if it didn't work out between you and James? I mean, look what happened with Theo."

"I doubt a lovers' quarrel broke Eden," Kieran said.

"I guess you're right." She considered it. "I just worry. After what happened with Lost and Found —"

"That was completely different."

"Was it? I seem to remember the dynamic being exactly the same," she countered.

He shook his head. "James is nothing like Jude."

"I know," she said, holding his eyes. "I'm fairly certain James loves you back." He winced. It was no secret that, after all was said and done, Jude hadn't really loved him. "I know that stings, but it's true."

"If anyone knows it's true, it's me," he said.

She rose from the floor, setting the packing tape gun aside. She came to stand in front of him and put her hands on his arms. "I don't say any of this to bring up bad memories. I say it because I don't want you to get hurt like last time. You're enough of a bristly pain in the ass without throwing a broken heart into the mix." He looked up at her, trying not to smile and failing. "You really love him, don't you?"

He nodded. "I'm as shocked as anyone else. I

would've thought this heart would have learned its lesson a long time ago."

She smiled. "You should see the way he looks at you when you're not looking. Phil's right; it really is disgustingly sweet."

Kieran snorted. "Oh yeah, about Phil —"

"Shut up," she said, shaking her head.

"He's a charmer, isn't he?"

She resumed her spot on the floor. "Just shut up and help me," she said, and he smirked.

* * *

A week later, James and Phil were working in the studio. Phil heard James's pause between songs and knocked on the door.

"Yeah?" James called, and Phil poked his head in.

"You hungry?"

James shrugged, putting the guitar he'd been using on its rack. "I could eat."

"Good, because I ordered pizza." James chuckled, and Phil added, "But I accidentally hit pickup. Would you mind picking it up?"

James frowned. "Just call the store. I'm sure they can switch it."

"See, that would've been the smart thing to do fifteen minutes ago when I placed it." James laughed, shaking his head. "Sorry. I was waiting until I heard you pause."

"I'll be back," James said, shoving his cell phone in his pocket and grabbing his keys. "It's under your name?"

"Yep." Phil watched James leave through the back door and pull away. He then went around to the front and unlocked the door.

"Hey," Kieran said.

"Hey yourself," Phil said.

"It worked?"

Phil locked the door behind them. "In spite of himself, he does get hungry from time to time. And I know he thinks I'm a dumbass. So yeah, it worked."

Ten minutes later, James came through the back door carrying two pizzas, plates, napkins, and somehow managing to balance the two-liter of diet cola on top.

"I'm back," he called. "What's with the vegan pizza? Is that some kind of —" James turned into the conference room and stopped short.

"Hey, babe," Kieran said. James gaped at him for a moment.

"Here, I'll take the food," Phil said, taking the boxes and the two-liter bottle from James's arms before he dropped it all out of shock, and placing everything on the conference room table.

And suddenly James was across the room, hugging Kieran, lifting him up in his arms. The only reason he didn't spin him around was because the conference table took up so much room. He placed him back on his feet, only to lean down and kiss him.

"What're you doing here?" James asked, more in awe than anything else.

"Well, you see, apparently, it doesn't take that long to get my shitty little life in order," Kieran said, and Phil chuckled.

"You're here to stay?"

"I am," Kieran said. "If that's still what you want." James nodded, pulling Kieran into another embrace.

"Better quit. We're embarrassing Phil." Phil shook his head.

James let Kieran go, turning to Phil. "You knew about this?"

"He called me a couple of days ago," Phil said. "Wanted to surprise you; asked if I thought you'd be okay with it." James looked back at Kieran. He was about to express just how okay he was when he heard the back door slam.

"I'm sorry, I'm sorry, I forgot my phone." A wave of adrenaline flooded James's system. Theo walked by the conference room, peering in. "I'll get my phone, and I'm g—" He paused.

No, James thought. Kieran and Theo's gazes met. There was an awkward moment before Kieran spoke up.

"Hello," Kieran said, diplomatic, smiling. Theo looked from Kieran to James. *Don't you dare*, James tried to convey with his eyes.

"Hey." Theo came into the room. "You must be Kevin."

"Kieran," Kieran said.

"Sorry," Theo said, holding out his hand, and Kieran took it, shaking with him. James felt his stomach turn. "Theo." Kieran nodded, and Theo added, "Nice to meet you."

James had to tear his gaze away from their hands. *The hand that struck me. The hand that twisted my arm behind my back so he could pin me...*

"Likewise," Kieran said. "I hope all is well for Eden."

Theo looked over at James. "No trouble in paradise as we speak," Theo said, and Kieran laughed politely.

James fought to keep the mask in place. He looked to Phil, finding him watching him, knowing he could see the horror and pain in James's eyes.

"That's good," Kieran said. After what felt like an eternity, their hands disengaged.

Theo turned to James. "I should get going," he said with a smile.

James managed a tense smile in return, and just as quickly as he'd come, Theo left.

After Theo's hasty retreat, James excused himself to the restroom, where he locked the door behind him.

Theo shaking Kieran's hand, like there was no reason why they couldn't be friends. *That hand...* The hand that had struck him in anger, then pinned him on his stomach, shoving down his jeans. James turned, kneeled over the toilet, and heaved as quietly as he could. Nothing came up. He hadn't had much of an appetite since he'd been back, and he hadn't eaten lunch that day. In spite of backing Theo into a corner, he still hated being around him, hated it anytime he had no choice but to interact with him. The nightmares and anxiety attacks were back, not as bad as right after the assault and accident, but more than they had been in recent months. He waited, making sure his stomach was steady before he stood.

He turned back to the sink to see the pale shadow of his reflection. Under the harsh fluorescent light, he looked every bit as exhausted and drawn as he felt.

"Pull it together, James," he said to himself, turning on the sink. He washed his hands, splashed cold water on his face.

In the end, he'd been able to eat. Kieran, Phil, and he ate around one corner of the conference table. To James's surprise, he managed to speak, to reinvigorate his excitement that Kieran was here to stay.

"I guess I should let you guys get back to it," Kieran said as they cleared away the trash.

"Yeah, right, like he's going to be able to focus on anything else tonight."

James smirked, said, "He's probably right."

"I don't want to disrupt your work," Kieran said to James.

"If you can cheer him back up enough, it would probably help more than hurt," Phil said. Kieran looked to James.

"I missed you," James admitted. Kieran smiled a smile that began and ended in his eyes.

"Take him home!" Phil called playfully through his cupped hands.

Back at James's apartment, Kieran dropped his suitcase and duffel in the corner of the bedroom. James put the leftover veggie pizza — Phil had taken the regular pepperoni — in the refrigerator. He cringed at how little food he had, almost none of it suitable for Kieran's diet. He was contemplating going to the store when a pair of arms wrapped around his middle.

"I'll go tomorrow while you're working," Kieran said as if reading his thoughts.

James closed the refrigerator, turned to Kieran, and smiled down at him. "Hey."

"Hey." Kieran leaned in, pressed a kiss to James's mouth, and James kissed back, threading his fingers through Kieran's hair. "Did I come too soon? Am I going to throw you off for the rest of the Eden album?"

James nuzzled Kieran's hair. "I'd have brought you back with me if you'd agreed to it. As rash as that would've been."

Kieran nuzzled him back. "I missed you," he said, hugging himself to James, and James kissed his forehead, his cheek.

"Missed you too," he murmured.

"How is the album going?" He must've felt James tense, because he pulled back enough to look up at him.

"It's fine," James said. Kieran studied him. He raised a hand to his cheek.

"That bad?"

"I just…really don't like working with him, you know?" He tried to sound normal, nonchalant.

"I know I don't know him, but he seemed alright," Kieran said. James saw Kieran's hand in Theo's, and his stomach lurched. "Jamie, have you lost weight? You seem thinner. And a little pale, no offense."

"I'm fine." He pulled away, feeling Kieran looking him over, analyzing him, seeking out the cracks. "I'm gonna take a shower. Make yourself at home."

Twenty-Two

James stood naked under the hot spray, willing the water to wash away the awful feeling from watching Theo shake Kieran's hand. *I let him touch Kieran. I let that happen. If I'd been honest with Kieran before...* He shook his head. *If I'd been honest, Kieran never would've moved out here with me. He wouldn't still be with me. Because how sick do you have to be to make music with the person who abused you? Who raped you.* He pressed his palms to the wall, dropping his head beneath the spout. Suddenly, he felt hands on him. He jumped and whirled around, almost losing his balance.

"Whoa, easy," Kieran said, bracing him. "Easy."

James laughed nervously. "You scared me," he said as Kieran stepped into the shower.

"Sorry," he said sheepishly. "Room for two?"

"Of course," James said, making room for him. He watched Kieran step under the spray, watched the water rain down on his long hair, his face, his thin, lithe form. Kieran opened his eyes, catching James ogling him, and smirked.

"Like what you see?"

James smiled. "You think?"

Kieran's eyes roamed over James's body, taking him in before returning his gaze to James's. He pulled him close. "Then put your hands on me," Kieran said. James's arms snaked around him, pressing their bodies together, and Kieran pressed his forehead to James's shoulder. "I missed you."

James squeezed Kieran's ass. "Oh yeah?"

"Please tell me you have condoms and lube around here." When he didn't answer right away, Kieran looked up at him.

"I'm sorry," James said. "I...I don't."

"No big deal. I got tested right before I came out to work with you guys. All clear."

"Mine was about two years ago. Right after..." James paused, tensing. "You know."

Kieran nodded, not a trace of disgust or even discomfort in his expression. "Have you been with anyone since? I was under the impression you hadn't."

"I haven't. Doesn't really solve the lube problem, though." Kieran smirked, stepping out of the shower. "Where—"

"Be right back!"

James laughed, watching the wet, naked man take off around the corner into the apartment. *Our apartment.* Less than a minute later, he returned with a small bottle of lubricant.

"Such a Boy Scout," James joked as Kieran handed him the bottle, leaning in to kiss him.

"You got me," he murmured against James's lips, and James snickered.

"Now who's the nerd?"

"Still you," Kieran shot back.

James opened the bottle and took some of the gel on his fingers, watching as Kieran leaned into the corner of the shower. He lifted one leg up, placing his foot on the edge of the bathtub, canting his hips upward. He reached down, stroked himself. James came to him, sliding his fingers between Kieran's cheeks, rubbing them over his hole. Kieran groaned, pushing against James's hand.

"You are a sight for sore eyes, you know that?"

Kieran relaxed as James pressed one finger into him. "Jamie," Kieran breathed.

"'S that feel good?" James asked as he turned his finger. Kieran gasped, and James froze.

"No, no, don't stop," Kieran pleaded.

"Am I hurting you?"

"No. Do it again." James retraced the spot, watching Kieran's face.

"Oh, wow, is that—" Kieran nodded, hips undulating as James stroked back and forth over his prostate.

"Another," Kieran gasped. "Add another." James withdrew his finger, then pressed two back inside, stretching him. "Oh fuck," Kieran moaned, bracing himself. James leaned in, pressed kisses to Kieran's throat, to his swollen, pink lips, his flush-warm cheeks. "More," Kieran panted. "One more."

"Because I'm big?"

Kieran smiled. "Yeah."

James pushed three fingers into him, ensuring that his lover was well primed.

"What, no smartass comeback? At a loss for words?" James's eyes sparkled as he looked him over. "That may be a first."

Kieran snickered, his laughter dying off into a soft whine. "Now you know where the off-button is," he joked.

James chuckled as he withdrew his fingers, took some more of the lubricant, and coated his erection, watching Kieran watch him.

"Watching me touch myself?"

"I told you, you're fucking hot. Look at what you do to me."

James looked him over, Kieran leaning back, leg up, hips turned upward, his face and chest flushed, reaching for him. James stepped close, taking his cock and brushing the tip over Kieran's hole, teasing him.

"How bad do you want me?"

Kieran stared up at him. "Bad," he croaked. "Please, Jamie." James positioned himself at Kieran's entrance and pressed inside. Kieran shuddered, fingers digging into James's arms as he pushed against him.

"You feel so good," James bit out. He drew back, thrust forward. He felt Kieran's legs shaking and slowed.

"No, Jesus, stop stopping," Kieran said with a touch of humor. James reached down and brought Kieran's legs over his hips, hitching him up against the wall, his back pressed into the corner of the shower. Kieran's arms wrapped around his neck, ankles locking behind James's ass. "You can't h-hold me up the whole time—"

James cut him off with a kiss. "Watch me." He began to move, muscles flexing, holding Kieran up by the sheer force of his strength. At this angle, with every thrust, James's abdomen brushed the sensitive underside of Kieran's cock. It was almost unnerving how well they fit together. "Look at me," James said. Kieran let his head fall back in the corner, looking down at James. "You're so damn beautiful like this, you know that?"

"S-so are you," Kieran panted. "Where have you been all my life?"

James kissed him, maintaining his rhythm. "Waiting for you, apparently."

"Mmm, 'm about to lose it," Kieran rasped.

"Then lose it," James said. "I've got you." He watched the crescendo of release sweep across Kieran's face, felt the way his body pulsed with his climax, drawing James in deeper.

"Jamie, oh fuck," he moaned, digging his fingers into James's shoulders.

"Right behind you," James said, driving upward into him with more power and intensity. All his muscles pulled taut, his hands biting into Kieran's ass. He came without announcing himself, save for a groan from deep within his chest.

"'S it," Kieran cooed. "That's it, Jamie." James felt him stroking his shoulders, his back, kissing his cheeks and forehead. He let himself be soothed down from his climax for a moment before he withdrew, placing Kieran on his feet.

Later that night, Kieran lay on his side, facing James. He was almost asleep when he felt James move. Kieran opened his eyes, noting that James had turned over on his stomach, his arms folded under him as if he were cold. Kieran saw his face twitching, drawn into a deep frown.

"Nnhh," he mumbled, flinching in his sleep. "No. Nnhho."

Kieran reached out and touched him. "Jamie? James. Wake up." He sat up, shaking his shoulder.

James snapped awake, looking around disoriented and near panic.

"Hey, it's alright. It was just a nightmare," Kieran said, trying to bring James out of it. He saw the fear and anguish in his face. James turned onto his back, hand on his forehead. Kieran looked him over. "You okay?"

"Yeah, sorry," he said. Kieran watched him try to

pass it off, even as his voice quivered.

"Must've been one hell of a nightmare." James looked over at him, studying him as if trying to ground himself by doing so.

"They usually are," he said, trying to laugh it off.

"If it was what I think it was, you shouldn't joke about it," Kieran said, and James closed his eyes.

"Don't tell me how to deal with it."

"James—"

"Just leave it alone." Kieran heard the edge in his tone and reached out to touch him. James sighed, but didn't push away.

"Look at me," he said, and James opened his eyes again. "Do you want me to wake you up if you start doing that again?"

After seeming to turn it over in his mind, James nodded. "I'm sorry. I didn't mean to snap."

Kieran reached up, smoothed down his short hair, looked over his face. He ran the pad of his thumb over the creases between James's eyebrows, watching his face relax.

"No, you're right," Kieran said, continuing to study him. "I forget you were surviving this long before I came along. I'm sorry. I just don't want you to make what you've been through into a joke."

James searched his eyes. "Where on earth did I find you?"

Kieran scooted into the crook between James's arm and the side of his chest. James wrapped an arm around him, leaning down to kiss his forehead as he laid his head against James's shoulder.

"I was a know-it-all asshole back then too."

James snorted.

The next day, as James was working, Theo sauntered into the sound booth.

"I thought we had an understanding," James said.

Theo tilted his head, feigning confusion. "An understanding based on what?"

James placed the guitar he'd been using back in its rack and stood up. "Did you think I was kidding?"

Theo leaned against the wall behind him, hands in his pockets. "How's your girlfriend?" James didn't look at him, didn't answer. "You know, he is kind of cute for a little guy." *He's trying to push you; just let it go,* James thought, remaining quiet. "He has no idea who I am, does he?"

"Just leave me alone," James muttered, willing his voice to remain steady.

"He doesn't," Theo said, confirmed by James's refusal to answer. He chuckled. "And why is that?" James felt his newly won power slip away. "Thought you were out and proud. Are you ashamed of me?"

"I'm not going to say it again. Leave me alone."

"No."

"What do you mean, no?" James looked at him in disbelief. "Do you want me to come clean about everything?"

"Come clean about what? Us?"

"About what you did to me."

Theo shook his head in disgust. "I never did anything to you that you didn't want."

James felt his stomach turn. "We both know that isn't—"

"Alright, Jamie." Theo took a step toward him. And to James's dismay, he felt himself take a step back. "What the fuck did I do, then? Why don't you tell me?"

"You know what you did."

"Are you really that much of a pussy?"

"You f-forced yourself on me."

Theo grimaced. "Are you stupid? You were hanging all over me back then. You were practically begging me to fuck you—"

"I was not!"

"You wanted it."

"Not like that."

"Oh yeah? Then why didn't you stop me, huh? Big, strong guy like you, you should have been able to stop me—"

"I told you no! I told you to stop. I shouldn't have to use force to make you—"

"Give me a break."

"You hit me. Remember? You blacked my eye. You damn near broke my arm holding me down," James said. His voice shook, but he didn't care. *He's going to hear me.* "I had those bruises for days."

"You were waiting for me in my room," Theo said. "What were you doing up there if you didn't want me to fuck you?"

"We'd never gone that far before. You know that."

"So let me get this straight," Theo began. "You come up to my hotel room. You get handsy with me, and then when I give you what you so desperately wanted, all of a sudden, I raped you?"

"Yes!" Theo laughed, and James gaped at him, bewildered. "You really don't believe you did anything wrong, do you?"

"I didn't!"

"I was fall-down drunk! You were my boyfriend—"

237

"I was not—"

"Yes, you were! And if not, then you were my friend! You were supposed to look out for me, protect me! Not take advantage of me when I was vulnerable!" James felt the tears welling in his eyes. "I trusted you!"

"I did not take advantage—"

"Yes, you did! I got mouthy, and you got pissed. You punched me in the face, and when I tried to leave, you pinned me down, and you—" James paused. "You raped me." Theo flew at him then, striking him in the mouth with his fist. James stumbled backward, managing to regain his balance without falling. He touched his mouth, his fingers coming away bloody. He looked up at Theo. "I'm not afraid of you anymore," James said. "I meant what I said when I told you if you hit me again, I won't hide it."

Theo began to charge at him again when Ed, David, and Phil rushed into the room, managing to pry them apart before any more serious blows. Immediately, James wondered how much they'd heard. Phil backed James up while David and Ed managed to keep Theo back.

"Easy, brother, easy," Phil said, holding him by the shoulders. Suddenly, all five men were looking at each other in disbelief, and James knew. They'd heard it all. A tidal wave of adrenaline washed through his system like a dousing of ice water, taking his breath away.

"Oh God," James said, running his hands through his hair. He felt the heat of embarrassment flush his face.

Ed asked, "Is that all true?" When no one answered, "I said, is that all true?" James swallowed hard and made himself look up at him. Ed was looking back, more in desperation than in disgust or anger.

"Of course it's not!"

David shoved Theo back into the wall, hands fisted in his shirt. "You shut the fuck up!"

"James?" Ed prompted again. For a moment James looked around at them; he thought they wouldn't believe him, just like he'd thought for the past two years.

"Tell him the truth," Phil said. James looked back at Ed and finally nodded.

"He's lying!"

On the heels of Theo's dissent, James expected doubt from Ed and David, questions, accusations that he was exaggerating.

"Jesus fucking Christ," Ed swore. James shoved his shaking hands into his pockets. "Is that why..." He trailed off. "Jesus Christ, that is why."

"You don't actually believe him, do you?"

David drew back and punched Theo in the face.

"David, stop." Ed grabbed David, pulling him back. Theo stumbled to the side, his hand coming up to his eye. Ed turned to him. "Get the fuck out of here. This album is off. No more Eden."

Theo gaped at him. "Ed—"

"I said get the fuck out."

"But he's lying—" Ed looked him in the eyes, and Theo took a step back.

"Get. The fuck. Out. If you come back here, I will press charges." Theo stared at the ground, then turned and left, slamming the back door behind him. After a moment, Ed turned to James. "How the fuck could you let me put this Eden thing together? Why on earth would you let me put you through that?"

"Hey, come on, sit down," Phil said. James sat down hard, leaning forward, his elbows on his knees. He was trembling, quaking, trying desperately not to cry.

239

"What's wrong with him?"

James winced. *What isn't wrong with me?*

"Are you having a panic attack?" Phil asked.

James put his face in his hands. "I'm okay, just…" James took a shaky breath. "Just give me a minute."

"Did you know?" Ed asked Phil. Phil looked at him, nodding. "Jesus fucking Christ!"

James couldn't quite pinpoint what had lent his admission credence. Whether it was because Phil backed up everything he said, or because Theo so vehemently railed against what James was saying, betraying his own guilt. Or perhaps it was that James was telling the truth and his friends believed him on his own merit. Whatever had led to this particular outcome, James was so thankful for it that he was near weeping with relief.

Twenty-Three

After calming down, James drove home. He trudged up the steps to his apartment, then stood outside the door, taking a few deep breaths before letting himself in.

"James?" Kieran called from the bedroom.

"It's me," James called back. He briefly wondered if he could make it to the bathroom to look at his lip before Kieran saw him. It'd stopped bleeding, but he could feel the scab forming. Kieran came down the hall, dashing his hopes.

"Hey, how —" He stopped short. "What happened to you?" He moved closer, looking at his lip. "You and Phil get into it again?" Kieran looked up at him, almost smiling. James shook his head.

"We need to talk," James said. "Let's sit down." Kieran eyed him, watching him sit down on the couch. After a moment, he followed, sitting next to James.

"What is it?"

James took a deep breath.

"Let me get you some ice first."

He tried to stand, but James reached for his hand. "Kieran, please."

Kieran sat back down "Okay. What's up?"

James leaned forward, elbows on his knees, rubbing his face with both hands. "I haven't been completely honest with you." He made himself look at Kieran and saw the look of fear in his eyes.

"What do you mean?"

"There's a piece of my past I didn't tell you. And now I…" He hesitated, taking a deep breath. "I need to tell you."

"You're scaring me."

"The guy I was with, the only other guy I've ever been with"—he took another deep breath—"it was Theo." James watched Kieran's eyes, first startled, then confused, before settling on anger.

"Theo?" James didn't answer. Kieran's eyes searched his face, but James had a feeling he wasn't really looking at him. He'd covered his mouth in shock. James felt the painful emotion flare in the back of his throat, because this was the reaction he'd feared so much. He'd feared it when he told Kieran about the abuse, the rape, the suicide attempt. With each revelation, Kieran had remained unwavering at his side. In a way, he was almost relieved to finally see the horror in his face, to finally have Kieran look at him like the messy, damaged thing he believed himself to be. "And you let me shake his hand? You let me stand in a room with him and make small talk?"

"I didn't *let* you do any of that. You were there, and he showed up. I didn't plan for that. I didn't know you were coming in early."

"How can you work with him? H-how… What about Phil? I know he knows. How the fuck is he okay with this? Jesus, how are you okay with this?"

James swallowed against his increasingly dry throat. "Eden makes a lot of money." He wouldn't have thought it possible for Kieran to look any more repulsed, but he managed it. Kieran closed his eyes, as if knowing how they were conveying his thoughts.

"Do you have any idea how spineless you sound when you say that?"

James looked away. "Spineless, huh?"

"Yes!" Kieran spat. "Which is not..." He shook his head, still processing it. "Like you."

"No?"

Kieran looked exasperated. "If you actually believe that about yourself —"

"What do you want from me? It happened. He was abusive. He raped me. But —" He paused, feeling cornered. "No one but you and Phil and my therapist knew until today."

Kieran frowned. "What do you mean, until today?"

"After he met you and realized you didn't know who he was to me, he came in, started taunting me, trying to mess with my head. I'd warned him when I came back not to mess with me or I'd out him too. And it worked..." James hesitated.

"Until he met me," Kieran finished. He looked out the window, although his gaze had turned inward. "Jesus Christ."

"We argued, ended up shouting at each other, and he h-hit me." James tried and failed to keep the tremor out of his voice.

"He did that?" Kieran eyed his lip, and James nodded. Kieran turned away, took a deep breath. James watched the angry flush creep up the sides of his throat. "He's hit you before, hasn't he?"

James swallowed hard. "Yes." He watched Kieran's hands, watched them clench into fists. "Kieran —"

"I think I need some air," he said, standing up, heading for the door. He grabbed James's keys.

"No! No, Kieran. Stop." James managed to get

between him and the door. "Don't."

"Let me out."

"I'm not doing that. You're way too upset to drive."

"Oh, I don't plan on going far," Kieran said. "Just far enough to find him." James put his hands on Kieran's shoulders.

"I can't let you do that." James felt the tightness in Kieran's shoulders, saw the splotchy flush that had crept up his throat and into his cheeks and ears, saw the uncharacteristic darkness in his blue eyes. He'd never seen Kieran angry like this. Irritated or pissed off, sure, but never so furious. "Please calm down. Please."

Kieran jerked away from him. "Are you kidding me? Calm down? After what you just told me?"

"I know. I know you're upset—"

"You think?" Kieran raked a hand through his hair.

"I know. I understand. And I accept full responsibility—"

"It's not your fault!"

"If I'd been honest with you—"

"I would've throttled him the minute he walked into that room."

"Give me my keys."

Kieran looked up at him then, his eyes still dark. Reluctantly, he handed them back to James. He looked around the apartment, then turned and walked back into the bedroom. James heard him go into the bathroom and shut the door behind him.

That night, after they'd both cooled off, James came into their bedroom. Kieran was already in bed. James lay next to him, looking over to see how far away Kieran was, that he had his back turned to him.

"Do you mind if I turn the light off?"

"Sure," Kieran said. James did so. He lay there for a long time, unable to shut his mind off. He knew he deserved every bit of frustration and anger Kieran had, but it didn't change the fact that he loved him. He thought of them making love in the shower the day before, thought of how pretty Kieran was, his looks at odds with his prickly wit. He loved and trusted him more than he had anyone, save for maybe Phil. *Oh yeah? Because you just showed him how shaky that trust still is.* He cringed.

Once he was sure Kieran had fallen asleep, James took his own pillow and went to the living room. There, he lay on the couch, facing the back. He folded his arms against his chest and tried to fall asleep.

At some point during the night, Kieran stirred. He turned over, scooting toward James's side, reaching for his warm, sleeping form. When he didn't find him, Kieran lifted up on one arm. He looked around, observing James's absence, noting that his pillow was also gone. He wrapped the throw blanket from the end of the bed around himself and padded out to the living room where he found James lying on the couch, arms crossed, facing into the back of the couch.

"Jamie, come back to bed," Kieran said, his voice raspy with sleep.

"I'm fine," James said. Clearly, he hadn't slept at all. Kieran frowned but knew better than to push. He knew James was likely exhausted and cranky. Instead, Kieran took the throw from around himself and draped it over him. He leaned down to kiss his temple and then went back to bed without saying another word.

James lay there, stunned. When he and Theo had an argument, it took hours, sometimes days, for Theo to come around. And when he finally did, it was never tender, never I-missed-you-I-still-care, especially if James had dared to be stubborn back. Kieran's sleepy words and kiss, his kindness in putting the blanket over him, spoke volumes about the kind of man he was.

James got up early the next morning, after sleeping only a couple of hours here and there, and decided to go into the studio. He knew he'd left the sound booth he'd been using a mess and needed to clean up. Then he wanted to come back and try to repair the damage with Kieran.

Before leaving, he peeked into their bedroom, finding Kieran curled up in the middle of the bed, all the covers bunched up around him. James smiled as he came in and sat on the edge of the bed.

"Kieran?"

Kieran stirred, looking around. "What time is it?"

"Early. I just wanted to tell you I'm going down to the studio to clean up a little. I left my stuff kind of a mess after yesterday."

"Is he—"

"No. Ed told him if he came back, he'd press charges."

Kieran nodded. "Okay."

James looked at him, his hair sticking up in spots, his body cocooned in the blankets. *One day, I'm going to be able to love him like he deserves.* He leaned over Kieran, kissed his cheek.

"I love you," James whispered. He was just about to sit back when Kieran grabbed the front of his hoodie and pulled him into a proper kiss. James snickered against Kieran's lips.

"Morning breath or not, you kiss me goodbye for real," Kieran said. "Peck on the cheek. What do I look like?" James chuckled.

"Thank you for not giving me the silent treatment."

"I'm still upset," Kieran said. "But I love you too."

"I understand." He sat up. "I'll be back in a couple hours."

Kieran stretched out in James's bed. "Alright." He yawned.

"I wish I could sleep half as well as you do," James said.

"Gotta save my strength," Kieran said, and James frowned. "If that was welcome-home sex a couple days ago, I can only imagine what make-up sex will be like."

James laughed in earnest then. "I'll see you later." He was still chuckling as he got in his SUV to leave.

James pulled up to the studio and shut his SUV off. Though it was still early—8:10 a.m. by the clock in his vehicle—he saw that both Ed's and Phil's cars were already there. He shrugged it off. Maybe they'd all decided to come in and straighten things up after yesterday.

He walked in through the back door, heading for the sound booth. He began straightening his guitars and notes, putting picks and cords away. He was winding up a cord when Phil happened past the door. He stopped.

"James."

"Hey, sorry. Didn't sleep well," he said. "Thought I'd come in and clean up a little." It was then that he saw how pale and tired Phil looked. "Are you alright?"

"You haven't heard?" James frowned at Phil just as Ed came up to the door. He looked back and forth between them.

"Heard what?" He immediately thought of Kieran. *No, he's home asleep in my bed. I just left him.*

"I think you better sit down, brother," Phil said.

"What's wrong?"

Ed took a deep breath, scrubbing his hand over his face. "Theo was in a car accident last night. He's dead."

Kieran had just gotten dressed and was in the kitchen making his morning tea, when he heard the door.

"Forget something?" he called out without looking.

"Kieran." Kieran turned at the sound of Phil's voice. James came to him, wrapping his arms around him immediately.

"What's wrong?" He brought his arms up around James, looking at Phil over his shoulder. "You guys are scaring me. What's the matter?" He managed to pull back enough to look up at James.

"Th-Theo, he, uh, he was in an a-accident last night," James said. "H-he's dead."

Kieran looked at the shocked, confused look on James's face as he heard his own words. He'd seen James cry. He'd watched him weather sadness, regret, confusion, even illness in the form of a hangover. He'd never witnessed the shocked grief he saw in his eyes right then. James reached up, rubbing his forehead. "I... I don't know why I'm s-sad. I don't..." He faltered, struggling to hold back his sorrow.

"No," Kieran said. "No, baby, it's alright. You're alright." He put an arm around him, trying to lead him to one of the kitchen chairs.

"I th-think I need to lie down," James said.

"Okay," he said. "Come on." He began guiding James to their bedroom.

"Kieran?" Kieran looked back at Phil. "Can I just… Can I hang around?"

It was then that Kieran registered the shocked grief in Phil's face. "Of course."

Once in their bedroom, Kieran helped him sit on the edge of the bed. James's hands shook, his eyes coming in and out of focus. Kieran sat beside him, stroking the back of his neck.

"I'm so sorry, James," he said, watching him.

"Why? He was an awful person," James said. "Why, why am I so…" He trailed off.

"Because you have one of the biggest hearts I've ever known," Kieran said, reaching for James's hand.

James chewed the inside of his lip. "He wasn't in my heart."

"Maybe not now. But a long time ago," Kieran said. James shook his head. "Jamie, you're in shock. You're grieving—"

"I am not grieving for him!" James flinched away from the suggestion.

"Just try to calm down," Kieran said.

"What's happening to me? I don't get it." He scrubbed his face with his hands.

"How do you feel?"

"I-I can't stop shaking. And my head hurts," he managed to say.

"Do you think you're having an anxiety attack?" James looked over at him, his eyes focusing on him for only the second time since he'd come home.

"Am I crazy?"

Kieran looked him in the eyes. "No, you're not. But I think you are in shock and you're very upset and confused. And I think if you wanted it, your medication would help calm you down." Kieran watched fresh tears well in his eyes.

"I'm sorry," he said, looking away again. "I'm sorry. I don't know what's wrong with me."

Kieran reached out, cupping his cheek, tilting his face back to his. "Nothing's wrong with you." He leaned his forehead against James's. "Let me help you."

James reached up, pressing his hand over Kieran's. "Okay."

"Where are they?"

"My nightstand."

Kieran opened the drawer and found the bottle. "Half?" James nodded, so Kieran broke one pill in half and gave James one half piece before putting the other back. He returned the bottle to the drawer and handed James the half-empty water bottle from the nightstand. James took the pill and drained the water bottle. "Come on, lie down." James let Kieran fuss over him. Kieran removed his shoes and hoodie, along with his belt. He then pulled the covers up over him.

"Lie with me," James said. "I just want to hold you." Kieran slid into the bed with him, and James wrapped his arms around Kieran's waist, pressing his face against his chest.

"I wish I was more solid for you," Kieran said. "Little more for you to hold on to."

"You're perfect," he said, his words muffled by how tightly he'd hugged himself to him. Kieran cradled him.

About an hour later, Kieran emerged from the bedroom to find Phil on the couch. He was flipping through TV channels with the sound off. He looked over when he caught movement out of the corner of his eye.

"Is he okay?"

Kieran nodded. "I got him to take his medication. He's sleeping. You okay?"

Phil looked over at him. "I'm in shock. I mean, he was an asshole, but…" He trailed off. "I guess he told you, then."

"Last night, after they fought."

"I wish you could've seen him at his worst to compare to now," Phil said. "He's come so far, and I'm so damn proud." He stopped himself.

"It's alright, Phil."

"It was almost him, you know? I thought…after the car accident, I thought for sure…" Kieran scooted closer, putting an arm around Phil. "It just makes me think of that, you know?"

"I get it."

"He didn't wake up for a week. They got everything stabilized, but then he just wouldn't wake up at first." Kieran watched him relive it. "When he finally did, I wanted to kick his ass for doing that to me." Phil chuckled.

"I can imagine."

"That man is my brother," Phil said. "And that fuck had him convinced he was worthless." Kieran felt his own rage from the night before flare, but he managed to stifle it. "I'm glad he's dead." Kieran knew Phil meant it. "Please don't tell James I said that."

"I promise I won't."

"I was the last person who saw Theo before he

attacked James," Phil said. "I ran into Theo on his way to his hotel room, and we argued. I told him I knew he treated James like shit. He told me to fuck off. But I never... I always sort of — "

"Don't, Phil. It wasn't your fault."

"I riled him up. I knew how he was, and I did it anyway. And then he took it out on h-him. I'm glad he's dead. And I hope it hurt like hell." Phil let out a shaky breath. "Sorry."

"Don't be sorry. If there are two people on this earth who aren't sad about this, it's you and me." Phil smirked. "I promise I won't tell him. Although I don't think he'd ever hold any of it against you. You're his brother too."

"So I take a nap and I come out to find my best friend in my boyfriend's arms?" Kieran and Phil looked over. James smiled, shaking his head.

"You know, I am starting to see what you mean about his dreamy blue eyes," Phil quipped, and James snorted.

"Shut up." James plopped down in the armchair, and Kieran got up and came over to him.

"How're you feeling?"

"A little better," James said.

"Hungry at all?"

"Believe it or not."

"Yeah? What would you like?" Just then, there was another knock. Kieran went to the door and peered through the peephole. "David." He let him in.

"Hey," David said. "Ed said you guys were over here."

"I guess you heard," Phil said. David nodded.

"I was just about to make breakfast," Kieran said. "Are we all hungry?"

"Is it going to be some weird vegan breakfast?" Phil asked.

"He does make a pretty awesome tofu scramble," James said, and Phil rolled his eyes.

"There's something I never thought I'd hear him say."

Twenty-Four

The morning of Theo's funeral, it rained. By the time Kieran woke, James had showered and was half dressed, standing over the stove, waiting for the kettle to steam.

"Hey," Kieran said.

James looked over at him. "Hey." Just-woken-up Kieran had to be one of his favorite sights. His blue eyes squinted at any light, and because he typically showered at night, his hair was a mess upon waking. His sleep clothes always hung off him, a size or so too big and usually threadbare.

Kieran shuffled over to him. "A watched pot never boils, you know." James put an arm around him, and Kieran's arms wrapped around his middle. James kissed his forehead.

"You don't have to go with me if you don't want to," James said.

"I know. And for the hundredth time, I'm going with you."

"I know."

"Are you hungry?"

"Not really."

"Too bad. I'm making oatmeal, and you're going to eat at least a little bit."

James smirked down at him. "Yes, dear."

Kieran pinched his ass.

"Hey!"

"Go on, finish getting ready," Kieran said. "Your tea and breakfast will be ready shortly."

When he came back, Kieran had oatmeal and tea waiting for him. Normally, James would've had coffee, but he found that at least for now, the caffeine made his anxiety and subsequent lack of appetite worse. He sat down, noting the diced apple and cinnamon in the oatmeal. Kieran scraped the last of his own breakfast from his bowl.

"Looks good," James remarked.

"So do you," Kieran said, winking as he licked the spoon clean.

James smiled, shaking his head. He knew Kieran had been working extra hard to make him smile or laugh, and one day, when it wouldn't choke him up to do so, he'd thank him for it. James took a bite.

Satisfied, Kieran rose. "Won't take me long." He leaned down, pressing a kiss to James's temple before going to ready himself.

The rain had slowed in time for the service, but hadn't entirely stopped. Florida might not offer every season in all its glory, but the drizzle combined with the chill in the air felt like autumn. Kieran stood beside James at the back of the small gathering at the graveside, Phil on his other side, David and Ed in front of them. He kept a close watch on James. Even behind the black suit and dark sunglasses, he could read his tension, anxiety, along with some form of grief that seemed to baffle James more than it did Kieran. As the casket was lowered into the ground, he slipped his hand into James's and squeezed.

James squeezed back. Kieran looked up at his profile, as set and calm as he could muster. But he could feel in the quiver of James's hand, in the chill of his fingers, what that stoicism was costing him.

Back at the SUV, Kieran let them in. James had agreed to let him drive, admitting that he wasn't sure how he would feel after the service. Kieran watched him climb into the passenger seat. He leaned back, his hands on his knees.

"You okay, Jamie?" James took his sunglasses off, and Kieran saw the tears.

"I don't know," James said, wiping them away. "I guess I don't know how I feel."

Kieran nodded. "Let's go home."

* * *

James sat across from Dr. Evans. As pleasant and pristine as always, she regarded him with some caution.

"Don't worry, Doc. I think the worst of the grief is behind me."

"It's okay if it's not."

"I'd rather not grieve over him any longer than I have to."

"I understand. But sometimes we can't control how long it takes us to process death. Especially one so wrought with complications."

He snorted. "Tell me about it."

"How do you feel about Theo's death?"

"I don't know how to answer that question."

"Answer it honestly."

James looked down at his hands. "If I say I'm sad, people would wonder why, given what he put me through. If I say I'm happy, I sound like a psychopath."

"There's more than just sad or happy."

"And what would be normal for someone like me?" he asked, looking up at her.

"There is no normal, James."

He sighed. "At first, I was very upset. Poor Kieran. I completely fell apart on him."

"And how did he handle it?"

"Amazingly. I don't know that I would've been so understanding in his place."

"With yourself? Or with him, if the tables were turned?"

He frowned in confusion. "I don't follow."

"Let's say your past was like Kieran's and Kieran's like yours. The person who abused and assaulted him dies and he grieves. How understanding would you be?"

"I hope as understanding as he was with me. I love him."

"So what you meant was if you had to console yourself, you wouldn't be able to do it?"

"It just didn't feel right, crying over his death like that."

"Before he hurt you, before he assaulted you, would you have called him a friend?"

"I guess so."

"You were close. Close enough to make music together. Close enough to develop feelings for each other—however problematic they became. Close enough to become intimate."

James felt exhausted thinking of it. He nodded.

"Do you think you might've been grieving for that time? For that version of Theo?"

He looked at her hard. "There was only one Theo."

"True. But we change as time goes by."

James tried to think back, but his mind and heart fought it. "I can't go back there," he said. "It hurts too much."

"I understand. And I'm not suggesting you go digging through your memories of him right now. But I want you to be aware that's likely where your grief is coming from. It'll subside on its own, in time. But I would encourage you to express it, not bottle it up." She paused. "How do you feel about the fact that he died in a car accident?"

He swallowed hard. "I don't know."

"I only ask because when you attempted suicide, it was with a car accident."

He rubbed his forehead. "It just feels so strange. That afternoon, he was alive. We argued. He was angry with me."

"I remember."

"The next morning, he was gone. Just gone."

"Does that scare you?"

"I wanted to die. I should've died. I jerked my car in front of a semi. I never should've made it."

"But you did."

"It's terrifying to think how close I came."

"Why?"

He met her eyes. "Because, I never would've made True North. I never would've found Kieran again. I wouldn't have gotten better. It could so easily have gone the other way for me."

"But it didn't. You're here. You have your band. You have Kieran. You are getting better. It's just making you consider your own mortality, which is completely normal."

"I'm so grateful I survived. I'm so happy to be alive."

She smiled. "I've waited over two years to hear you say that."

He looked up at her, smiling back. "Does that mean I'm finally fixed?" He winked, and she laughed.

"You're getting closer all the time, James."

James walked through his apartment door to find Kieran standing over the stove.

"Hey," Kieran said, turning to face him, leaning against the counter.

"Hey," James said, hanging his keys on the hook. He walked to Kieran, then leaned down to kiss him.

"How'd it go?"

"Okay," James said.

"No startling revelations?"

"Not this week," James said with a smile. Maybe someday he'd tell Kieran about how much Dr. Evans had helped him. But for now, he just wanted to let it be. "What're you making?" James looked over at the large pot on the stove.

"Vegetable soup," Kieran answered. "Easy on the stomach." He patted James's trim waist for emphasis as he turned back to cooking. He insisted that James eat more regularly, so he bought and cooked things that were easier on James's nervous stomach.

James leaned against the counter, watching him. Since he'd moved in, James had become aware of just how small his apartment was. He'd waited for it to get on their nerves, waited for them to get on each other's nerves. Somehow, it hadn't happened yet. He looked in the living room, at the stacks of partially unpacked boxes and miscellaneous furniture that belonged to Kieran. Whereas they seemed to fit well with each other, their stuff needed more room. Kieran followed his gaze.

"I know, it drives me nuts too," Kieran said. "And I'm the slob."

James looked back at him. "You're not as bad as you think you are. But I think we are going to need a bigger place."

"I still need to find work. I haven't exactly been looking," he admitted.

James came up behind him, wrapping his arms around him. "You've been too busy taking care of me," James said, resting his cheek against Kieran's hair, and Kieran leaned into him.

"I don't mind," he said. He turned, wrapping his arms around James's waist. James cupped his face, kissing him once. Twice.

"I love you," he said.

"I love you too," Kieran responded, and James kissed him again, deeper.

"How much longer does that need to simmer?"

Kieran smiled against his lips. "A couple of hours at least."

"Good." James lifted him, and Kieran wrapped his arms and legs around him. "Because we're due for some make-up sex."

The swiftness with which James undressed both of them excited Kieran. He turned toward the bed, but James stopped him, pulling him back against him. His hands were everywhere, smoothing and feeling and squeezing him.

"Jamie." Kieran leaned back, feeling the length of James's body pressed against him from behind. James nuzzled his shoulders, the back of his neck.

"Get on the bed," James murmured in his ear. There was urgency in his voice that sent an erotic shiver through him, making him break out in goose bumps. He crawled onto the bed, and he felt James follow him. He went to turn over when he felt James's hands on his hips. "Stay like this," he instructed. James hovered behind him, running his hands over him. He brushed Kieran's hair aside, and his mouth grazed his nape, nipped his shoulders. Kieran pushed his ass into the cradle of James's hips. He felt the heat and rigidity of James's cock, heard James groan, his teeth latching on to his shoulder a little harder than before. "You're such a tease," James said, chuckling.

"Who's manhandling who?"

"I just can't get enough of you," James said. Suddenly, his mouth was gone, as was the heat of his chest as he'd loomed over him. Kieran turned to look over his shoulder when he felt James's hands on his ass. His big hands grasped his cheeks, squeezing. Kieran loved it, loved how James touched him. And then he felt James's mouth grazing the smooth curve of his ass as he dragged his lips along the soft flesh. "I just can't get enough," he repeated. Kieran felt him spread his cheeks, and without warning, he felt James press his mouth against him.

"Oh fuck," Kieran swore, folding his arms and resting his forehead against them. He felt James's tongue tracing his hole, flicking back and forth over it. One of James's hands continued to stroke over his ass and lower back, almost comforting him. He pulled back, and Kieran felt him tease him with his fingers. "Jesus, Jamie," Kieran breathed.

"You like this?"

Kieran felt his mouth again, his tongue pressing, soft but insistent. "Uh-huh," Kieran panted, nodding, even though James couldn't see him do it. James alternated between using his mouth and his fingers, playing with Kieran, opening him with maddening slowness.

After several minutes like this, he became aware that James had gotten up. He heard the nightstand drawer, heard the sharp *pop* of the lubricant cap as he opened it. He felt James resume his place behind him, felt him apply the lube, his warm touch ensuring that Kieran was thoroughly prepared. He'd never known a more careful, generous lover.

"You're trembling," James said.

"You're making me crazy," Kieran said, managing to stifle his emotion. He heard James snicker as he bent over him, placing himself at Kieran's entrance.

"I just figured you were due for a little ass-kissing," James said in his ear. Kieran snorted, chuckling as James pressed inside, his laughter dissolving into a groan as he pushed back against him.

James gripped his hips, drew back, thrust forward. Kieran lay prone before him, wriggling as he moved, whimpering into his folded arms. Suddenly, James paused, reaching for him, pulling him up against him.

Kieran let himself be manipulated into a sitting position, his back against James's chest, James buried firmly inside him.

"Jamie," Kieran breathed as one of James's arms locked around his waist, anchoring him against the bigger man. His free hand was everywhere, feeling him, fingertips brushing over his nipples, stroking down his stomach. Kieran reached behind him, his hands on James's hips, grasping him as he continued to rock back and forth within Kieran's body.

"How does it keep getting better with you?"

Kieran had no explanation. He hadn't experienced this level of intimacy with anyone else. "I don't know," he admitted. "But it does." He grabbed James's free hand, wrapping it around his cock. "Touch me." James stroked him in time with his thrusts, and Kieran rode the waves of pleasure, increasingly shattered and shaking. He felt himself spiraling closer, his cock twitching in James's hand. James let go of his side and turned Kieran's head, seizing his mouth just as he came. Kieran moaned against his lips.

It took Kieran several seconds to come back to himself, but once he did, he didn't miss a beat. He began to fuck himself on James's cock, rocking and rotating his hips, drawing short, gasping breaths from his lover. He felt James's fingers digging into his hips, felt the wall of muscle pressed firmly against his back begin to tense. Kieran kissed him in quick, fleeting kisses.

"K-Kieran, I'm—"

Kieran felt the vibration against his back as James groaned with his release. His head dropped to Kieran's shoulder, and Kieran felt the sharp bursts of heat as James filled him with his seed. James gripped him for nearly a minute, hips jerking as his orgasm played out. After a few moments, when James didn't move, Kieran became concerned.

"You okay?" No answer. "Jamie?" James moved then, lifting Kieran, withdrawing from him. The ache of that emptiness was compounded when he saw the look on James's face as he fought tears, the emotion there unmistakable. "James—"

"'M okay," he said, fighting to get control of his

voice. "Sorry. I'm sorry." He rubbed his forehead. Kieran guided him down to the bed with him, pulling the covers up around them.

"It's okay," Kieran said, scooting close. "You've been through a lot."

"It's not that," James said. "I'm just, I—"

Kieran ran a hand over his short, dark hair. "You can tell me."

"I'm just so damn happy to be alive." He chewed the inside of his lip. "Is that awful?"

"Of course it's not."

"I... I didn't really know I felt that way until he...until Th-Theo..."

Kieran pulled him closer, wrapping his arms around James, pressing his forehead to his. "I promise you, that doesn't make you awful," Kieran said. "That makes you human."

At that, James finally let go. He cried for a long time, and Kieran didn't interrupt. He held James, pressing kisses to his hairline, holding him tighter when the sobs wracked him, smoothing his hands over his back.

After a time, when James's tears had dried and his sobs quieted, they found that neither of them wanted to let the other go.

Epilogue

A year later...

For the first thirty seconds he was awake, James forgot where he was. Again. But it came back to him, like it always did. He was home. They were home. They'd found a house not far from the studio that suited them better than James's old apartment.

He heard the soft, droning snore coming from his side and looked down at Kieran. *A bomb could go off, and he'd sleep right through it.* Kieran's breath puffed against James's side, his long, messy hair tickling James's shoulder and arm. He could feel Kieran's hands pressed against his side as well. James cuddled him close. To his surprise, the slight movement woke Kieran, who peered up at him through sleepy blue eyes.

"Hey," Kieran croaked.

"All this bed, and you still end up right here," James teased.

"I like invading your personal space," Kieran joked. James laughed, looking him over as he lifted up on one elbow.

"That's some great hair," James said, and Kieran smirked.

"You know, I try," Kieran said, making no move to smooth it down. James leaned in to kiss him, then pulled him on top of him.

"So, little elf, what would you like for Christmas?"

"If I'm an elf, what does that make you?"

"Santa?"

"Now *that* is a very different story from what they tell kids," Kieran quipped.

* * *

After working on some music for the new True North album, James came by the vocals ISO booth.

"I'm going to go pick up Addy," James said, shrugging into his jacket.

"Enjoy your bonding time!"

James leaned in to kiss him. "Will do."

Adrienne climbed into James's SUV. "Hey!"

"Hey," he said, briefly leaning in to kiss her cheek. "How was your flight?"

"I slept through most of it."

"I can't sleep half the time in my own bed, but you and your brother can fall asleep anywhere. It's almost unfair," he said, and she laughed. "I want to do something before I take you back to the house, if you're not too tired."

"Ha-ha. Where are we going?"

"Lunch, but I want to do something else first."

She narrowed her eyes.

"It's a surprise."

When James pulled into the parking lot of the jewelry store, Adrienne looked over at him, eyes wide. He smiled.

"I know you guys aren't exactly close with your

folks, so I...wanted to ask for your blessing," he explained. "I know you didn't trust me at first, but I hope I've earned your trust. Because I love him, Adrienne. I want to marry him." He watched her as she bit her lip, fighting the tears welling in her eyes.

"Are you asking me for his hand?" she tried to tease through her tears.

"I am." He took a nervous breath. "I'm not exactly sure how he'll react. We've never really discussed it." He looked down at his hands, and she reached over and squeezed his arm.

"He'll love it," she said. "It might shock the hell out of him, but he will."

"Do I have your blessing?"

She nodded, wiping her eyes. "You do."

He beamed. "Alright, come on. Now I want your opinion."

Inside the store, James approached the counter, Adrienne at his side.

"Mr. Morgan," the man behind the counter said.

"Hey, Roger."

"Have you finally decided?"

James looked over at Adrienne. "I brought help. Can we look at the rings I picked?"

"Of course." Roger turned, then brought the small tray out. Three sparkling rings sat in the grooves of the velvet tray. "All fine choices."

The first ring featured a square black-onyx stone flanked by two smaller diamonds. The second featured two equally shaped and sized aquamarines. The third and final featured three identical diamonds. Each ring was set in platinum, each shining brilliantly beneath the store lights.

"My God, James," Adrienne said. "They're all beautiful."

"Which one do you think?"

"This one," she said, pointing to the one with the three identical diamonds. "This one's most him, for sure." She smiled up at him, and he nodded, looking to Roger.

"That's the one," he said.

She looked at them again. "Are you sure? That's just my opinion. They're all amazing—"

"That's the one, Addy. You're absolutely right. It's him." She beamed.

"You have excellent taste, miss," Roger said. He took the ring and placed it in a red velvet box. When he rang it up, Adrienne's jaw dropped.

"He's worth every penny," James said before she could say anything. After he'd paid and they walked back out into the cool, early winter air, she stopped him. "Addy—"

"No," she said. "No. I just wanted to thank you. He's never been this happy. Ever."

"I want to make him happy."

"You do," she said. "You will."

He nodded, shivering. "Come on, then, it's freezing out here."

She laughed. "You think this is freezing?"

He chuckled. "You sound like Kieran." They climbed into his SUV, and he handed her the bag.

"Hide it in your stuff," he said. She hesitated, her expression similar to the one she'd made when he'd paid for the ring. "He won't go through your stuff. We just moved, and I have no idea where to hide it from him."

She softened. "Alright. I won't lose it, I swear."

He smiled. "I know you won't."

Somehow, in the midst of moving into the new house and working on the new album, he and Kieran — with Adrienne and Phil's help — found time to decorate their living room for Christmas.

Their tree, artificial this time — *"Next year, it's going to be a live one,"* Kieran had insisted as they'd loaded the box into James's SUV. *"This just feels like cheating."* — was decorated in white lights, with strings of silver and gold beads and ornaments in red, green, silver, gold, and blue. At the top sat a five-point star glowing softly white.

James sat back in the far corner of the sofa they'd brought with them from his old apartment, Kieran nestled in beside him — at least until it was time to give James his present.

Kieran hopped up, the white ball on the end of the Santa hat he wore bouncing as he did, and hefted one of the bigger boxes from under the tree. He plopped it down in front of James with a huff at the strand of hair that'd fallen in his face.

"For you," he said.

James placed his coffee cup on the end table. "I must've been a good boy this year," he joked, pulling the box toward him. Kieran, Phil, and Adrienne watched him tear the wrapping paper before opening the thick cardboard box within. He looked inside, then smiled up at Kieran.

"For my favorite nerd."

James lifted the two books out of the box.

"What books are they?" Adrienne peered over, trying to get a look at the covers.

"Stephen King?" Phil asked with a smile.

"And Peter Straub." James looked them over. *"The*

Talisman and *Black House*."

"Check the copyright pages," Kieran hinted from his perch on the arm of the couch.

James looked up at him, eyes wide. "You're kidding."

"Check them."

James flipped the first book open, then the second. "They're first editions. Kieran — "

Kieran cut him off, stifling the impending protest with a kiss. "Just enjoy them, would you?"

James looked around. "Where're my glasses?"

"I knew I should've ordered the large-print editions," Kieran quipped, and James shook his head, putting the books back in the box.

"You next. Although, I'm definitely not sure if you made the nice list or not," James said. He got up and took the wide, flat box from beneath the tree. "From me and Phil," he said as he handed it to Kieran. Kieran looked between them with mock suspicion before opening it. Inside, he found a brochure for the same company that made most of James's guitars. James resumed his spot on the couch beside Kieran.

"I'm not sure I follow."

"I have my signature drum set," Phil said.

"And I have my signature guitar," James continued. "And we want you to create your own signature guitar."

Kieran smiled, flipping through the brochure.

"Does this mean you're keeping him?" Adrienne winked.

"This means we want him to play guitar with us on this album," Phil said.

"And live," James finished.

Kieran bit his lip. "I don't know what to say."

"Merry Christmas, Kieran," Phil said. "And welcome, officially, to True North."

"Thank you, guys." For a moment, it seemed like he might get emotional. But then he smirked up at them, winking.

"You're such an asshole," Phil said.

"This really is awesome," Kieran said.

Adrienne caught James's eye, and he gave her a slight nod.

"Alright, I'm going to start breakfast," she said.

"I'll help," Phil said.

Kieran continued to leaf through the brochure.

James stood, stretching, eyeing the tree. Adrienne had placed the small, red velvet box between its branches, far enough back that it wasn't noticeable unless you were looking for it. He looked back at Kieran.

"Hey," James said. Kieran looked up at him. James reached for him and he rose, putting the brochure on the coffee table.

"Hey," Kieran said.

James wrapped his arms around him, pulling him into a kiss. "Merry Christmas," James said, squeezing him, hoping Kieran couldn't feel his heart pounding. He pulled back, looking down at him.

"Merry Christmas to you," Kieran said. "What's with the goofy grin?"

"Well, I may have one more present for you," James said, and Kieran rolled his eyes.

"Yeah, yeah, well, I'll be sure to unwrap that package when we're alone," Kieran teased, and James smiled, shaking his head.

"Funny," James said. "But seriously, I do."

Kieran frowned as James reached between the

branches of the tree and extracted a box. By the time James went to one knee, he could see all the white around Kieran's irises.

"Holy shit," Kieran swore.

"Kieran Jackson, will you marry me?"

Kieran looked down at him, and for once, James felt like he'd caught him off guard. His hand went to his mouth, his eyes darting back and forth between the ring and James's face.

"Holy shit, James."

"If you need time to think about it, I understand. You don't have to answer right now," James said, but Kieran shook his head.

"No, no. I don't. I know." He nodded. "Yes, I'll marry you."

James smiled, taking the ring and sliding it onto Kieran's finger. He stood and wrapped his arms around Kieran as he leaned in, seizing his mouth.

"I love you," James said fiercely.

"I love you," Kieran responded, almost in disbelief. "Jesus fucking Christ," he swore again, hugging himself to James.

"So was that a yes?" James and Kieran both turned to find Adrienne and Phil standing in the dining area, watching them. Phil had recorded it all on his cell phone.

"Oh my God, you proposed to me while I was wearing a Santa hat?" Kieran jeered at James before turning back to Phil. "And you recorded it?" They all laughed, including Kieran, who passed a hand over his eyes, wiping away tears. "Yes, it's a yes," he said, flipping off the cell-phone camera.

Phil chuckled. "Charming."

"Isn't he, though?" James beamed at him, reveling in the moment. *Nothing can feel as good as this. Absolutely nothing.*

Acknowledgements

To my mom, Lola Baisden. You've been right beside me for this whole journey. When the anxiety rolls in, you always keep me steady.

To my sister, Victoria Baisden. You've supported me in the same way I've always tried to support you, only you do it better. You definitely should've been the older sister.

To my best friend, Chelsey Hutchings. You talked me out of giving up on this thing and myself so many times. This book would not exist without you, no matter what you say.

To my beta readers, Victoria Baisden, Chelsey Hutchings, Brittney Hooker, and Krystal Dean. I'm sure you all knew I was terrified to let anyone read this. Your excitement and encouragement helped me through that very scary step.

To those who helped with the research for this book, specifically Alex Douglas and Brittney Hooker. Anything I got right, they helped me understand. Anything I got wrong is on me.

To my editor, Keren Reed. I've never worked with an editor before, but you made the process as painless as it could be. I learned so much with your help and I know this book is better because of your work.

To my proofreader, Judy Zweifel of Judy's Proofreading, for that final polish. I've never worked with a proofreader either and you made it incredibly simple. Thanks for answering all of those questions on a Sunday evening and putting this first-timer at ease.

To my family, friends, and day-job coworkers not

mentioned above, you rock! It's been an amazing experience writing this book and even the smallest interest and/or encouragements have truly meant the world to me. On the chance that this book takes off, I promise not to forget the 'little people'.

And last but not least, to you, dear reader. I have waited my entire life to thank you. I hope you enjoyed reading *Credence* as much as I loved writing it.

Delphia Baisden is a first-time indie author. In 2016, she finally decided to use her passion for writing to tell the love stories of her heart. She is an avid rock 'n' roll fan who feels most comfortable in a band tee and a pair of jeans. She currently lives in a small town near Columbus, Ohio, with her mom, Lola, and their three cats, Cassy, Maggie, and Charlie.

For more information, please visit <u>delphiabaisden.com</u>.

Printed in Great Britain
by Amazon